CASH CITY

CASH CITY

A NOVEL OF CAIN CITY

Jonathan Fredrick

MYSTERIOUSPRESS.COM

ISBN: 978-1-5040-7557-2

This edition published in 2022 by MysteriousPress.com/Open Road Integrated Media, Inc.
180 Maiden Lane
New York, NY 10038
www.openroadmedia.com

For Quincy

CASH CITY

CHAPTER ONE
THE CAMMACK BUSINESS

Until he came knocking on my door, I had never seen Joe Cammack.

Small towns like Cain City, West Virginia lull a person into believing that they've rubbed elbows or traded a light concern about the weather with nearly every citizen. You think because you know Tom and Mary walking down the street, and you know their parents, their kids, their cousins, their cousins' cousins, that's all there is to know. It's a quaint little notion, and I understand the peace of mind that it might provide, but it's false and it's dangerous, and it allows for some nasty vices to trot right into a town, unannounced and unnoticed until they've already taken root. And the good citizens cry out—how could this be happening in our town, in our neighborhood, in the house next door? They complain of the entire world going to rot. They throw up their hands as if the moral and physical decay were an act of God, as if their own apathy had nothing to do with it, never realizing their sense of safety was nothing but a shared mirage.

Not that I particularly gave a fuck about Cain City or anybody in it.

I was standing at the windows in my office taking a call from a potential client and watching the cars swish by down on the avenue. An ugly piece of weather had moved through in the morning, leaving behind clogged drains, swamped streets, and lashing winds that rattled the windows in their frames.

"Listen, lady," I said into the phone. "I don't mind scavenging alleys and trees and gutters for your precious cat—excuse me, Lucy—but I gotta charge you like I'd charge anybody, you gotta understand that. Time is money. If you wanna pay somebody thirty bucks to find her then talk to whatever kid lives on your block. I'm sure they'd be happy to do it for half that."

The woman prattled on for a bit about the finer points of the cat's personality and how that might help find her. I began to wonder if I should take the thirty bucks and treat myself to a nice lunch.

A shy tapping on my office door turned my head. I interrupted the lady.

"Good luck to you, then. Call me if you change your mind."

I cut the call, crossed the width of my office in a few strides and opened the door. A big, solid guy stood hunched in the middle of the hallway, head bowed as if he wanted to conceal his face.

I said, "What can I do for you?"

He lifted his head and in doing so straightened out to his full, considerable size. He had ruddy features that bulged forward as if they were clamoring to get off his face. The face itself seemed locked in an urgent and pained expression. The leather creases of his skin put his age about sixty, but faces in this corner of the world tended to erode rapidly. I guessed him to be around forty-five.

"My name is Joe Cammack," he stated with the bent twang of a native.

I volunteered my name and repeated my initial question.

"I'm looking to hire you," he answered.

"Them's the magic words."

I grinned and showed him in. The heel of his right boot tracked wet mud across the wood floor. I wouldn't complain about it until I was certain he was wasting my time. By the looks of him, he didn't have any money, so that might be soon.

He said he was pleased to meet me and extended his hand. I offered mine; he took hold of it and yakked it up and down. His palms had the course, thick texture that came from a life of labor.

I sat down and invited Cammack to do the same, referring him to either of the two chairs on the visitor's side of my desk. He nodded his head but remained standing, agitated over whatever business he'd come for. His manic energy made me a little uneasy.

"How do we do this?" he asked.

"Well, you explain what you need me for, or think you need me for, and I decide if it's something I am able and willing to do. Then I determine how much it would cost you and we go from there. Now, how can I help you?"

Cammack either didn't hear the question or evaded it on purpose. In substitute for an answer, he informed me that he worked on the loading docks down by the river for the Swann Hauling Company and that it was good, steady work and he'd been at it for nearly sixteen years.

I congratulated him.

"I just wanted you to know that I was employed."

Cammack smacked his jowls loose as if to continue speaking, but no words formed in his mouth, just a series of stuttered syllables. I stayed seated in a casual manner and waited for him to settle down and string together a few noises that made sense.

Cammack looked like he might have a little Indian blood in him, or maybe Mexican. His right eye floated outward quite a bit so I couldn't tell if he was eyeing me or the liquor stock on the shelf to the left of me. Either way he looked red and thirsty.

"Would you like a drink?"

"No, sir," he shook his head, resolute. "I'm fine."

But he needed one. You could smell the need seeping from his big ruddy pores. I favored getting a fast one in him. A bit of liquor might calm him down and get him speaking English instead of hemming and hawing around, grinding his muddy boot into my rug.

"I'm having one so you might as well," I told him, thick and pleasant.

"Okay then, if you're having one."

Technically I was having a third, but fuck it, I looked like I had my shit together and looking right is the most important component of getting business in this business. I snagged a couple of highball glasses from the cabinet beneath the shelf, poured two healthy servings of bourbon, and offered one to Cammack. He accepted graciously. The glass trembled in his hand, but he managed to hit his mouth hole. The drink appeared to steel him a bit.

"I heard tell you was the person to call when there ain't no one else to call."

Now, there are a few ways I could digest this fresh little piece. Any way you slice it, I'm a last resort. As fortunes fell, somebody was always in need of a last resort.

"Who," I said evenly, "paid me that fine compliment?"

"Carl Turnbull told me about you. You know Carl?"

"Sure, I know Carl."

"He said you was a lifesaver with that—-uh, little situation he was in a couple years back, the restraining order thing with his missus."

"He was easy to help, because he didn't do anything wrong and his wife was seven shades of bat-shit crazy."

"Yeah, she had some things."

"Let's get to it then. What is it I can do for you specifically?"

He gulped down another swallow and I waited for a spell while he gazed at the drink and built himself up to something.

"You heard about the girl went missing two weeks ago?"

"I saw something about it in the papers."

"Ain't been no story in the papers."

"Maybe it was the news."

"Ain't been nothing on the news neither." Cammack fixed a suspicious eye on me. His wonky one continued to take in the scenery. "I don't know, we could've maybe missed it on the news. But I don't think so. Somebody woulda told us."

"That doesn't surprise me. A lot of times, incidents like that get kept under wraps. Thataway, parents still send their kids to the college, townsfolk feel nice and safe and stay oblivious to the true goings-on, and everyone skips merrily on their way. That is, until they don't. You hear whispers about these things though, in my circle."

Cammack seemed to buy that inspired line of bullshit. He nodded his head at me like he knew what I was talking about with the cover-ups.

"That girl is my daughter," he said. "Trisha."

I sat a little straighter in my chair.

Cammack swigged down the last of his bourbon. I got him fixed with a second and he started on that one.

"She is my only child, Mr. Malick, and I—I . . ."

Cammack shuddered. Fat tears welled in his eyes. He looked about to crumple right there on my freshly muddied rug, but he blinked the tears away, sucked in some air and regained his composure.

"I'm sorry, it's just that I been down to the police station every day since my baby disappeared and every day they tell me they handlin' things. They tell me that things are comin' along real well with they investigation, but they cain't give me no information. Day after day they cain't tell me nothin' about nothin'. Finally, I got so fed up I raised my voice at 'em. Way I see it, if things was comin' along nicely, like they say, they should have had something to tell me long time ago, and I said to 'em something like that."

"Didn't take it too well, did they?"

"Tossed me out on my ass and told me not to come back. Said they'd phone me when they had something. Been six days. Nothin'. I don't like dealin' with them police."

"We have that in common."

"So I ain't doing it no more. But after they booted me, I'm startin' up my car and pullin' away when the secretary they got over there comes hustling out the doors and flags me down. She must of felt sorry for me cause she tells me they ain't even really lookin' for Trish. Says they think she was probably on drugs or some nonsense like that or maybe just run away with some dude or something. She says girls go missing all the time round here and ninety-nine percent of the time that's what's usually happened, so the police don't pay it much mind. But I know my baby didn't run away. We talk on the phone every Wednesday and we eat together every Sunday afternoon, my wife and Trish and me. I know my daughter, she ain't gonna up and leave like that, without no word to her mother or me. She was the type that told me and my wife everything. But the police won't listen to me. They just nod along with their fake grins like I'm the one who's cuckoo."

"Did you get that secretary's name?"

"Not off the top of my head. Nice woman. Had short brown hair, wore glasses, sort of a rounder lady."

"I know her. Sandra Nicely."

"Nicely." He raised a finger. "That's right. You'd think I'd remember that."

"This is delicate, but I have to ask. Was Trish into anything seedy? Drugs? Anything like that?"

He shook his head emphatically.

"Not a chance. She was perfectly fine and healthy every time I seen her, didn't seem to have a care in the world. Brightens up a room. She's that type, you know what I'm sayin'?"

Cammack raised a hand in the air as if he were either professing scout's honor or praising Jesus, then balled the hand into a tight fist and brought it down hard on the back of a chair.

"Can you help me? Tell me you can help me. Her mother won't even bring herself to leave the house for fear that Trish may show up. First couple days she run the roads all hours day and night lookin' for Trish, callin' out her name like Trish was some stray dog or some such thing. But now she won't even leave the house. Only goes in three rooms, the bedroom, the bathroom, and the kitchen. Just sits by the phone waitin' for Trish to call and say everything is all right, that it was just a big misunderstanding. That she just run off with some dude on a wild ride. Whole body jumps every time the phone rings."

Cammack set his drink on the far side of the desk and put his left palm down to steady himself. He reached into his shirt pocket, took out a photograph and reached it over to me.

"Your wife could be right," I told him. "This could all be an innocent misunderstanding."

"I wish I could believe that, Mr. Malick. I really wish I could."

I took the photograph and glanced at it.

"Pretty girl," I said offhand, as one does about other people's children or pets, regardless if they are adorable or hideous.

"Thank you." Cammack's chin inched forward.

"Is this current?"

"Pardon?"

"The picture, was it taken recently?"

"Oh, yes. That's from last Fourth of July."

I inspected the photo. Trisha had inherited her father's olive skin and thick nose. Coupled with what I assumed were her mother's features—curly auburn hair, doe eyes, high cheekbones—the sum was more than pretty. She was stunning. In the photo she was sitting on a lawn chair holding a cup of tea, wearing high-cut white shorts and a navy off-the-shoulder t-shirt embossed with an American flag. Her thin lips curved into a vague smile for the camera. Trisha looked, as her father proclaimed, fine and healthy. She also looked familiar, but I couldn't pair the face with a setting. I didn't mention it to Cammack.

Cammack looked beyond me out the windows onto the street, drew in a deep breath, closed his eyes and let loose his air. The poor bastard was so broken up he was starting to tug on the two heartstrings I had left.

"Tell me you can help me," he appealed for a third time.

"That depends on some different things, Mr. Cammack."

He opened his eyes. "I ain't got much money."

My cue. I started to tell him where he could take his muddy boots, but then he dug into his pants pocket and withdrew a loose wad of cash. That shut my mouth.

"I asked Carl how much something like this cost," Cammack explained as he piled the money on my desk. "He told me he thought it was a sliding scale depending on the type case and what not, so I cobbled together as much as I could from family and some co-workers. This is what we came up with."

I began to thumb through the bills.

"That there's five hundred," Cammack said. "Took me a little while to get that much. That's why I'm just now coming to you, but I'm sure I can scrounge up more for you if you think you can help me out."

I peeled five twenties off the stack and slid them across to him.

"I'm not gonna take every dime you've got. For four hundred, I'll take a crack at it and see if I can find something out for you. If I can, and I'm sure I can, then you and I will renegotiate. How's that?"

"Is that how it works?"

"That's how it works." I pocketed the cash. "Now I'm gonna ask you some questions so you might want to have that seat."

"Sure." Cammack fit his big body into the seat and got situated.

"Let's begin at the beginning," I said, putting a fresh drink in his hand. "What day did your daughter disappear?"

CHAPTER TWO
HER FAVORITE COLOR

Fortified with liquor, Cammack got chatty. Around his fourth serving of Maker's Mark, I got the impression that he envisioned me as his personal savior, emerging from the depths of his darkest hour to deliver his daughter home safe and sound and lovely as the day she was baptized. I try to temper a client's expectations, but a switch had clicked over in Cammack that couldn't be unswitched. The desperate ones come in want of miracles. I take their money and they get what they get.

Cammack provided the details of Trisha's life as he understood them. Some were useful, some were not. I ticked off the useful ones in my head. As a child she went for a swim in the river and contracted spinal meningitis. Recovered eventually, but it left her immune system weak and susceptible to various ailments. Despite frequent truancy, she received decent grades in school. Ran away a few times as a teenager, an experience that ultimately brought them closer together, Cammack insisted. He and his wife had persuaded Trisha to have an abortion when she was seventeen, five years ago, a regretful mistake that Trisha had learned from. Cammack didn't know who planted the seed, claimed Trisha would never tell him.

After high school, she started up at Cain City College. Made it through her freshman year, but decided to take the fall semester of her sophomore year off. That was six semesters ago and her sabbatical was still going. She rarely brought home or discussed any friends. Bizarre for a pretty twenty-two year old, I thought, but Cammack claimed Trisha had always been a solitary girl, had always favored her own company above that of others.

I learned where Trisha liked to eat, drink, dance, shop, bank, and get her teeth cleaned. Six months ago, she obtained a job as a receptionist at an auto body shop downtown that she was plenty excited about. Her father still thought she was selling short her potential. No steady boyfriend since her college year, a local fellow she had brought around now and again. Older kid that Cammack had liked well enough. Name was Norman Hinkle. Hinkle came from a solid family that lived on the Southside. His father was some kind of surgeon.

From there Cammack began to run on in a non-linear manner, sharing anecdotes about Trisha's disposition as a baby, her grade school hijinks, her ability to twirl a baton, and her favorite color, blue. Seeing as he just put four hundred dollars in my hand, I let him ramble, but after a while I got restless, stood up in the middle of one of his sentences and assured him that I had enough information to start. After all, time was of the essence in these matters.

I got his information, told him that he and his wife would be kept up to speed on any progress, and ushered him out the door. Two thumbs of Maker's remained in his glass so I married that with mine and rinsed his empty in the kitchenette sink. As I was stacking the cleaned glass in the cupboard, that same timid knock sounded at the door. I stepped over and twisted the knob. Cammack stood there looking dumbstruck, his head swiveling back and forth down the hallway.

"This place is like a maze."

"Happens to everybody," I said. Especially the lushes, I thought. "Give me a second and I'll show you the way."

I left Cammack in the hallway, knocked back my muddled drink, splashed some water on my face, brushed my teeth, strapped my SubCompact Beretta into my shoulder holster, threw on my coat and flat cap, snatched my wallet, cell phone, and keys off the counter, stepped out and locked the place up.

Cammack was fiddling with one of the old metal lockers that still lined the halls. He saw me approaching and closed it.

"I used to go to high school here," Cammack said. "Forget which one was my locker."

"Yeah? Forget how to get around, too?"

"Thirty some years ago. Looks different. Smells the same though."

"Trish go to the new one?"

"Yep. She was here for her first year. New one opened up when she turned sophomore."

Cain City consolidated its two public high schools a few years back, leaving both old ones vacant. Cain City East got the wrecking ball. In its place they erected a Big Lots. But Southside High was the original, constructed back in the twenties, and considered something of a landmark, so they converted the three upper floors into apartments and set aside the first floor for business offices. The auditorium still held the occasional concert or recital.

The first floor, of which I was the sole resident, was nearly two stories off the ground. The basement was half above ground and half subterranean. I think there was a local art gallery down there along with a boiler room. I'd never been. I rented what used to be a small classroom and teacher's office, and used the classroom for my workspace. The old teacher's office had enough space to fit a bed, a chair, some drawers, a mini-fridge, and a tiny bathroom with a shower. The best thing I could say about the place was that it had good water pressure; shower stung the skin. And rent was cheap. The city half-assed the refurbishing job because they didn't want to knock any asbestos loose that they would later be forced to clean up or answer for.

A right down one hall, left down the next, and another right brought us to the front exit. Cammack and I pushed through the double doors and stepped out onto the veranda. The day was brisk and overcast. The air was clean from the storm; the wind clawed at your body. The veranda and steps down to the street were still slick from the rain. I said so long to Cammack and watched him tramp down the steps.

Dark clouds had gathered over the rolling hills to the south. The sky to the north was clear over the river valley and the hills that way. A few people were going into the yogurt place at the strip mall across the avenue, but it wasn't quite lunchtime and only a handful of cars were sprinkled throughout the lot. Last night, someone had thrown a rock through the plate glass window of Sole Brothers, a shoe store, and burgled the place. The owner was out front now patching the window over with plywood. The Rent-To-Own shop next to that had been out of business for a long time and the movie rent al place at the far end of the row had been vacant for a month. No businesses were in any great rush to take their place.

Behind me, a tennis ball thudded rhythmically against the wall of the school. A squeaky voice barked at me from that direction.

"Hey, playa. Can I holler at you for a minute?"

I ignored the silly voice trying to sound tough, buttoned up my coat, and started down the steps.

"Yo, man. You know I'm talking to you."

The voice belonged to this little half-pint latchkey punk that always loitered around the school. He pocketed the tennis ball, yanked his pants up high enough to walk without tripping, and trotted after me.

"Hello? I know you hear me."

"Scram, kid. You're bothering me."

"C'mon, man. You look like a real cool guy."

"I'm not even a little cool."

"Hold up, maybe I can help you out with that."

The kid skipped down the last few stairs and caught up to me. He was wearing a hooded sweatshirt and a side-cocked Cincinnati Reds cap, the bill flat across and stupid looking. He must have been about twelve, maybe thirteen. He was small, but rangy, overdue for a growth spurt.

"Where you going?"

"See child services about a pickup."

"Ha-ha. See, that's funny. You funny, too. Let me ask you something."

"No."

"Why you always got weird funny people coming to see you? That dude was a giant."

"Don't you have anyone else to hassle?"

The kid grinned.

"You the only one around."

I grunted. At the bottom of the steps I turned left onto the sidewalk. The kid stayed with me.

"Yo, how bout I give you some money and you go down to the gas station and buy me some brew?"

"What's your brand?"

"Co-ro-na."

As the kid elongated the syllables he made some silly gesture with his hands flitting up and down.

"No."

"Aw, man. At least buy me some cigs or condoms or something."

"Condoms, really?"

"Hells yeah. I ain't no virgin. I gets mine."

"Why do you talk like an idiot?"

"Talk like what?" The kid feigned as if he were insulted. He tapped on his chest with his fist and shrugged. "This is how I do. Recognize."

"Sure, kid."

"C'mon man. I'm too young to be a daddy. Dumbass teenage sex is how I got here. Kids making kids ain't no good for nobody. I don't get some condoms, there's gonna be three of me hanging round here before long. I know you ain't gonna like that. So it's preventative."

"Decent sell, kid. Lead with that and maybe you can sucker the next guy. Take a hike."

The kid stopped walking.

"You take a hike you old honkey."

A car driving by splashed gutter sludge all over the kid's pants.

"Fuck," he spat.

I kept walking.

"I thought you was cool, man," he hollered after me.

"Told you different."

CHAPTER THREE
STUPID FACE

A light drizzle took a personal interest in me as I walked three blocks south and crossed the street heading west on Twelfth Avenue. Four more blocks and I arrived out front of my destination, a modest red brick house in the middle of a block of modest red brick houses. Matching green and black SUV's were parked at the curb along with a silver Civic. The whole family was home. I climbed the four steps to the porch, brushed the pellets of water off my shoulders and cap and knocked on the door.

Inside, the muffled voices of a man and two women bartered over who was going to answer it. Heavy footsteps approached and the door swung open. Bruce Hale led with his big hard belly and I saw it before I saw him. His head was craned back toward the interior of the house as he chuckled at something that was said, but when he turned forward and registered the visitor on his doorstep he stopped laughing and straightened up.

"What are you doing here?"

"I missed your stupid face."

"Don't get cute, Nick."

"No one's ever accused me of being cute."

Hale put his hand over his mouth and squeezed his cheeks as if he were trying to keep from getting mad.

"Is this how you want to start with me?"

"We can skip the pleasantries."

He glanced back into the house to make sure no curious eyes were coming up behind him to see who'd come knocking, then shook his head and faced me.

"How's life in the cheating spouses business?"

"Lucrative as ever," I said, with an exaggerated grin. "Doesn't pay quite as well as crime, though, round these parts."

Hale chafed.

"Why are you here?"

"I don't mean to put a kink in your cozy weekend, Bruce. Just need to run something by you from a case I'm working."

"If you wanna talk to me on a professional level then call me. Don't show up at my house."

"Would you have taken the call?" Hale didn't answer. "There you go."

"You shouldn't have come here. Cynthia will have a conniption fit if she sees you."

"Doesn't time heal all wounds? I believe you've mentioned something like that to me before."

"Not for women. They're different when it comes to that kind of thing."

"My recall might be a little fuzzy, but isn't she the one who broke my nose with a fucking serving plate." I pointed at my nose. "Got the scar to prove it."

"That's because you slugged me in the gut, Nick. For no good reason. In the middle of a barbecue at my house."

"No good reason? My memory must be going. I thought I had a phenomenal reason."

"And what's that, huh? That I was trying to talk some goddamn sense into you? Jesus, why are you bringing this up?"

"Talking sense? That's what you were doing?"

"That's exactly what I was doing."

"Still, not really an eye for an eye when it's all measured out. Look, I didn't come here to stroll down memory lane."

"Good, come out with it then." Hale again peered behind him.

"Girl named Trisha Cammack went missing last week. What do you know about it?"

Hale got very still. "What do *you* know about it?"

"Nothing yet."

From back of the house somewhere Cynthia yelled out, "Who is it, Bruce?"

"I'll be right in, honey," he hollered back. "You're on the Cammack case?"

"As of thirty minutes ago."

Hale looked hard at me for a minute. I could practically see his mind churning. He said, "We can't talk here and you can't come in."

"We're not pals anymore?"

"Shut up."

Getting Hale riled up was something of a specialty for me, though it was almost too easy to be fun. Almost.

"Make something up for the old lady and come have a drink with me."

Hale's forehead rolled up into three fat rolls. He smoothed his eyebrows over with his thumb and middle finger, dragged his hand down over his face and sighed through his nostrils.

"I'll pay, you drive," I offered. "That sweeten the deal?"

"All right, give me a minute."

Hale disappeared inside.

"Easy enough."

The front door was left ajar just enough for me to listen to Cynthia's protests. Something about plans to barbecue that afternoon. Then he must have spilled the beans that not only was he leaving the house, but it was me he was leaving with, because she started to lay into him. Cynthia grew up on the other side of the river where the accents were even more pronounced than the ones in town. The more she yelled the more backwoods hers became. I took a moderate amount of pleasure at having caused them some slight marital discord.

"You told me we would never see that son of a bitch again," she screamed.

"It's a small town," Hale countered. "Of course we're gonna see him again."

"Not on our fucking front porch, Bruce. I don't care what you do. Get that man off my porch. You better not come back here three sheets to the wind either, or else."

"Or else what?" Hale replied lamely, no doubt for my benefit.

I walked down the steps and waited by his black SUV. Hale emerged from the house seconds later, hurried over to the car and unlocked it.

"All good?"

"Get in," he barked, scoping me from head to toe. "Why do you always look like you're about to queue up in a goddamn bread line?"

"I aim for a classic style."

He started the car and said, "You put the ass in classic."

CHAPTER FOUR
A FINITE WORLD

We headed east, back toward my place. Catty-corner from the viaduct into downtown was a crap bar that I frequented called The Red Head. Weekend nights, the place was overrun with college kids, but the rest of the nights and during the day it was a fine spot. Also, it was three blocks from my place, the drinks were cheap and stiff, and the doors opened at noon. We were the first patrons of the day.

We sat at the far end of the bar, away from the slats of gray daylight streaming in through the front windows. Tadpole, the bartender, greeted us and launched into one of his jokes.

"This blind guy strolls into the bar and sits down, right where you're sitting, and he says to me, 'I've got the greatest blonde joke ever told.' And this lady sitting beside him says, 'Well, I'm a blonde and my friend here, who happens to be a fourth degree black belt, she's a blonde. And the woman on the other side of you is blonde. And the two women in the booth behind you are both body builders who are also blonde. You sure you still want to tell that joke?' And the blind guy says, 'Well, not if I'm going to have to repeat it five times!'"

Tadpole slapped the countertop with his bar rag and laughed at his own joke until he started coughing.

I complimented the joke and ordered a Maker's. Hale asked for a Heineken. I paid with one of the wrinkled twenties Cammack had given me. Tadpole slid thirteen-fifty back across the counter and plopped a bowl of peanuts in front of us. I left him a couple bucks and the quarters.

After Hale got a couple of sips down I started in on him.

"What's your official line in this Cammack business?"

"Are you gonna spend the very little currency you have left with me for *this* case?"

"I didn't know I had any currency left with you."

"You don't if this is it."

"Fine by me," I said truthfully. "So what's your line?"

"Don't have a line."

"Don't give me the shit runaround, Bruce. You know that I know a missing girl falls straight into your fat lap. Are you the one that's been talking to her father?"

"That guy," Hale groaned. "All of us have been talking to her father. Her father made sure that all of us were talking to him. He's a goddamn nuisance is what he is. Needs to let us do our job. How'd he come across you?"

"Beats me. I thought you might have told him."

Hale snorted.

"Why would I give myself that headache?"

"Musta been the yellow pages then. Anyhow, he thinks I'm his great last hope at finding his daughter."

"People will latch onto anything when they're desperate."

"He's certainly desperate."

"I feel sorry for him, I do. My heart goes out."

"If you guys handled him the way he says you handled him then that's a pretty shitty way to show you feel sorry for somebody."

"You don't know what you're talking about," Hale bristled. "You weren't there."

"Maybe. Seems to me like the guy just wants some honest answers about his missing daughter and no one will give him squat."

"We tried to give him honest answers. He doesn't want to hear them."

"Give them to me?"

"You want me to shoot you straight?"

"No, jerk me around a little."

"All right, Nick. I'll level with you about this thing since it seems like you're gonna be circling it for a while. But after this conversation I'm done with it. This case is a waste of everybody's time. That girl—" Hale pointed at the front door. "She will turn up when she turns up. She's not the type of girl who posts a status update every fifteen minutes so every asshole knows what she's up to. We're not gonna find her by following some neat little accumulation of evidence."

I said, "Let's hear it," and ordered another round for the both of us.

"The Cammack girl is an addict, big time. Whatever she can get her hands on."

"Pops neglected to tell me that."

"Doesn't shock me. Her father refuses to believe anything that resembles reality. He insists that he knows his daughter better than we do and that we—" Hale put a fist to his chest and belched, "—are flat wrong. Girl's been an addict since she dropped out of college. Got hooked on crack, meth, the works, by some sleaze boyfriend she had back then."

"Hinkle?"

"Yeah, the Hinkle kid."

"You pick him up?"

"We talked to him. Runs a little landscaping thing on the Southside. Pretty certain he's a low-level dealer, too, but we can't pin anything and have too many bigger fish to fry to waste any juice on him. Says he hasn't seen her in months. Maybe that's true, maybe it isn't."

"Does the father know Hinkle got his girl hooked?"

"Doesn't seem to. He's delusional about that girl. And we didn't tell him."

"Anything to this new job she got at a body shop?"

"Doesn't exist."

"What do you mean, doesn't exist?"

"The body shop. No such place. She made it up for her parent's sake. Works at the Midnight Run downtown."

"She works at the Run?"

"Sure does." Hale shook his head and popped a peanut into his mouth. "Been working there two years. Applied to all the legit clubs outside city limits too, but they don't hire girls they know for certain are messed up and everybody knew this girl was messed up, no matter how hot she is. Went down to the Run last week a couple different times. Talked to each of the girls and employees down there. Course, no one had anything worth a goddamn nickel to tell us."

"You get a private dance?"

"Should've."

"Shut the place down?"

"Naw. Me and Hive just chatted with them. That place is the least of our worries."

"Bigger fish to fry," I offered, taking a drink.

"That's right."

I thought for a second.

"I know a girl that works there. Maybe I can get her to tell me something."

Hale popped another peanut in his mouth and dusted his hands off.

"Which one do you know?"

"Never got her real name. Stripper name is Gum Drop."

"Aisha Bryant," Hale clucked, cocking an eyebrow. "Not bad if you like 'em brown. You fuck her?"

"No."

"Don't give me that look. Which one of 'em would you plow, if you had to pick?"

"I wouldn't."

"Don't kid a kidder."

"You can get your kicks however you want to get 'em, Bruce. I prefer to piss without a burn."

Hale chortled. The beers had loosened him up.

"Yeah, I guess they're a rough lot down there, aren't they? Half those girls are totally buckled. But you seen one down there goes by the name Fantasy?"

"No."

"C'mon, you can't miss her."

"I haven't studied their fucking bios."

"She's a firecracker, I'm telling you. I'd slice that pussy in half. You can smell that tang from the stage. Nice looking snatch. Big old titties that still kinda hold up too."

He demonstrated with his hands the size he meant to convey and made a goofy face that failed to sell the appeal.

"The dutiful wife not doing it for you anymore?"

"Don't judge me. I have the sex life of a goddamn seventh grader. I beat my meat a lot and every so often I get thrown some kisses, a few pecks on the cheeks if I'm lucky. What kind of life is that? Marriage is like this club you join that nobody tells you about, this club of mutual suffering. You get a house, couple cars, insurance, joint fucking bank accounts and you're stuck in it. Then you have kids and *pfftt*, that's it, that's the kicker. You know what I'm talking about."

I shook my head. "Must not have been in the club long enough."

"Lucky you." Hale swigged his beer. "To put the real cherry on top, as I get older, my dick looks more and more like a fucking button on a fur coat. It's no good."

"I don't want to hear about your shortcomings."

"Gum Drop. What kind of a stripper name is that anyway? Worth a shot I suppose. No one will talk to us so we got nowhere to go. No leads, nothing."

"You tell her father about the Midnight Run?"

"Negative." Hale turned his palms up in a gesture of apathy. "By that point, we didn't feel the need to upset him for no good reason. Details been kept out of the papers for the same purpose. He'd probably just call us liars again anyhow."

"Doesn't sound like you guys turned too many stones over."

"Can't turn 'em if they don't budge. Feel free to shake as many trees as you want. I hope you find her, I do. But I don't think you will."

"No? Why's that?"

"Things in this town aren't like they used to be, Nick. If you can't see that you need to turn the lights on my friend. All you have to do is flip on the local news. Lead story is the same every night, somebody getting robbed by some junkie. Every single night. Nobody wants to say this out loud because that makes it too real, but drugs and drug dealers are taking over and we don't have enough manpower to do anything about it. There's a new pipeline coming in from Detroit. You heard about that?"

"A little."

"Hell, you can see it. Count the number of Michigan license plates you see next time you walk down the street. It's a goddamn infestation. We started pulling over every car we came across with Michigan tags, but there's too many of them and they're smart enough not to keep the stuff in their own cars anyway. And arresting them does no good. They're like the gray hairs on my head; pluck one of 'em, three more spring up in its place."

"Maybe you should pluck the black hairs."

"Way it works is this: somebody in Detroit figured out that they could sell drugs here for triple the amount they sell for there. On the flip side, they found out they could purchase guns on the cheap down here and turn those for triple the amount in Detroit."

"Sounds like a prize gig."

"Oh, it is. This is big business we're talking about. The fucking American dream flipped on its ear. This town is in a combustible situation, only nobody's privy to it. Look here, there's a tick under fifty thousand people living in Cain City, right? Our patrol unit is what, eighty men? Eighty men." For emphasis, his eyes got big and his chin jutted out. "That used to be plenty to keep things straight. It's not even close to enough now. Best of situations we have thirty, thirty-five guys on the street at a given time. Drug Unit and Felony Unit have one sergeant, six detectives between them. That's it. Feds and DEA have, at best, a token presence. It's a fucking joke. We can't put a dent into anything serious. We can't keep up and we can't keep a lid on this thing for long. Even if we keep the bulk of it out of the papers or off the news, pretty soon people are going to notice somebody's getting shot every other weekend."

Hale was working himself into a tizzy now, talking like a man who needed to be unburdened. As fortunes fell, I happened to be the nearest cleric.

"Things weren't like this when I was growing up. This was a great town to live in. You shoulda seen it."

"Everything changes. It's a finite world."

"You ain't kidding."

"Things were already going downhill when I got here. Remember that riot when the steel mill shut down?"

"Hell, yes, I remember it. We had to break that fucker up. What was that, fifteen years ago? We were just pups."

I nodded. Hale looked past me as if he were visualizing the memory, then snapped back to the present.

"That was the fuse on this cluster-fuck. It's a major part of the problem, no jobs and nobody can get a job. All these people robbing places are unemployed and have to find some way to get their fix. It's gotten so rotten, they've taken to robbing old ladies in the parking lot of grocery stores. Pull right up to 'em in a car, knock 'em down with the door, snag their purse, done deal. Hell, sometimes they take the time to ransack the old lady's trunk. Who's fucking there to stop them?"

We ordered another round. Other patrons had shuffled into the bar by this point so we turned the volume of our conversation down. Three guys at the front end of the bar kept yelling at the baseball game playing on the TV. A table of women took turns dialing up country songs on the jukebox.

Hale continued to wallow in his lament.

"This drug ring is renting property all over town now, too. Landlords have so many vacancies they'll rent to anyone who'll pay and these guys have no problem paying. Straight cash, off the books. More and more of them keep matriculating and now they're entrenched. At least in other places, other towns, you have your good neighborhoods and you have your bad neighborhoods, right? You can delineate between the two. We used to have that here. Not anymore. Now there's no disparity whatsoever, it's all mixed up."

"Speaking of landlords," I brought it back around, "Where did the Cammack girl live?"

"There's another mystery. She didn't have a paper trail to anywhere. Her listed address was her parents' house."

"That's interesting."

"I hope you can find that girl. I do. We just don't have the numbers or the time to commit anything to it. We're up to our eyeballs as it is."

"Eh, maybe she'll just turn up from some bender like you say. I'd appreciate it if you keep me up on anything that comes across your desk about it."

"I will. I'll do that. I promise. You know what, Nick. I'm sorry for the way things have gone between us."

"Here we go. Jesus Christ, get a couple beers in you and you turn into a sap."

"I'm being serious here."

"Don't be. It was my fault. I punched you, remember?"

"I had it coming."

"You'll get no objection from me."

"To be honest with you, Nick—"

"Now I know you're drunk."

"Let me finish here. This thing frightens the shit out of me. I've got a family here. If you were still in the game maybe you'd know how to go about it."

"Lucky for me." I tinked my glass against his. "I'm not still in."

I drank.

"You're satisfied with what you're doing? Background checks, tailing husbands and wives, sleuthing for bicycle thieves, all that nonsense."

"Very content."

Hale cast a shrewd eye on me.

"I don't believe you."

"You can believe whatever the hell you want."

"How come you don't work with any of the lawyers? Lawson does real well working for them."

"He can have 'em. I'd rather shit in my hands and clap."

"Pays good."

"Not good enough."

Hale narrowed his eyes to very determined slits and reflected on that or something else for a minute.

"What are you still doing in this town? If I were you, free as a bird, I'da been long gone."

"You know why," I answered him curtly.

"When does Kincaid get released?"

"You know when."

"Scheduled for just over a year from now."

"That soon?"

"Don't fool around." Hale jabbed a finger at me. "What are you gonna do when he gets out?"

"Welcome him back into society. What do you think?"

"I think you're gonna go after him." He waited a few beats for me to confirm his crack prediction. When I stayed mum, he sighed, "I'll have to stop you."

"You can try."

"What if he's not the guy?"

"He's the guy."

Hale looked at me irritably but didn't pursue the topic further. Brought it back to his problems.

"These fucks are running the place, Nick. They just don't know it yet. I'm scared to be around when they figure it out. I don't know what happens then."

We sat there for a while after that, silent, drinking our drinks and watching the ballgame, stuck listening to a never-ending queue of achy-heart music from the jukebox.

Hale polished off his beer and drummed the bar with his fingers.

"I better get home."

"You've got some grilling out to do."

"We're celebrating." Hale gave his hard paunch a little slap. "Found out yesterday Charity is the valedictorian of her class. Can you believe it? With my blood running through those veins?"

"Congratulations."

"She'll be giving a speech at graduation, has her choice of schools, fucking amazing. They grow up so fast."

"I bet they do."

"You want me to drop you at your place?"

I told him no, I was going to stay at The Red Head for a bit.

"Okay." He slid off his stool and clawed my shoulder. "Let me know if you get anything out of Gum Drop," he said, scoffing to himself.

CHAPTER FIVE
THE TWO DRINK DRUNK

I finished my drink and signaled Tadpole for a third, or a seventh, depending on the count. He scooped some fresh ice into my glass, added the bourbon and brought it to me. Outside, the clouds had parted and bursts of sun came through the door each time it swung open. I paid no mind to those who came or went, because the only thing occupying my mind was the family Cammack. The more Trisha Cammack came into focus the fuzzier she looked.

Somebody climbed onto the vacant stool next to me where Hale had been. I glanced sidelong. Lying flat on the counter was a miniature set of pale hands attached to miniature pale arms attached to a miniature pale person.

"Jesus, kid. Quit haunting me, will ya? Go off somewhere and grow."

The kid cocked his head at me as if I needed to be more specific.

"I waited for that po-po to leave. Figured I'd come in here and keep you company."

"I don't need any new friends, kid."

The kid looked around the bar.

"Don't look like you got any friends."

"Friends are over-rated. How'd you know he was a cop?"

"License plate has that little star on it."

"Hmm."

The pre-pubescent attracted Tadpole's attention and he strolled over to our end of the bar.

"This your kid, Malick?"

"You'd think."

"If it ain't then he gots to go."

"Now Tadpole, I'm sure this fine young man has some identification proving he's of legal age. How about it, kid? Got some ID?"

The little grifter reached into his back pocket and dumped a wad of knickknacks onto the counter. He sifted through them and plucked out a driver's license. With the confidence of someone who had done it a thousand times, he took the license between his fingers and extended it to Tadpole.

Tadpole examined the license.

"All right, Tremaine Miller, what can I get you?"

Tadpole handed the ID over to me. The photo was of a humorless thirty-one year old mixed guy, six feet tall, a hundred and eighty five pounds with a crescent shaped receding hairline.

The kid said, "I'll have what he's having." He delivered this line like he had seen it on TV and practiced for just such an occasion.

Tadpole smirked, "Don't push it, kid. Come back in a decade."

I shrugged.

"He has legitimate identification. I see no reason to withhold service from the man."

Tadpole's face went sour, but he played along, poured the kid a Maker's, diluting it with a spritz of water. He fit a wedge of lime along the rim and slid it across the counter to the kid. The kid removed the wedge and dropped it in his glass so it was like mine. He didn't wince when he took the first sip, but you could see him working hard to keep his face straight.

"That's four bucks," Tadpole told him.

The kid made a show of feeling through his pockets before he looked up at me real sheepish and friendly.

"Yo, can you float me? I'll get you back."

"Sure. This once." He was an amusing little shit, I'll give him that. "No Co-ro-na?"

"Naw." The kid took another sip. "What kind of gat you got under your jacket?"

"How do you know I have a gat?"

"I saw it when you were buttoning up your coat outside the apartments. The wind flapped it open and I peeped your gat."

"In case."

"In case of what?"

"In case I run into somebody I don't like."

That must have been a sufficient answer. He didn't pursue it.

"Can I hold it?"

I laughed at him.

"No."

"Where you from?"

"C'mon, kid, what's with the interrogation?"

"You just don't sound like you're from here, that's all."

"I'm not."

"Where you from then?"

"Chicago."

"Chi-caa-go." The kid's voice raised an octave on the second syllable to make it sound northern. "What the hell you doing here?"

"You're the second person who's asked me that in the last half hour."

"What'd you say to the first time?"

"None of your business. Don't you have a mother?"

"Everybody has a mother."

"Where's yours?"

"Work."

"Father?"

"Somewhere. Where's yours?"

"Somewhere."

The kid didn't have anything clever to add. He tugged at his bourbon a little more. He was starting to get the hang of it and the liquor was going down easier. Before long he was ordering a second.

I told him, "You better slow down."

"Man, please. I handle my liquor."

"Uh-huh."

Four minutes later the kid was rushing out the door with cheeks full of bourbon, breakfast, and stomach acid.

Tadpole watched the kid scat, then looked at me like I was the dullest bastard on the planet.

"What the fuck, Malick."

"You served him." Tadpole didn't see the humor. I put my hands up. "All right, I've got it."

"I better not see that runt in here again."

"That was the whole point, Tadpole."

I settled the tab for the bourbons and beers, exited the bar and entered the big bright world. The kid was in the passage between buildings, bent at the waist, gagging and heaving. I waited for him to finish.

"You want something to eat?"

He straightened up and wiped the chunks off his mouth. His face was sweaty and purple and bloodless.

"Nuh-uh."

"C'mon. It'll make you feel better."

The kid was woozy. I guided him by the elbow across avenue traffic to a hot dog stand, bought him a big slushie and a plain dog and got myself one with sauce. It was warm in the sun so we sat at a picnic table out from under the awning. After the kid got a couple bites down and stopped looking clammy I asked him what he was trying to prove.

"To who?"

"To the world."

"I don't got nothing to prove to nobody."

"The way you dress, the way you talk. You waltz into a bar and order a drink when you've never had a drink in your life."

"I've had a drink before."

"Right, kid. You're an idiot."

"I don't know who you're calling an idiot. You're the idiot you drunk-ass motherfucker. I'm smarter than you and I'm only in seventh grade."

"If I'm the idiot, being smarter than me doesn't exactly make you smart, does it?"

The kid squinted like he was trying to think up a thought.

"Get away from me," he muttered. "Just leave me alone."

"I'll make you a deal. I'll leave you alone if you leave me alone."

"Whatever."

"Don't follow me anymore either or you're going to find yourself in a real situation. Puking your guts out will seem like a pleasant memory."

"Whatever."

I left the kid nibbling on his hot dog and headed back to the high school. Along the way I made a mental checklist of the items I needed to accomplish, in the order I wanted to accomplish them: talk to Gum Drop; find out where Trisha Cammack slept at night and haunt that place; track down the Hinkle kid and see what angle he's taking on her disappearance. Between those three things some kind of play should open up. The Midnight Run didn't start purring till ten. I had time for a nap.

CHAPTER SIX
GUM DROP

When I came awake it was black outside. Blue light flickered from the TV and lit up the otherwise dark studio. The glow made my head throb, as did the ceiling fan whirring above me. I rolled out of bed and turned the TV off, the fan off, and switched the lamp on. The clock read seventeen past ten. I slapped myself in the jowls a couple times to no effect, so I poured myself a bourbon and carried it into the shower. The hot water coupled with the drink rallied my senses and shook off my lethargy.

Afterwards, feeling clean, I wiped the moisture from the mirror and inspected the reflection. A recurring fantasy of mine was that one day, upon looking in the mirror, I'd find a wholly different person staring back. But today was not that day. Today I was still me. The cheeks were a bit puffy from the sleep and liquor. The hair was getting a bit wild, little curls had started to sprig up along the edges. I couldn't remember the last time I had a shave. And I was still me.

After sorting myself out for a night on the town, I stuffed the essentials in my pockets and hit the door. The temperature had sunk with the sun. The air was frosty. Each breath I took clouded out and evaporated in front of my face. Some azaleas were planted in a little patch of dirt at the base of the stairs. I couldn't give a shit about flowers, but for some reason I stopped and looked at them. A warm day had tricked them into blooming early and now they were stiff with the cold, fated to die having scarcely tasted life.

My Skylark sat in the corner of the school parking lot that was zoned for residents. Another dozen cars were scattered across the lot, none of them within five spaces of the Skylark. The other residents treated it like they would get hepatitis or lockjaw if they happened to graze it with the back of their hand. I understood that the car was covered in bird shit, took a bottle of oil every other week, had a busted AC belt, radio that only picked up AM stations, and paint that was peeling off like a third degree sunburn, but the damn thing wasn't infectious. I climbed behind the wheel, got the engine chugging and steered her north under the viaduct into downtown.

The Midnight Run was located on a seedy little stretch of Third Avenue, situated between Jimmy Jammer's tattoo parlor and a vacant building that used to be a realty office. The street was deserted. The guard at the front of the Run always patted for weapons so I stashed my Beretta in the glove box and locked it up.

I walked down the street keeping an eye on the shadowed nooks and dark gaps between buildings. Reaching the Run, I thumped on the sturdy door and stepped back. The slot on the door slid open. A pair of fat eyes looked me up and down and then to the left and right of me. I said, "Just me," and the slot slammed shut.

The precaution was necessary. Strip clubs were illegal inside city limits though, to my knowledge, the Run never received too much hassle. A few deadbolts clunked and the door swung open. The fat eyes belonged to a fat man sporting a handlebar mustache that extended down below his third chin. He wasn't the most welcoming fellow I'd ever met. Forced me to turn sideways to fit past him in the doorframe.

"Arms up," he ordered. He gave me a pat down, then said, "No hats."

I complied, tucking my flat cap into my jacket pocket. Upon entering, a pungent smell, reminiscent of a wet animal, wafted into my nose and stuck there. My eyes adjusted to the dimness and smoke of the place as I weaved through the clientele, mostly biker types, past the bar and pool table and onto the main floor.

By their nature, strip clubs are bleak, desperate places, and they didn't come more bleak or desperate than the Midnight Run. Every strip club on earth had mirrors plastered over every surface; walls, private booths, ceilings, but there were no mirrors in the Midnight Run, not even in the bathrooms. Requisites for employment seemed to be seven tattoos, minimum, stretched out over saggy, pock-marked folds of flesh. The Trisha Cammack from the picture in my pocket was too young, too beautiful, too classy, too much potential for the Midnight Run. She belonged in the light of day, not in this dungeon.

On stage Gum Drop was on her knees, gyrating. I took a seat at a small round table in the back, away from the stage. Since entering the place, I'd attracted a lot of eyes. I feigned interest in the performance and soon enough those curious eyes went back to wherever they were looking prior to my entrance.

Compared to the rest of the talent milling about looking for laps to grind, Gum Drop was Best in Show. Her thick ass bouncing up and down looked like a tidal wave, gathering momentum on the way up and then crashing down onto the shores of her ample thighs. She swayed her tits and her hips, flung her curly weave into her eyes and then out of them, then climbed to the top of the pole and glided upside down to the floor. They didn't have a pole last time I was here; that was new.

An old pervert and a couple college kids, stupid grins wide on their faces, sat with their elbows on the stage and tossed dollars at her. One of the boys crowed, "Midnight Run, here we come!" and high-fived his buddy. Gum Drop dipped her ass in their faces and smacked it hard, leaving a nice flush handprint. She spun around and twisted her nipples. The hyper boys commanded her to play with her pussy. She obliged them.

A girl with sloppy tits moseyed over and asked sweetly if I would like a private dance. I pointed to the stage. "Waiting for her." The girl dropped the smile, slunk away to the next sucker and picked it back up. Another squatty girl that didn't bother with the sweetness approached and informed me that she would make me cum in my pants for twenty dollars. I gave her the same bad news.

Two tables over, a bleached blonde was hitting up one of the biker types for quarters. I thought it odd until the music from the jukebox stopped and stayed stopped. The only thing grimmer than a strip club without mirrors is a strip club without music. The whole place seemed suspended in time. Previously loud voices quieted to a murmur. And when they weren't in motion, when they were just standing there chomping their gum, the girls were somehow more hideous. Gum Drop collected the dollar bills scattered at her feet and stomped the stage to signal the next dancer.

The blonde spoke to the biker in a breathy, exaggerated voice.

"I got to dance right now, sexy. Maybe after we can take a trip to the V.I.P. room. Here's a preview."

Blondie sauntered past me. She was wearing those tall clacking hooker heels and each step she took looked on the verge of breaking an ankle. She slammed into the jukebox like a beginner on roller skates who hasn't learned to brake, thumbed the biker's quarters into the slot and punched some buttons. A reggae type song got the place humming again. Blondie mounted the steps to the stage and commenced her routine. It was a lot nastier than Gum Drop's. The college kids ate her up.

Gum Drop slinked off the far side of the stage, stepped into her neon orange panties, shimmied a transparent negligee over her head and sashayed my way.

"Buy me a drink," she said, motioning to the waitress as she sat in the chair next to mine.

"Sure."

The waitress brought us a vodka-soda and a Maker's.

"You haven't been to see me in a while," she said, her tone glazed and neutral. "No slutty husbands to chase down?"

"You tell me. Did somebody miss me?"

"Of course. To what do I owe the pleasure this evening?"

"No pleasure, just business."

Gum Drop adopted a teasing, winsome manner, batted her false eyelashes and shook her head deliberately back and forth.

"Tsk, tsk. Always business, never pleasure." She leaned in as if to disclose something. "Good thing for you, pleasure is my business."

I removed the picture of Trisha Cammack from my pocket and placed it on the table.

"You know this girl?"

"Put that away," she snapped.

Her flirty face morphed into something poisonous and her eyes darted around furtively. I tucked the picture away.

"I'll take that as a yes. When's the last time you saw her?"

"I've already told the police everything I know."

"I doubt that."

"Buy a dance from me."

"I don't want a dance. I want you to answer the question. Who are you scared is listening?"

"You play my game and I'll play yours."

"How much?"

"Forty for one in back, twenty for one here."

"Here will be fine."

"I recommend the back."

I repeated myself. Gum Drop's flirty face returned. She stood up and stuck out her hand. I subtracted the twenty from my wallet and pushed it into her palm.

"We'll wait for the next song," she told me.

We made faces at each other for a long minute until the reggae song ended and *Paradise City* by Guns N' Roses began. She started the dance where she stood, running her hands over her breasts and down to her hips to in between her legs. She let the straps from the negligee fall off her shoulders and slid it down her body to the floor. Stepped out of it and kicked it up to my face.

"Do you know why they call me Gum Drop?"

"No idea."

She snickered like this meant something—an inside thing for herself—slunk toward me and tilted her lips to my ear.

"How come you never ask me out?"

She spoke loud enough to split my eardrum, and for anyone within earshot to hear her clearly. Far as I could tell, no one else cared about what came out of her mouth. Then again, I wasn't exactly seeing straight because a flimsy nipple was doing its best to poke my left eye out. Gum Drop smelled of sweat and onions mingled with an exorbitant amount of something flowery. I liked it.

"Too much competition."

"I know that's not true. You're not the jealous type."

She knelt between my legs and made some friction with her chest there. She looked up under her eyelashes at me.

"You don't like dark girls? You probably like them skinny-minnie little things, don't you?"

"I don't discriminate when it comes to women. Which one of these girls is called Fantasy?"

"The blonde on stage. She more your flavor?"

"Just curious. You know I only have eyes for you."

"Then what's the problem?"

"I'm damaged goods."

She threw her head back and let loose a derisive, throaty cackle.

"Honey, it don't get no more damaged than this right here."

I nudged her on her elbow and guided her up to me. Her lips brushed against mine and she straddled me. Her meaty thighs pinned my legs tight and she grinded against my groin.

"You like that? You can grab my ass if you want to."

"My turn," I whispered. "When's the last time you saw Trisha Cammack?"

She tickled my earlobe with her lips. If it was a show she was putting on for the voyeurs, it was a good damn show. The thought of a backroom performance caused me to shiver.

"Oh, I don't know."

"Take an educated guess."

"Been a while. What day is today?"

"Saturday."

"No, the date."

"May sixteenth."

"Had to be last month because we had a big party for Cinco de Mayo and it was a while before that."

Gum Drop kept the sexy charade going, affecting a baby voice, sticking the tip of her tongue between her teeth and arching her eyebrows as if everything were a proposition.

"Did you know her well?"

"Not well. Lots of these heifers round here didn't like her because they thought she was trying to steal their shine. But I liked Trish. She was a sweet girl. Dumb as fuck, but sweet."

"What do you mean, was?"

"I don't mean nothing. Once they gone from here honey, they gone."

"How big of a junkie was she?"

"She was a fiend." Gum Drop made an audible sound sucking air in through her teeth. "Just like me."

She reached between my legs. I swiped her hand away.

"Where did she stay?"

"On her back."

"Don't toy with me."

I grabbed the back of her hair and pulled it tight. Gum Drop didn't blanch. She fought against it so I'd pull harder. *Paradise City* ended. I let loose of her hair. Blondie collected her tips and stomped on the stage to signal the next performer. Gum Drop gave my lap one last grind and pushed up off of me.

"I want another dance," I said, putting another twenty in her hand. "And straight answers."

The next dancer featured was the sloppy-titted one. She got the jukebox going and Gum Drop picked up where she left off.

"Tell me where she stayed."

"She bounced around with whoever fuck her, stuck her, and fed her."

"Who was the last person to do that?"

Gum Drop shook her head and looked away from me. She knew the answer and was thinking over whether or not to give it up.

"La-di-da, you sure you want to travel down this road, baby? It's a one way street."

"I asked the question, didn't I?"

Her eyes got serious. Everything else on her body stayed loose.

"You're getting involved in a game I'm not sure you're ready to play. This ain't like no cheating fools. This is some living or dying shit."

"Sounds dramatic."

"It is."

"I've got nothing better to do."

"I don't really know for sure. Girl couldn't keep her pussy in her pants, but last shift I worked with her she left with a guy named Tremaine."

"Tremaine what?"

"Tremaine Miller."

"I know that name," I muttered, more to myself. "I know that name."

She traced the contours of my face with the long nail on her middle finger. Then it came to me—the kid, his fake ID.

"You tell the police this?"

"Do I look a fool to you?"

"You told me."

"You ain't the police."

"True."

She lost the baby voice. "I can trust you, right?"

"Haven't you always?"

"This is different."

"Where does Tremaine live?"

"I don't know that one and I don't wanna know."

"Where does Trisha get her drugs?"

"Same place. A lot of the girls here score from Tremaine."

"They probably don't know where he lives either, do they?"

She closed her eyes, clasped her hands behinds my neck, arched back and emitted a low moan.

"Do you score from Tremaine?"

"I don't do that shit, honey. I've got kids."

"Good for you. He sleeping with any of these other girls?"

"Not that I know of. But look around, would you sleep with them?"

"Only you, sweetheart."

"Why don't you take me in the back room and sample this pussy? I wasn't playing earlier. I can feel that nice cock under them pants and you're kind of hot, in that damaged sort of way."

She winked.

"Well, there's no accounting for taste."

She laughed.

"You're funny."

"Not really. What I have to offer, Aisha, you don't want."

Her eyes widened. She liked that I knew her real name.

"How do you know what I want?"

The song on the jukebox was winding down. The college kids and the pervert applauded the sloppy-titted dancer as she scooped up the four dollars they left her onstage. Gum Drop tapped the tip of my nose with her forefinger.

"The offer is on the table."

"How many guys get that offer?"

"You're the first tonight."

"I'm flattered. Did Trisha have any regulars that came to see her?"

"Look around, honey."

I glanced around the place to placate her. Two of the strippers had a hold of the college kids' belts and were leading them through a beaded curtain into the backroom.

"What about the Hinkle kid, he ever show up?"

"Norman?"

"Yeah, Norman."

"Norman came in now and again whenever he got fuck-hungry."

"He give her drugs, too?"

"I'm sure."

The song ended and was followed by the hollow thud of another stomp on stage. Next girl up.

"Game's over."

"Anything else I might need to know?"

"I didn't hang out with the girl," she said, slipping her top over her head. "She wasn't a bad dancer."

"Thanks, Aisha."

"Any time, Slick Nick," she cooed. "Any time."

Aisha pinched my cheek and lifted off of me. I downed my drink, set the empty glass on the table and got to my feet. My legs were stiff and bloodless from having had her weight on me. I shook them a little to get them tingling.

"Come back and see me sometime," Gum Drop said.

She pivoted on her heels, whipped that weave in my face, and stalked away without ceremony. No looking back.

CHAPTER SEVEN
THE SHALLOWS

I was three gulps into my second drink at The Red Head, watching a few locals play shuffleboard, when I got the call from Hale. I stepped outside to take it.

"Found her," he said.

"Where?"

"The river. You don't need to come."

"I'm coming."

The entrance at the floodwall was cordoned off so I parked the Skylark across the street at the post office lot, walked over the train tracks, ducked under the yellow tape and was approached by two young uni's I didn't recognize, a man and a woman.

"Crime scene, can't come in here, sir," the woman said.

"They know I'm coming."

The man put a stiff hand into my chest that stopped me.

"Who are you?"

"Malick."

"We can't let anyone past here without clearance."

"I'm cleared. Radio your boss."

They got on the horn, confirmed my clearance, mumbled an apology and pointed me in the direction of the crime scene.

At the far reach of the parking lot were half-a-dozen squad cars and two tech vans, all sitting empty. Beside the tech vans was an ambulance where two EMT's were lowering a gurney from the back hatch. Midway down the hill between the floodwall and the river was a paved walkway. I started down it. A series of lamps illuminated the path. Every other lamp was defective leaving large gaps of black between the cones of light. The river, high from the rains, glistened with movement but was noiseless. The only sounds to be heard were my footsteps on the pavement and the hard air flowing in and out of my lungs.

I moved in and out of the shadowed gaps and cones of light, passing an empty playground, an amphitheater, the docks, and an old barge that used to house a decent restaurant called Cheeky's. Fifty yards beyond the barge the walkway came to an end at a long, open field. I stood beneath the last lamp and gazed into the cool black expanse of the field.

Way in the distance was the main bridge into southern Ohio. A lone pair of headlights glided across the bridge and into West Virginia. To the right, down the slope of the hill, was a wooded area silhouetted against the dull glow of the moon. The temperature was dropping by the minute and colder still from the knowledge of what waited on the other side of those woods.

I stepped away from the light and into the field. The grass was high and coated with dew, making the footing slippery. It took a minute for my eyes to acclimate to the dark and find the beaten trail that sloped down through the woods to the river. As I made my way down the trail flashlight beams sliced through the crowd of trees to my left and faint voices became audible. I cut over toward them and as I felt my way through the trees, a sudden cold sweat broke out all over my body. My throat clamped tight and my stomach curdled into a knot. I put my hand against a tree to steady myself and forced a few deep breaths in through my nose and out through my mouth until the hyperventilating subsided and I felt sturdy again. Moving forward, I emerged into a small clearing about twenty yards from the swollen river's edge.

A gray fog hovered above the smooth, rushing water. Hale was away to the side of the scene having an animated conversation with the crime beat reporter, Ernie Ciccone. About twenty other police personnel were milling about. Lit flares were spread over the ground, casting a macabre red glow over the proceedings. I stepped out from the tree line and came upon two uni's who were facing the river. One of them was snickering to the other about how Trisha Cammack was the best-looking corpse he'd ever seen and how he wouldn't mind riding to the morgue with the body.

I looked past them and saw the body. Of all the professionals circling the scene, collecting evidence, snapping photographs, theorizing about crimes and criminals and victims and motives, faces creased with serious and determined scowls, no one was paying any mind to the dead girl splayed out in the middle of it all. She lay on the mud bank of the river, face up, both knees angled to the left, and her toes, pointing down, skimmed the edge of the lapping water.

I went over to her. Her slender body was naked save for a sheer pair of blue underwear. Blue—her favorite color. Her skin held no color; it was the color of ice. On the inside of her left arm fresh track marks covered faded ones. Her right arm was tucked at an awkward angle under her body. Her auburn hair was spread evenly around her head forming a kind of dark halo. One eye was closed. The other was half-open and looked to be staring directly at me.

The asshole uni I passed at the edge of the wood may have been crass, but he wasn't wrong. Trisha Cammack was the prettiest dead girl I had ever seen. Death had yet to distort her striking features. And one thing was certain, she may have been missing for over two weeks, but Trisha Cammack had been deceased for less than twenty-four hours. I gazed down at the corpse of that young girl and thought about all the different paths she could have taken and all the different lives she could have lived. This was the one she got.

A voice beside me said, "Hello, Nick."

No need to look over. I knew who it was.

"Hive."

"Bad business here."

"Indeed," I glanced sidelong his way. "I guess they'll make anybody a detective now."

"What can I say?" The corners of Willis Hively's mouth curled into a somber half-grin. "Slim pickin's out of this lot."

Hive had the nervous habit of working over a pet rock in his hand and he was working it over now as we both puzzled over the body.

"I remember my first homicide. You told me that everybody's story ends in death, but some stories begin there."

"Sounds like something an asshole would say."

Hive chuckled at that.

"How've you been?"

"Putting one foot in front of the other. No more undercover for you I take it."

"Got the family now. Wife was pestering me to go a safer route, you know how it is."

"How are the girls?"

"Ornery as shit. Growing up fast."

"I hear they do that."

"Hale tells me you were working the vic."

I grunted in the affirmative.

"You know her?" I asked.

"No, not this one. After my time."

"Rigor set in?"

"Starting to in the head and neck. She hasn't been gone long. What do you make of it?"

"I'm sure you've already run all the scenarios with the boys. What's the going theory?"

"Drugs. Or a sex thing."

"On the face of it, sure, she had to get naked somehow." I looked down at the body. "But it's a little funny."

"How so?"

"There's no visible wound or abrasions other than the track marks on her arm. No blood, correct?"

"Correct."

"So, for shits and giggles, let's assume it wasn't a sex thing, that it wasn't murder."

"Then we're talking overdose."

"Easy to make the jump. She was a junkie, very possible that's what happened. But why then did somebody go to the trouble of dragging her all the way down to the river to get rid of her? Plenty of places to dump a body that are easier than this to get to. It's funny."

Hive scratched at his chin with the hand that wasn't working the rock.

"She's with someone who deals or someone who can't afford to be found with a dead body. Makes sense to me."

"Sure, but why not finish the job? You get her all the way down here and you've got her almost to the river, then you have a change of heart. Why?"

Hive shrugged.

"Maybe you lose your nerve."

"Maybe, but that doesn't sing to me. I didn't see any tire tracks in the field. That means, at minimum, you've already dragged a body all the way from the parking lot down the path, across a soggy field and through the woods. That's a long way to go only to lose your nerve at the finish line."

"So what sings?"

"I'll know it when I hear it, but not that." I gestured toward the shoreline. "This is the best spot for fifty miles in either direction to get rid of a body."

"How do you figure?"

"You put a body in this river anywhere else it's going to surface somewhere. Maybe close, maybe a dozen miles away, but it's going to come up. But you walk a body out and let go of it at the edge of these shallows, that body is going to float a hundred yards downriver to a spot where the crosscurrent is so strong, sucks a body down to where it ain't never coming up."

Hive arched his eyebrows.

"I didn't know that."

"I don't think too many people do. But you knew not to swim here growing up, didn't you?"

"Only redneck kids swam in here. Black folk are smart enough not to put a toe in this nasty-ass river. We go to the public pool. Like civilized people."

"Fair enough. But I bet every little redneck kid knows where the swimming holes are, and this isn't one of them."

"How do you know about it?"

"Jake was found upriver, not too far from here."

"Aw shit, Nick. I'm sorry," Hive said, shaking his head to scold himself. "I wasn't thinking."

"Forget it."

"No, for real, forgive me."

"Forgotten is forgiven. Now listen, point is, it'd be an awful big coincidence if she was brought here by someone who didn't intend to put her in that crosscurrent."

"Coincidences sometimes happen."

"Maybe, but you can't investigate a coincidence."

"Then it would have to be somebody who knew the river."

Hive looked down at the rock in his hands and folded his lips behind his teeth. While he organized his thoughts

I watched a barge hauling a pyramid of coal float by and sound its foghorn.

"That rules out anyone from Detroit," Hive said. "Have to be a local."

"Maybe, maybe not. Could be more than one person. Can't be easy to carry a body all that way. Even a little body."

Hive frowned.

"No drag marks. One pair of boot tracks leading to the body and walking away. Big ones, size thirteen. You don't think it was murder?"

"Could be. Sloppy finish if it is."

"Most murders are sloppy."

"Not the fun ones." I pointed a thumb up the slope, "You rouse the bums that sleep against the floodwall?"

"Three up there when we arrived. Questioned them, none of them saw anything. One admitted to hearing a vehicle come and then go, but says he didn't even peek out from beneath his blanket."

"Who found her?"

"Man out for a late rendezvous with his mistress on his pontoon boat. Woman insisted they call it in."

Hale snuck up behind us and must have overheard our discussion. His thick hand clapped my shoulder and lingered there.

"Two things in this world that make a man fuck up," he smiled jubilantly, "Money and pussy."

Hale seemed recovered from the pessimism that consumed him earlier at The Red Head. For some people, having a dead body dropped into the mix invigorates them, cleanses the palate. I glanced past Hale's shoulder and noticed Ciccone, the reporter Hale had been chatting up, slinking away into the trees by the path.

Hale said, "Told you she'd turn up."

"You're a regular prophet."

"When I'm right, I'm right. Sorry it ended this way for you though," he said, sounding anything but sorry.

I shucked his husky paw off my shoulder. My feet were suctioned to the mud. I grabbed my thigh to yank them free and turned to face Hale.

Hale's expression turned smug.

"So much for Mr. Cammack's great last hope. I guess this is the end of the line for you on this one, Slick."

"Don't look so heartbroken."

"Say, you get around to questioning Aisha Bryant yet?"

"Earlier tonight."

"She good for anything?"

"I'm sure she is, but nothing to do with this," I lied.

Hale made a clucking sound with his cheek.

"That's a shame. I was hoping you had a lead for us. We'll just have to rush the autopsy and the tox report and see what was floating around in this little girl's blood."

"What then?"

"We trawl the pond, see whoever's moving a similar product and hone in on them. We'll get 'em."

"I won't hold my breath. Do me a favor and keep me posted on your findings. I'm sure the Cammacks are going to want to know what did her in."

"We'll take care of the Cammacks," Hale said.

"The last person they want to see is you. Besides, I want to get to them before they read the morning paper."

"This isn't going to make the paper."

This information slipped from his mouth. If he could have caught the words as they escaped and stuffed them back in he would have.

"Why not? I just saw Ciccone. They don't go to press for another hour."

I looked over at Hively but he kept his face neutral and gave nothing away.

Hale said, "Ernie is doing me a favor, holding off for a day or two. We'll see if anybody slips up, knows she's dead before the rest of the world. Besides, we don't want to get the whole town worked up over one dead girl."

"Of course not," I said, with an extra dollop of sarcasm. "God forbid people know what's really going on. It may cause mass hysteria. Let's wait 'til the bodies start piling up."

Hale's left eye twitched but he kept his smile carved tight.

I said, "Get a tarp or a partition over here. Don't leave her on display. And let me handle the parents."

"Sure, Nick," Hale said, "Sure, you handle the parents. One less thing for us."

CHAPTER EIGHT
THIRSTY GRIEVERS

On my way back to my car the sky closed up and it began to sleet. The two uni's keeping watch at the floodwall were nowhere to be seen, having taken cover somewhere under a tree or in one of the cruisers. I dipped under the crime scene tape and hustled across the street to the post office lot and got into my car. There, I sat behind the wheel listening to the sleet pelt the roof and windshield and hood and I thought about Trisha Cammack's body lying bare in the mud, pummeled by jagged little spits of ice. This is life.

I drove back under the viaduct into the Southside and turned west on Twelfth Avenue. Thunder clapped overhead. Streaks of lightning animated the desolate West End. If Cain City was an afterthought to the world at large, then the West End was the afterthought of Cain City. The potholes on this side of town were bigger, the grass browner. There were as many cars parked haphazardly in yards as there were on the streets. A bunch of lawns were littered with plastic snowmen and reindeer, left over from Christmas, battered and dirty from being displayed for months on end. One lawn had a whole damn nativity set still out.

At three-fifteen in the morning, I parked out front of the Cammacks' house and cut the engine. Their lot was one of the better-kept in the neighborhood, adorned with a single manicured bush. At six-forty-seven the storm broke and the orange of the sun bled over the horizon. At seven-thirty a light shone in the corner window on the second floor of the house. I gave them a few minutes, then, at seven-fifty, rang the buzzer.

Mrs. Cammack, a freckled little woman with pinched features and orange hair, opened the inner door inward, the screen door outward, and greeted me with a polite expression despite her obvious wariness and confusion as to who I might be.

I removed my hat and said, "Hello, Mrs. Cammack. I'm Nick Malick."

Mrs. Cammack clutched her robe together over her chest. For an instant she seemed perplexed, then startled, saying, "Yes, yes," holding the door open for me. "Come in."

My shoes were caked with mud from the river so I removed them on the porch before I entered the house. The front room was tidy. Clusters of framed pictures, mostly of Trisha at various ages, filled the space on the walls, tables, and mantle. A glass cabinet against the far wall displayed a sizeable collection of Hummel figurines.

"You must want to speak to my husband."

She called out for Joe once and, after clearing her throat, a second time. He grumbled a response from somewhere in the bowels of the house.

"Mr. Malick is here to see you," she hollered.

Mrs. Cammack offered me a glass of water, which I declined. We stood silently until Joe Cammack materialized in the doorway that led into the kitchen. He was rubbing the palms of his hands on the front of his jeans in an effort to dry them.

"Mr. Malick, welcome to our home."

He lurched at me and seized my right hand in his damp one, jerked it up and down and dropped it.

"I have some news for you," I said. "May we sit?"

Both their eyes alighted and they traded glances with one another.

"Certainly," Mrs. Cammack said, making rapid conflicting gestures with her hands like she needed to move but didn't know where to go. Cammack wrapped his arm around her shoulders and guided her to a floral couch against the wall. I crouched on the edge of the matching ottoman to the side of them.

There is no way to give this news and no way to take it, so I just gave it.

"I'm sorry. Your daughter was found deceased early this morning down by the river."

"She's dead?" Mrs. Cammack asked, needing to hear it twice.

"Yes, ma'am."

They were both as still as statues to start, but then Mrs. Cammack's lips began to quiver and the quivering spread to her limbs on out to her hands. Her breathing went fast and shallow. Her mouth opened up to scream but the sound was delayed coming out. When it did come, it was terrible and swallowed the whole room. Joe Cammack held her tight to stop her shaking. Her body went limp and slid through his arms to the floor where she became wedged between the couch and the coffee table. Cammack lowered himself down behind her, stroked her hair and made shushing noises in her ear. I looked away from them.

After a time her sobs ceased and her shallow breathing evened out. Her chin was tucked down against her chest and her hair lay draped over her face. When she finally spoke her words were clear and deliberate.

"Joe, will you get me a glass of water? My mouth is dry."

With the words her hair billowed out like a curtain in the breeze.

"Sure, sure," Cammack said, getting to his feet. When he was gone from the room, Mrs. Cammack parted her hair to get it out of her eyes and gazed at me as if I might not be real but imagined.

"I knew it," she said thinly.

Joe hustled in with a glass of water and put it in her hands. She coughed up the first sip. A second sip held.

"What happened?" Cammack asked me.

"Maybe I should talk to you in a different room."

"I want to hear," Mrs. Cammack insisted. Joe gestured for me to proceed.

"We're not sure yet. Could be murder, could be an overdose. Could be both."

"Both? How could it be both?"

"No," Mrs. Cammack pled with her husband. "No, she said she didn't do drugs anymore. She said she was done with those ways."

Cammack hoisted her to her feet.

"Let's lay you down in the bed, okay?"

Mrs. Cammack didn't protest. Joe shuffled her into the deep part of the house. When he returned he had a drink in each hand and handed one over. He looked steadier and calmer than I'd seen him to this point. The rum was of the cheap, fruit-flavored variety. I nipped on it to be polite.

"Thank you for finding my baby."

"I didn't have much to do with it."

"So, you're done now?"

"I am. I wish there was a different ending. I'm very sorry for what you're having to go through."

"So am I, Mr. Malick, so am I. I can't—" His sentence trailed off. "You deal with this sort of business all the time, death, dead people."

"Every now and again."

"Probably numb to it, ain't ya? Probably lost count of all the dead people you seen, can just wash it right out your mind."

"I should be going."

I set my glass down on the end table and stood. Cammack stood with me.

"Tell me, do you think I'm a bad father?"

"I have no idea what kind of father you were."

"Of course not."

I reached the door, every instinct in me begging to walk right through it without so much as a glance back; go home, sleep for three days, and never again think of this house with the thick air of loss and anguish, the Hummel figurine collection and the single puny bush on the lawn. But my feet didn't obey the commands from my head.

I turned and faced Cammack.

"Sometimes things happen. You could have been the worst father in the world or the best one, and it may not have mattered. You can't live their lives for them. All you can do is your damnedest to protect them, but you can only do so much. And then sometimes we fail. It may not even be our fault, but we still fail."

"I did do my damnedest."

"I believe you."

I pulled open the door. Cammack rushed toward me and pushed it shut.

"I have to go now, Mr. Cammack."

"No, please," Cammack panted. "I need to ask you a favor."

I dropped my head and looked at the top of my socks and silently cursed my feet.

"What is it?"

"I want whoever did this to my daughter to be punished. I want them found and I want them punished. Will you help me do that?"

"That's police work, Joe. That's not what I do."

"You and me both know that my girl don't mean nothing to those police, just some low-life trash junkie. They may go through the motions, sure, but in the end, *pfftt*, they just gonna let it drop."

He had me there.

"What if she wasn't murdered?" I offered.

"She was murdered. One way or the other, somebody did this to her. If I could find 'em myself, and thought my wife would be okay, I would stop them breathing with my own two hands."

Cammack shook two clawed fists in front of his face.

"Now, I ain't got no money right now, you know that, but I can go around and raise some more, and I get paid at the end of next week. You can have my whole check, I don't care. Just help me find who did this to my baby."

I looked at Cammack and shook my head.

"Nothing you do is going to bring her back. Nothing you do will ever make you feel better about her being gone. Whatever satisfaction you think you'll get from revenge or whatever you have in mind, you're wrong. It's meaningless."

"Why don't you leave that for me to decide? Please, Mr. Malick, I know you're a good man."

"No, I'm not."

"Yes, you are. Whoever did this can't never be allowed to do it again. If you was a father, you would understand. Please, help me find them. Please."

I felt like punching him in the face and afterwards punching myself in the face. Telling him, I *was* a father you prick fuck. Instead, I said, "I'll tell you what, I'll dig around a little bit and see what I can see, but I can't promise you anything."

"I'll pay you as soon as I can."

"I don't want your money. I told you, this is not me taking on your case. No promises. I'll see what I can see and I'll let you know. If I do find anything we can figure out the money part then."

"Thank you," Cammack gushed. "This means everything to me."

"Yeah, yeah."

Back in the Skylark, I slammed the door shut and punched the steering column four or five times until one of my knuckles split. Finished with that, I started her up, drove home, tossed my muddy shoes in the sink, and lay there on the bed until my brain shut the hell up and I went to sleep.

CHAPTER NINE
SPILT MILK

At two p.m. I went outside to see if the kid was out there panhandling for condoms and beer. He wasn't. He wasn't loitering around down by The Red Head or the gas station either. I went back into the high school up to the second floor apartments and commenced to knocking on doors.

None of the five people who answered their doors knew who I was talking about when I described a short kid, all limbs, twelve or thirteen years old, always bouncing balls off the front of the building and generally being a nuisance. One of the more prudent residents questioned what I wanted with a boy that age before they dismissed me.

At the foot of one door was a pile of newspapers, still rolled. I removed the rubber band from that morning's paper and thumbed through it looking for anything on Trisha Cammack's body being discovered. Nothing doing.

Up on the third floor, I amended my description to include the Cincinnati Reds baseball cap the kid sported. Still that got me nowhere until I reached the third to last door. An old man told me it sounded like the kid who lived at the end of the hall in apartment 312. He didn't know the kid's name. I thanked him, bypassed the next apartment, thumped on the door to 312 and stood aside so the kid wouldn't be able to spy me through the peephole.

A television blared from within the apartment. A moment later the door came open and the kid poked his head out. Seeing me standing there, he hurried to slam it shut. I lowered my shoulder to stop the door from closing and the rebound bounced the kid off his feet back onto a small coffee table. One of the legs buckled and the kid tumbled over the table onto the floor, spilling a bowl of Lucky Charms all over him. I stood in the open doorway and watched the kid scramble to his feet. The crotch of his pants was soaked with milk.

His face flushed with anger or embarrassment or both.

"What the hell are you doing?" he yelled. "Get up out my house, dog."

"Where's your mother?"

"I swear to God I'll call the cops if you don't get out of here."

I stepped toward the kid. He cowered. I grabbed him by his arm and jerked him toward me.

"You listen to me, kid. I'm not here to play with you. Do you have a mother?"

"What? Yeah, I got a mother."

"Where is she?"

"Where she always is, damn."

He wiggled to get away from me so I gripped him harder.

"Ouch, man, what's your problem?"

"I'm not fucking around. I have a couple of questions to ask you and you're gonna answer them. Now I'll let go of you if you'll be cool. Are you gonna be cool?"

"Yeah, whatever."

"Come again?"

"I'll be cool, I'll be cool."

I shoved him back onto the couch. He huffed and flared his nostrils to let me know he was pissed, but he wouldn't meet my eyes. He just stared at my chest like he wanted to bore a hole through it.

"What's your problem?" I asked him.

"I thought you were supposed to steer clear of me and I was supposed to steer clear of you. Ain't that what you said?"

"That's over with. Turn that TV off."

Some music video was grating my ears. The kid picked up the remote and aimed it at me.

"You're in the way," he said. I stepped aside and he flicked the TV off.

"Where's that ID you used at the bar yesterday?"

"In my other pants," he mumbled.

"Speak up."

"In. My. Other. Pants."

"Where are they?"

The kid pointed to a pair of jeans atop of a pile of clothes across the room. I jammed my hand into the pants pockets and rooted through the collection of shit he had in there: a rabbit's foot, loose Skittles, a school hall pass, library card, half a roll of Rolo's, some nickels and pennies, a crunched up cigarette. I found Tremaine Miller's ID and tossed the other garbage on the floor.

The address listed on the license was Block C, number 114, Malcolm Terrace Housing Projects.

I held the ID up for the kid to see.

"Where did you get this?"

"Suck my dick, bitch," the kid spat.

I stepped toward him. The kid jumped sideways to the far end of the couch.

"All right, all right, I'll tell you, damn."

The kid waited to make sure I wasn't coming at him. Then he continued.

"I swiped it down at the gas station. Tremaine was paying for his gas and some beer and shit and the dude behind the counter asked to see his ID. Tremaine handed it over and while the dude was scoping it out Tremaine started throwing down some game to this fine honey that was in line behind us and he kind of forgot about the ID. So when the dude slid it back across the counter, Tremaine didn't see it. He just grabbed his bags and left. But I saw it, and I swiped it. You happy?"

"Ecstatic. What are you doing hanging around with him?"

"Nothing, man. Tremaine's cool, he'll hook me up from time to time."

"Hook you up with what?"

"Not what you're thinking. I don't do that stuff. He tried to sell me some shit at first, but I told him I didn't have any money, so then he just gave me some for free, but I'm not stupid. I knew what he was doing. He thought if I liked it, then I'd find a way to get money to buy it. But I ain't playin' that. I seen them dudes."

"What did you do with it?"

"With what?"

"The stuff he gave you."

"Oh, nothing. I asked some homeless dude if he wanted it and gave it to him."

"What was it?"

"Crank, I guess."

"You didn't take it?"

"Naw."

"You didn't sell it?"

"Naw."

"What else does Tremaine hook you up with?"

"He's cool, you know."

"Yeah, he's the coolest."

"Once he figured out I was too smart for his game, he told me he liked me. He would ask me what I wanted and he would get it for me. Like Milk Duds, Sprees, shit like that. Nothing serious."

"He ever try to get you to sell in your school?"

The kid shook his head.

"Naw."

I gestured to the driver's license.

"Is this where he lives?"

"How should I know?"

"You know how to get a hold of him, a phone number, something like that?"

"Naw. I just know it from the gas station, that's it."

"You leaving anything out?"

"That's it."

"Don't lie to me, kid. If I find out you're lying to me, I'm coming back."

"Whatever, I'm not scared of you."

I pocketed the ID.

"What's your name, kid?"

"What's yours?"

"Nick Malick."

"Davey Huckabee."

"Change your pants, Davey Huckabee. You look like you pissed yourself."

The kid got red. Once I was out in the hallway and there was a nice sturdy locked door between us, he had some choice words for me.

CHAPTER TEN
TRIGGER FINGERS

The Malcolm Terrace Housing Projects were squeezed into a spit of land on the east side of town between the hospital and the railroad track. It was comprised of twenty-eight housing blocks that were laid out in squares, eight units to a block, half of which faced the street. The other half opened to the interior courtyard.

Unit 114 of Block C opened to the interior courtyard, but it was at the end of the building so a walkway between courtyards provided a clean view of Tremaine's doorway from where I was parked on Clifford Avenue. In the hour that I sat there eating hot dogs, swilling coffee and watching his door, seven people came and went, none of them staying more than a couple minutes. Three of the seven I recognized: a dentist named Garvey who once filled a cavity in one of my molars; a car salesman I knew from local advertisements; and a woman who worked the desk at the YMCA. Anybody could tell you the woman was on the junk, but Garvey and the car salesman were both curious revelations. Twice, Tremaine popped his head out the door to smoke a cigarette and have a look around. He was doing just that when my phone vibrated in my pocket. It was Willis Hively.

He said, "Pathologist just finished the preliminary autopsy. Thought you might like to hear. Nothing conclusive as to whether she was murdered, no visible external or internal trauma, nothing obvious under the fingernails. She did have blood in her lungs. That, coupled with some fresh needle marks, has the pathologist thinking heroin overdose. We've seen a lot of those lately. There's a new brand on the street, calling it Motor Seventy-Five. Name stems from the Motor City combined with the interstate they travel to get here."

"Practical."

"Yeah. Just starting to pop up on our radar, which means it's been in circulation for months. There was an overdose last week, some waiter down at Easy Earl's Barbeque, same thing, blood in the lungs. That's what he had in his system. There'll be more. People round here are used to shooting a certain amount and most of them aren't smart enough to ease back the dosage. Who knows how many are gonna croak before it's over."

"Thanks, Hive. Let me know if anything else works its way to the surface."

"You still working this?"

Tremaine flicked his cigarette into the grass and went back inside his place.

"I might poke around a little if that's all right with you, see what I can stir up."

"Fine by me. Hale seemed to think you'd be done with it after last night."

"Him and me both. But what the fuck, I don't have anything else better to do."

"One other thing, Nick. They found semen in her from three different sources."

"Three? Jesus."

"Two different people had vaginal sex with her. A third just oral. Some small abrasions, but nothing to indicate rape. Thought you should know in case you walk into anything."

"They running DNA on the semen?"

"You know how it is. Nothing right now points to foul play. That changes, they'll run the samples. Until then, it'll get buried in the backlog like everything else. Hey, if you're going to be seeing this Cammack thing through, how about we play a little you show me yours, I'll show you mine?"

"Why not. One more thing—I know it's not in the papers, but anybody know she's dead yet? The information made public or on the street?"

"Not yet. We're keeping it in whispers for now. If we can't get anywhere, the word will be out there in the next day or so anyway. We'll see what shakes loose."

I hung up. Paying Tremaine Miller a visit seemed like a popular thing to do so I got out of my car, crossed traffic, and strolled casually between the buildings and across the courtyard. As I walked I thought about how to play it; what lies to tell, how to tell them, and how to keep track of them.

From the vantage of my car, it didn't seem as if any of Tremaine's visitors had used any special knock or code word to gain entry. I pressed the buzzer and stepped back from the stoop. On a porch adjacent to Tremaine's, a craggy old lady sporting a helmet of gray hair, a milky eye, and lips tucked tightly in her mouth, stared at me as she pitched back and forth in a wood rocker. Nobody but her was around. Tremaine's inner door was ajar, but his screen door was thick with dust and lint making it difficult to see inside. Some shapes in the back of the place started moving and the outline of a figure emerged as it approached the door.

Tremaine, fatter and balder than his license picture, unlatched the screen and flung it open. He wore a gray sweat suit, a gold tooth, and a deep scowl that made him look like he had just taken a shot of vinegar. He said, "Who you?"

I affected the manner of a jovial, well-meaning doofus. "Are you Mr. Miller?"

Tremaine looked me over and repeated, "Who you?"

"My name is Nick Malick. I was hired by the family of a missing girl to try and find her whereabouts. Do you know a girl named Trisha Cammack?"

"Naw, I don't know nobody by that name. Get the fuck outta here."

"Please, Mr. Miller. Your phone number was in her phone records numerous times. I'm not here to cause trouble for anyone. I'm just here to try and find Trisha Cammack and get her home safe and sound to her folks."

"What'd I just tell you?"

"I understand that, but there has to be a reason she called your phone. Maybe it was by mistake or maybe she thought you were someone else. Maybe she was interested in you and tracked down your number—I don't know. Whatever the reason, I just need to ask you a couple of questions in case it could help us find her. We have to try everything, you understand. We're tracking down everybody she made phone calls to in the last two weeks. You might have some information that you don't even realize could lead me in her direction. Please, if I may come in, I won't take too much of your time and the family would be truly grateful. They're very worried about their daughter."

"You can't come in here."

"Then how about we go somewhere and talk," I grinned. "I'll buy you a cup of coffee."

"Get the fuck outta here."

"Mr. Miller, if—"

"Don't you listen?"

Tremaine stepped down from the stoop and right into me where I could smell the funk of his breath and see the murky yellow of his eyes. I let him stay there and even slumped a little to give him the confidence of power.

"I said I don't know no girl by that name. You best be getting the fuck up outta here before I fuck your little white ass up."

I raised my hands passively.

"I'm just doing my job, Mr. Miller. If you don't answer a few questions from me, my agency will just keep sending people here until you do answer them. That's a hassle for everyone."

Tremaine's lips stretched tight over his teeth.

"You gotta be kidding me with this shit."

"It's just a few questions to see if we can glean any information from you that could be useful in tracking her down. After I'm done, I cross you off a list and no one else will bother you, I promise."

"Cross me off now."

"Now, I can't do that. Oh, I almost forgot. There's also a reward if what you tell me leads us to find Trisha."

"How much?"

"Five thousand dollars."

"Man, that ain't shit."

"Please, if I may come in, I promise not to take too much of your time."

Tremaine growled, "You've already taken too much of my time." He glanced around the courtyard and then fixed his yellow eyes back on me. "Why can't you ask me what you got to ask me right here?"

"That'd be fine for me. However, it may take a few minutes and I thought we'd make it as pleasant as possible by sitting down and just having a discussion. As I said, I'm more than willing to go somewhere and buy you a cup of coffee."

Tremaine sneered, "I don't want no goddamned coffee."

"I also wouldn't want anybody to hear what it is that we're discussing." I nodded toward the old woman on the stoop. "It is a bit sensitive."

Tremaine glanced at the woman, smacked his lips together and flicked a finger toward the apartment.

"We can talk in the kitchen."

The front room of the unit was sparse; a futon, lamp that sat on the floor, recliner, an unframed *New Jack City* movie poster hanging on one wall and an eighty-four inch hi-def television mounted to the other wall, hooked up to a PlayStation. Stacks of DVD's were in the corner. Tattered gray carpet covered the floor. A thin hallway led to the back of the unit. If anyone else was in there they weren't visible from the entrance.

Tremaine led me to the adjoining kitchen where there was a fold-out table in the middle of the linoleum floor along with three folding chairs. I sat in one of the chairs. As Tremaine moved around the table to take the seat across from me, I caught sight of the square bulge under his sweatshirt at the base of his spine.

Tremaine said, "Yo, ask what you got to ask. Let's get this thing started so we can get it over with."

"Of course. I apologize for the intrusion. Now, you say you don't know anybody by the name of Trisha Cammack, yet your phone number is all over her records. I'm sure there's an explanation, Mr. Miller, I just need you to tell me what it is."

"I don't know what you want me to tell you. I don't know the bitch."

"Maybe you run in the same circles? One of your friends may know her. It could be as simple as that. I'll show you a picture."

I took the picture her father had given me from my pocket and placed it in front of Tremaine. He picked it up and stared at it for a long time. Swift thinking must not have been his strong suit.

"You know what?" he said, looking up. "I have seen this bitch. I think she hangs out with a homie I know."

"That's great. I'm gonna need his name."

Tremaine put on a sly grin.

"I don't know him that well really. People call him Cupcake. I see him around here and there. She's always with him."

"Do you know his real name?"

"Naw."

"Do you know why they call him Cupcake?"

"You should ask him."

"That's okay. That's more information than I've gotten from anyone else. When's the last time you saw Trisha in the flesh?"

"Maybe a week ago. Saw her at a party down around the way. Her and Cupcake."

"You ever talk to her?"

"Girl that fine, yeah, I hollered at her a little bit."

Tremaine was starting to get rolling into his story now. I let my face light up.

"That must be where she got your number then. That makes sense."

"Yeah, that's right. I remember now. I'd forgotten her name though. She's been calling me a bunch, but you know, I don't fuck with another man's girl."

"You talked to her on the phone?"

"Like I said. That's Cupcake's girl. I don't fuck with that. But you know, we talked a little bit."

Tremaine handed the photograph of Trisha back to me.

"Fantastic," I beamed. "Do you remember what you talked about?"

"Nothing, really. Just talking like a man and a woman talk, you know."

"Did you get a sense like she was gonna leave town for a little while or anything like that?"

Tremaine's lower lip jut out and he shook his head.

"Naw."

"You've been a tremendous help. Now, I'm just gonna go over a few other facts that we know about Trisha and see if they match up with what you know about her. Then I'll get out of your hair. If you have anything to add, please do."

I fished out a steno pad that I kept stashed in the inside pocket of my coat, removed the short pencil from its binding and pretended to analyze a list of facts on the blank first page.

"Trisha Cammack worked at the Midnight Run as a stripper, is that correct?"

"Yeah, that's right."

I made a checkmark next to nothing.

"She lived alone in an apartment downtown on Third Avenue and Twelfth Street?"

"I don't know where the bitch lives."

"Ever seen her dance at the Midnight Run?"

"Couldn't tell you."

"All right." I scribbled on the notepad. "She was a drug addict and had recently started using a potent form of heroin with the street name Motor Seventy-Five."

"I don't know nothing about that."

"That wasn't a question. I know that's true."

Tremaine's expression didn't change, but his hands, lying face down on the table, now curled up ever so slowly into fists. A letter was etched on each of his knuckles.

I nodded toward the knuckles.

"What does that spell?"

"What does what spell?"

"On your hands there, what does that spell?"

Tremaine brought his two fists together to let me read the tattooed words:

C-A-S-H C-I-T-Y

"That have a special meaning?"

"You could say that."

I jotted "Cash City" on the notepad.

"You say she was dating a guy named Cupcake?"

"That's what I said."

"Okay. One more thing," I looked up from the notepad and leveled my black eyes with his yellow ones. "You supplied Trisha Cammack with the drug called Motor Seventy-Five that was the direct cause of her death last night."

"What?" Tremaine stiffened. "I don't know what the fuck you talking about."

"Again, not a question. That one's true, too."

"What else do you know is true motherfucker?"

"I know that you had sex with her last night, most likely before you put the junk in her veins that killed her. Then you dumped her body."

Tremaine's face twisted into that of a coiled and venomous snake, ready to lash out. His nostrils flamed in and out with his breathing as his body tensed for action. Then, all at once, he became controlled. His body relaxed, but his eyes remained violent.

"Is that how you want to play this motherfucker?" Tremaine said.

"I'm playing it, one way or another. Here's the thing I don't get, Tremaine. The other two guys that fucked her last night—now, did she fuck them before or after she fucked you? Or did the three of you just run a train on her and then dispose of her body together?"

Tremaine cocked his head sideways, looking momentarily confused, but then he started to cackle. Apparently, he liked the sound of it, because his cackle sprang an octave higher.

"I could shoot you right now and no one would ever find you, or even care about finding you. You'd just vanish like a puff of motherfuckin' smoke."

"Plenty of people know that I'm here."

"Don't matter. I could tell the whole world it was me who dusted you. No one would touch me. No one would lay one fucking finger on me. You don't have a damn clue. We can do any fucking thing we want to do here. You come in my house like this, like this," he gestured at me with both hands. "And you think you gonna walk out?"

Having observed him lying for the majority of our conversation, I was sure these last words out of his mouth were genuine. He was either thinking about shooting me or already set on doing so and sorting out how to go about it.

"The police might have something to say about that."

"The police? The police?" Tremaine mocked. "Who you think control the police?" His face contorted into a ruthless leer. "You scared now, huh? You know you fucked. You like questions so much, riddle me this motherfucker. What's it like knowing you about to be snuffed out? That this the last face you ever gonna see?"

Way I figured, I had two options. Neither or which seemed too pleasant. One, I could run and likely get shot in the back, or two, go for my gun and risk getting shot in the front.

"You gonna shoot me?" I said, staying very still. Tremaine didn't move either, not visibly, but something in him tensed. The linoleum floor beneath his chair creaked. His hand twitched. I said, "Do it."

In the flicker of a moment, Tremaine reached back and had his pistol in his hand swinging it round toward me. I thrust all my weight forward into the table, crashing it into his sternum. The pistol discharged. The bullet zipped past my left shoulder and plugged into the ceiling.

Tremaine staggered backwards against the sink. I pulled the table back and rammed him again. Air exploded out of him and he folded forward. I vaulted across the table and, drawing my Beretta, cracked the butt of it against his temple. His legs went weak and I cracked him again. Tremaine crumpled to the floor, choking for air.

I jammed a knee into his spine just below his neck, ripped his pistol from him and stuck it into the back of my pants.

"You wanna shoot somebody you son of a bitch?"

I slammed the butt of my gun into Tremaine's trigger finger, hearing it and feeling it crunch against the floor. Tremaine screamed. I grabbed the finger and yanked it sideways and he screamed again.

"Tell me what happened last night."

Tremaine struggled to suck some oxygen in his lungs.

"Fuck you," he panted. "You dead, you dead."

I took hold of his thumb and peeled it back until the ligaments tore loose and the bone dangled free of the socket. Tremaine winced and emitted a pitiful little moan.

"Last night," I said.

"She—she was—she was here."

"And?"

"I fucked her, like you said, but that's—that's it."

"Give me your other hand."

"No, no!"

Tremaine thrashed beneath me and got his left hand tucked under his chest. I kicked him in the ribs. He whimpered and I pried his hand loose, pinning it under my foot.

"Okay, okay, I gave her the drugs. I gave her the drugs, but I didn't kill her. I didn't kill her!"

"Who did?"

"How do I know?"

I separated Tremaine's left trigger finger from his other fingers and reared back to smash it.

"Wait, wait," he bawled. "I swear to God. She was over here for days getting high as a motherfucker. She kept offering to fuck if I kept feeding her the dope. But last night, she was taking too much. She just kept wanting it and wanting it and I finally told her she couldn't have no more. She was shooting up all my shit."

"Then what?"

"She got mad as hell and stormed up outta here. That's it. I didn't even know she was dead, I swear to God. I thought she'd be back round today for more. That's how she be. Relentless after the shit."

"Where'd she go?"

"How the fuck should I know? To get fucked by two other dudes I'm guessing, fucking ho."

"What about this Cupcake? He real?"

"Naw, naw. I was just fucking with you, I swear," Tremaine pleaded.

"Was anyone else here last night?"

"Some clients and shit, but wasn't none of my boys here. Nobody hangin' with me or nothing like that."

"What time did she leave?"

"Bout eight o'clock. Eight or so." He hesitated. "Yeah."

Someone must have heard the gunshot and called it in because an approaching police siren became audible.

"You done did it now," Tremaine said.

I brought the gun butt down on his off-hand trigger finger, wrenched it back at the knuckle and watched him writhe in agony. Then I called Willis Hively.

CHAPTER ELEVEN
PISS AND VINEGAR

By the time the police arrived, I had already frisked the apartment and discovered a trove of heroin, crack, meth, pills, and was waiting on the stoop with Tremaine hog-tied and sprawled across the ground at my feet.

"In the back bedroom," I directed Hive, who had shown up less than two minutes behind the patrolmen. He sent two of the uni's inside and ordered the other two to take Tremaine into custody.

"This some bullshit," Tremaine protested as they hoisted him to his feet. "He attacked me. What you charging me with? This my house. He came up in my house and he attacked me."

"He plant all those drugs, too?" one of the patrolmen remarked.

Tremaine, now sporting three crooked fingers and a golf ball sized welt on his temple, twisted his torso and spat a glob of bloody mucus in my direction. He mouthed the words, 'You're a fucking dead man.'

"You catch that?" I asked Hive as I returned Tremaine's death glare.

Hive shook his head facetiously.

"Seemed like something nasty."

Tremaine turned his attention to Willis Hively.

"Fuck you, little Willie. Fucking traitor."

The patrolmen led Tremaine away.

"You two know each other?"

"Since third grade. Grew up in the same courtyard as him. Vicious fucker, even back then. You should have told me you were having a go at him."

"What good would that have done?"

"I would have warned you off of it. These guys don't play by the rules, Nick. You can't take a run at guys like that on your own."

"I'm still here."

"Yeah. What happened to his fingers?"

"He took a shot at me."

I pulled out Tremaine's pistol and handed it over.

"His gun. Not mine."

"Jesus Christ. What the hell are you doing mixing it up with Tremaine Miller?"

"Heard a rumor that he might be the guy who dealt to Trisha Cammack."

"Was he?"

"One of them anyway. I don't think he killed the girl, but he definitely kept her in the smack and so far he's the last person to see her alive. Had her hopped up for sex off and on for the last couple weeks. Is there anybody involved in this mess goes by the name of Cupcake?"

"I've heard the name. Why?"

"Tremaine tried to point me in his direction when I asked about the girl, but took it back when I got the better of him. Said he just made the name up."

"No, he's real, far as I know. I've never seen him."

"What does 'Cash City' mean?"

Hively frowned.

"Tremaine have the tattoo?"

"Across his knuckles. Nice looking job."

"It's what they've dubbed Cain City. Cash City."

"Cute."

"It's kind of like this Detroit line's version of the made man here. You have the tat, you're in, you're one of them—on your way up. Tremaine must have been a little higher in the chain than I thought."

"You guys knew he was involved?"

Hively nodded.

"We suspected as much, but couldn't pin anything on him. Thought he was low-level."

"I sat in my car for an hour and watched seven people purchase drugs off him."

Hive started to respond but then stopped. He stood there looking forlorn. I could tell he was trying to fit some pieces together in his mind because he had his pet rock out and was working it over.

"Tremaine is local," he said, more to himself, then looked up at me. "I haven't heard of them giving those tats to locals. Usually they keep it to the guys who come down from Detroit."

"Only a couple places in town he could get a tat of that caliber. Check out The Farcyde and Jimmy Jammer's Tattoo Palace, see if anybody else has had one done."

"Yeah, I'll do that." Hive looked down at me and scoffed. "Jesus, Malick, when's the last time you were shot at?"

"Been awhile. Chicago. Where's Bruce?"

"En route."

As if on cue, Hale emerged between buildings, spotted us, and came charging across the courtyard like a bulldog frothing at the mouth.

"Speak of the devil," I said.

"You goddamn bastard," he raved, wagging a finger in my direction. All the blood he owned looked to have pooled in his face. I half expected smoke to puff out from his ears. "Do you have a brain sprain? Do you have any idea what you've just done? There's a reason we don't just barge in and arrest any ol' person we want. This job ain't about piss and vinegar."

Willis Hively stepped into Hale's path to keep him from getting at me.

I said, "No thanks necessary." That stoked Hale's fury good. Hive called another officer over to help keep him at bay.

"There are repercussions," Hale seethed. "You'll see. You'll see you little smartass. You'll see."

Hale screamed and cursed some more eloquence, something to the effect of me being a waste of flesh who turns everything I touch into pure shit. His blustering was amusing for a minute, but when he said that I had been dealt exactly the hand I deserved in life, I considered breaking his face to shut his yapping. Hive got him under control and persuaded him to examine the crime scene inside Tremaine's unit.

Two doors down, the gray-haired old woman rocked away, lips flopped out in a toothless grin. Some of the other residents were outside now, too, delighting at the spectacle. The police coming around was high entertainment, as long as they weren't the ones in trouble.

When it became evident that Hale was not going to have another go at me, Hive said, "I'm gonna need a statement."

I gave him the broad strokes of the thing, putting the sequence of events in order, leaving out the bit Tremaine shared about the Detroit pipeline having the police in their pocket, and we called it official.

"Maybe you should lay low for a while," Hive said to me as I moved to leave.

"Sure."

"Nick," he cautioned. "Lay low for a little while."

I immediately disregarded this advice and went looking for Norman Hinkle. Willis Hively had assumed, mistakenly, that Tremaine Miller was a low-level player. Hale had used the exact same language the day before, "low-level," to describe Hinkle. I suppose his knuckles would tell if that story were true or not.

The number for Hinkle's landscaping business was in the yellow pages. I called it and got an automated out-of-office message. I headed down to the Southside and cruised the avenues and streets, past Hale's house on Twelfth Avenue, Hively's on Ninth, past my old address on Sixth Street. I'd heard the defensive coordinator for the college football team had moved in. The house looked the same, maybe a little nicer. Someone had planted a tree in the front yard and put a new awning over the porch. Out on the lawn a woman, little older than me, mid-forties or thereabouts, was on her hands and knees fooling with some flowerbeds. There was no sign of Hinkle anywhere. The door at his parents' house, his listed residence, went unanswered.

Weighing it all out, I figured that was enough pro bono work for one day. I drove home, parked the Skylark in the corner of the school lot, trekked the two blocks up to The Red Head, had a Maker's, listened to a goofy drunk on the stool next to me jabber on about the evils of modern technology, had another bourbon, fended off the clingy advances of Cara Adkins scamming for a free drink, decided that I didn't want to be around people anymore, paid Tadpole and left.

In the alley between the hot dog stand and the gas station, a mangy orange cat was lapping up murky water from a ditch. It fit the description of the missing cat that loony woman had phoned about. I remembered the name, Lucy, and called it out. The cat stopped its licking. Its eyes darted sidewise as it ducked its head below its hunched shoulders.

"Lucy," I said again. "That you?" The cat raised its neck and appraised me with an alert, guarded expression. I took a couple steps toward it, squatted down and held out my hand. The cat slunk over and circled round my hand and my feet. The cat had tags with its name, Lucifer, and the owner's name and phone number.

I picked her up.

"So Lucy's just a nickname, huh?"

Back in my office, I dropped the cat on the floor and ran some water in a bowl for her. Then I plopped into the chair behind my desk and fixed myself a drink, drank it, and fixed another. The cat explored the nooks and crannies of the place. When she hopped up on the desk I took another look at her tags and dialed the number.

"Hello, this is Nick Malick . . . that's right, the investigator. I've found your cat. I have her here in my office . . . Yes, she's perfectly fine . . . No, I can't bring her to you, but you're welcome to come pick her up anytime . . . Yes, well, I understand . . . thirty bucks will be fine."

A crisp knock sounded on the door.

"No thanks necessary, I'll be around all evening . . . Uh huh, goodbye."

Another sharp knock. I put down the phone, got up and answered the door. Standing in the hallway was a woman, dressed in a Big Tom's grocery uniform, brown slacks and a brown collared shirt. Her nametag, pinned to the right side of her chest, read Karla.

"Can I help you?" I offered.

No inflection in her voice, she said, "Are you Nick Malick?"

"That's right, and you—"

She slapped the shit out of me, catching me flush with the solid part of her palm, knocking my jaw out of whack. I whirled back and started to say, "Who the hell—" but she cut me off before I got any more out.

"I'll tell you who I am," she erupted. "I'm the mother of the little boy you bullied this morning, that you got drunk yesterday. That's who I am. Who do you think you are, coming into my home, picking on a thirteen-year-old boy, pushing him so hard you make him fall and break a table? How dare you? I should call the police right now and have you arrested for assault and for breaking and entering and for plying a minor with so much alcohol that you made him sick all night, puking and dry heaving."

As she squawked, my anger tapered off and I took in the full composition. Her sandy gold hair was pulled back in a careless ponytail, a loose wisp of it trailing across her forehead and down her check. Her voice had a southern lilt that deepened as she got more worked up. The dull work uniform failed to hide the full figure beneath it. Her face was a bunch of mismatched features that should not have fit together: round cheeks and long nose, big bluesy eyes with a pert little slit of a mouth. She possessed a moody, lived-in quality, the type of woman who had seen some things, things that had taken their toll.

"I don't know if you're a pervert or what you are," she continued. "But you listen to me. Stay away from my son, you hear me? If I catch you anywhere near him again I will not hesitate to get a restraining order and press charges and do whatever I have to do to get you locked the fuck up. Do you understand me? Am I clear?"

I stretched my jaw and felt the bones in there clicking back into alignment.

"Are you through?"

"No. I want the money to replace my table."

"Finished?"

"That depends. Are we clear?"

"Oh, we're clear, lady. You're not exactly mincing words. But before you flounce off on your merry little way thinking you came down here and gave me the business, let me clarify a little something for you. Your runty little angel up there seems to have omitted some essential details from the story."

The muscles in her jaws bulged into little knots and she crossed her arms defiantly over her chest.

"I'm the one trying to stay the hell away from him, not the other way around. He's the irritant, following me all over, coming into the bar after me. And the fake ID he had—yeah, he had a fake ID—belongs to a local drug dealer who's a suspect in a murder that I'm investigating. Your boy stole the ID from him. These are the types of people you should be worried about your son hanging around and emulating, but it seems to me like you're too much of an absentee mother to see what's going on six inches past your nose."

She blanched at this.

"Furthermore, the only reason I entered your apartment was to retrieve the ID from your son and find out how deep he was involved with said dealer. The table got broken because he tried to keep me from getting it so, no, I'm not gonna pay for your goddamned table, and I suggest you learn what's what before you go around slapping people. As for him getting drunk, I didn't feed him anything. He ordered his own drinks. You're lucky if liquor's all he's into."

Off the look in her eyes alone I would have put down money that she'd slap me a second time. Instead, she said, "I don't care what you say. Stay away from my son."

"Gladly."

With that, she stomped off down the hall. I went back into my office, sat at the desk and drank myself into a nice, numb stupor.

CHAPTER TWELVE
ONE BODY, TWO BODY

The rumble of my phone pulled me conscious. I pried my eyes open and lifted my head from the desk. The corners of my mouth were split and raw and my head felt like it had been blended in a juicer. It was still dark outside. The digital projection from my phone read 4:17 a.m. Three missed calls in the last hour, all from Willis Hively. I dialed him back.

When he picked up I said, "What now?"

"Another vic."

He must have been outdoors because an ambient static on the line made it hard to hear him.

"At the river?"

"Downtown."

"Overdose?"

"Not this time. Double tap. One to the chest, one to the head."

"Who is it?"

"Did you meet with a woman named Aisha Bryant two nights ago?"

"Fuck."

"Yeah, fuck. You better come down."

The alley between Fourth and Fifth Avenues was barricaded at both ends of the block by squad cars, lights throwing reds and blues against the rear faces of the buildings. I parked at the bottom of the sloping avenue and walked up. The same two cops who had tried to keep me from Trisha Cammack's crime scene the night before were warding off Ernie Ciccone, the reporter, as well as some stray drunks seeking some late night excitement. A news crew was setting up outside the barricade. The cops recognized me and didn't stop me from slipping past the perimeter.

"Why does he get to go in?" Ciccone whined. "Hey Malick, you know what happened down there?"

"Yeah."

"Can you give me a statement?"

"No."

An EMT truck was parked at a slant in the middle of the alley obscuring any public view. I squeezed past the front fender and surveyed the scene.

Willis Hively was huddled over a pool of blood with two veteran detectives from the Felony Squad, Jerome Kipling and Red Lewis. A string of the blood ran from that main pool to a dumpster where the blood was smeared up the side. Four crime scene techs were scouring the pavement for evidence. The EMT's were loading a gurney into the back of their truck. Beneath the gurney's sheet were the contours of a body.

Leaning against a doorframe on the other side of the alley was a pregnant teenager, pretty far along, chomping on gum and looking generally dissatisfied with everything happening both inside and outside of her. A female uni stood watch next to her. Hively, Jerome, and Red noticed me. We exchanged nods. Hive came over with his shoulders hunched and his hands jammed into his pockets.

"I wish this weather would warm the hell up already," he shivered.

I tipped my head to the gurney.

"Gum Drop?"

Hive nodded.

"The one and only. Far as we can tell, she was shot over by that doorway, dragged to the dumpster where they stuffed her in there face down. Prostitute named"—he flipped through his steno pad—"Katrina Phipps found her, saw the legs jutting out of the dumpster."

I gestured to the teenager.

"Who's the girl?"

"Aisha's daughter."

"Her daughter?"

"She lived in an apartment on the third floor of that building." Hive pointed to a lit window two buildings over. "Had earbuds in, didn't hear the shots, but heard the commotion when the cavalry showed up and came down to check it out. She identified the body."

"Jesus."

"Four more kids up there, ages three to eleven. This one's the oldest. Fourteen."

"Gum Drop had five kids?" I looked again at the pregnant girl. "The dads or any other family around?"

"Don't think so."

"Fuck's sake. She sell her ass, too?"

"Claims she doesn't."

Aisha's daughter's arms were folded atop her round belly. The cold of the night had her nose running and she kept wiping it on the back of her hand. She exhaled as if she were bored and hocked her gum onto the ground. She caught my staring and stared back at me, an exaggerated version, bugging her eyes out, already full of contempt for the world and all its inhabitants.

"Suspects?" I asked.

"Throw a rock." Hive lofted his little pet rock in the air and caught it. "You and me need to have a talk. Follow me over to the Jolly Roger's."

"You finished up here?"

"Yeah. Red and Jerome are the leads on this one. I'm just here because of the connection to our case."

"You mean me."

"Yeah, you."

Jolly Roger's Donuts was one of only a handful of places in town open all night and it was the closest. I followed Hive west on Third Avenue for half a mile, then south a block on Eighth Street. He bought us both coffee and we sat at a small table by the window, me drinking my coffee, him blowing on his to get it cooler. We were the only customers. Outside, the sky had turned from black to a deep blue as night gave way to day. Moisture on the glass blurred our view of the avenue.

"What did Aisha Bryant give you?"

"Tremaine Miller. Told me Trish scored her drugs from him, slept with him."

"That's it?"

"That's it."

Hive winced as he sipped his coffee.

"Nothing else?"

"No." I shook my head. "Nothing."

"You think that's what got her killed?"

I shrugged noncommittally.

"Who knew you talked to her?"

"Nobody. Bruce knew that I talked to her. That's it. Where is Bruce tonight?"

"Didn't want to deal with you. Told me to take it. Wanted me to make sure you understood that this is what he meant by repercussions."

Hive went silent and thoughtful for a bit. The counterman Santos came over and refilled my cup. I looked out the window and listened to the electric drone of the place. A streak of orange yellow slid up over the horizon. Hive shook his head, cocking his mouth sideways.

"Did anyone see you, overhear you talking to her?"

"All anyone saw was me getting a lap dance. She put on a pretty convincing show while we chatted."

"Would she have told anyone?"

"She wasn't dumb. She knew the consequences of being caught snitching."

"Doesn't make a lick of sense." Hive rubbed his eyes. "How could they have tracked her? Maybe she's unrelated, totally different angle."

"You know how I feel about coincidences."

"Yeah, that'd be a big one. She didn't give you anything else?"

"Nothing you didn't already know about."

"Like what?"

"Like the Hinkle kid."

Hive's eyes got big.

"Have you talked to him?"

"Not yet. I'm planning on it."

"From here on out I need to know everybody you're talking to and when you're talking to them. I need total transparency from you."

"I like you, Hive. You know I like you, so I'm going to be honest with you."

"Don't do me any fucking favors."

"I'm going to do what I'm going to do. If it benefits my client to clue you in, I will. If it doesn't, I won't."

Headlights glided across Hive's face from a car turning the corner on the avenue. He stared out the window and followed the car until it was past him. Then he focused back on me and said, "This is serious now, Nick. People are getting killed. People that you talked to are getting killed, more than likely because you talked to them."

"Maybe I'm contagious."

"Jokes? This is how you're going to play it?"

I leaned forward.

"You think I don't realize that body is on me? You think I don't realize the ramifications?"

Hive jammed his finger down on the table.

"I've shared everything I've gotten with you."

"And I appreciate that."

"I expect the same courtesy."

"I'll think about it."

"You'll think about it," Hive repeated. He was getting cranked up now. "I'm the one ally you've got on the whole damn force, Nick. You want that to change? If there's a development in your case, any development, large or small, I need to know about it. I'm not asking you."

"You're not telling me either. Look here." I leaned in and lowered my voice in case Santos was eavesdropping. "I'll share with you what I'm comfortable sharing with you. That's more than anybody else is gonna get from me. If I talk to someone and they give me something that may put them in danger, I'll let you know. If I find something that I think will help you on your end, if it doesn't compromise me, I'll let you know. Otherwise, I'm under no obligation to tell you a goddamn thing. I was hired to do a job and I'm gonna do it however I see fit."

Hive sat back, deflated, started to take a drink of coffee but then set it down and let it be.

"You're a stubborn son of a bitch. Whoever did this could come after you, you know."

"I'm in the Yellow Pages."

This struck Hive unexpectedly and he coughed up a laugh. Santos glanced over at us from behind the counter. I asked, "Did you check out the tattoo parlors?"

"Yeah. Jimmy Jammer's was the place. Head artist that works there, Leonard something—"

"Schaffer."

"He says there's been at least six guys have come in there and gotten the tattoo across their knuckles. Said he would call if anyone else showed up wanting it done. Only name of the six that stuck with him was Tricky."

"Tricky Jackson?"

"You know another Tricky? Also, Tremaine Miller told us the same thing he told you. Admitted to the sex and the drugs, but denied dumping her by the river. Said she was breathing just fine when she left his place."

"And then there were two."

"Two who are in need of some antibiotics. Trisha Cammack had three active STD's and a fungal infection at the time of her death. Chlamydia, syphilis, warts, and thrush."

"Jesus."

"Releasing her body back to her parents today. Unless something else turns up we're calling it an accidental overdose. For now, insufficient evidence to support any other conclusion, homicide or suicide."

CHAPTER THIRTEEN
THERE GOES BREAKFAST

A decade ago, I arrested Tricky Jackson for an armed robbery that sent him to Moundsville on a five-year stint. Since being released he'd held down a job delivering food and kept out of trouble or, more likely, kept the trouble he was involved with out of sight. I liked Tricky well enough and kept tabs on him from time to time so I told Hive to let me track him down and see what there was to see. Hive kidded me not to break any fingers.

When I got back to the office, the cat was seated in my chair behind the desk, tail swaying lazily, as if she had been planted there all morning waiting to show me that there was a new boss in town. I swiped her off the chair and dialed the number from her tags again. A man picked up. I asked for a Mrs. Higginbottom. The man, who identified himself as Mrs. Higginbottom's neighbor, informed me that she had been found dead on the floor of her foyer late the previous evening, wearing a coat and clutching her purse as if to leave the house. I uttered some condolences, explained to him about the cat and that somebody needed to come get her.

"Oh, Lucy," the man said. "What a wonderful cat. She gave Martha so much joy and companionship in her declining years. Martha was very distraught when Lucy went missing. I'm sure she was extremely relieved when she turned up." He gasped suddenly. "I hope the excitement didn't cause her passing. That would be tragic. Such a fine cat."

"You want her she's yours."

The man covered the phone and there was some muffled talk before he got back on the line. In a low conspiratorial voice, he said, "My wife is allergic to dander so adopting the cat is out of the question."

I inquired as to whether there was any family to take her in. He explained that Mrs. Higginbottom was the last of her people.

Politely, I said, "What the hell am I was supposed to do with a dead old lady's cat?" to which he offered no solution. I hung up the phone and stared at the cat, who was stretching and sharpening her claws on my rug like she didn't have a care in the world.

"Well, fuck."

Sifting through my cabinets for something edible and finding nothing, I flopped down on my bed and clicked on the television. The news was starting. Lead story was on a hold-up of the Roll-A-Rama, a roller-skating rink downtown, during a nine-year-old kid's birthday party. Next was a short segment about Gum Drop's body being found jammed into that dumpster. After those came a handful of breezy stories, one on the health benefits of blueberries and another on a new, state-of-the-art teeth-whitening technique being offered by a dentist in town. No mention on the telecast of Trisha Cammack.

The cat hopped up on the bed and I shoved her off. This repeated several times until I just let her stay up there and nuzzle into my chest.

"I can feed you or kill you, which do you prefer?"

The cat looked at me contentedly, knowing an empty threat when she heard one.

After a shower I walked upstairs to the second floor. The stack of unread newspapers was still in front of the one apartment. I plucked today's paper off the pile and took it back downstairs to read. Still nothing there about Trisha Cammack either. The back page had a small blurb about Aisha Bryant being killed, but that was it. Keeping Trisha out of the news for a day, I could justify that, but two days was pushing it. Her funeral arrangements would probably be announced in the next morning's paper. And murders, even working girl murders, usually garnered more than a back-page mention.

This spate of crime either had the powers that be very frightened, or something a little dicier was going on. I brought the Internet up on my phone and scrolled through the *Cain City Dispatch*'s web archives. Plenty of crimes had been reported in the last couple months, robberies, some B and E's, assaults, one homicide that looked to be domestic in nature, a handful of overdoses, but nothing outrageous, nothing to indicate the city's impending demise.

I gathered my things and headed out to purchase some breakfast and cat food. The day was bright and fresh. I stood on the veranda and leaned my head back to catch the sun full on my face. The sky was a clean sheet of blue that felt like an electric blanket casting warmth over a cool day.

The thud of a ball turned my head and I saw the kid, Davey. He saw me too, but refrained from saying anything annoying. He kept on tossing the ball at the wall, a little harder now for my benefit. I walked over to him.

"Aren't you supposed to stay a hundred yards away from me or some shit?" the kid said.

"Aren't you supposed to be in school?"

The kid dropped his head and pocketed the tennis ball. "I guess."

"Relax, I'm not gonna turn your little truant ass in."

Davey eyed me curiously.

"I don't get you, man."

"Yeah, well, join the club. I'm going to get some food. You hungry?"

He mulled over the offer.

"I could eat."

On the way to the gas station the kid chatted me up.

"So you're like a private detective or some shit?"

"That's right."

"That's fucking cool."

"Sounds cooler than it is."

"Maybe I could do that, too."

"You've just about got the brains for it."

The kid bristled.

"What does that mean?"

"Nothing."

"You packing that heat?"

"What do you think?"

"Can I hold it?"

"Sure, let me turn the safety off."

"For real?"

"No."

"Can I touch it?"

"Quit asking stupid questions."

"Man, dang," the kid shook his head. We crossed the street at the light. "Yo, sorry about my moms and all that. She was going nuts and coming at me about the table and everything else and I had to tell her what happened."

"I didn't figure you for a tattler."

"It just came out. I didn't even know what I was sayin'. You don't know what it's like when she comes at you. Shit gets intense."

"I've got a pretty good picture of it," I said, catching myself smiling at the memory of her slapping me. "You get in trouble?"

"She took away my PlayStation, but that's all right. I know where she hides it. And she yelled at me for about ten hours. Then she started crying so that made me feel bad as hell. You kinda ruined my deal telling her I'm hanging out with drug dealers and lady murderers and shit. Good lookin' out."

We reached the gas station and I told Davey to pick out whatever he wanted to eat. He piled two armfuls of junk food onto the counter in addition to an extra-large Slushie. I grabbed a bag of cat food, poured myself a black coffee and selected a ham and egg muffin from beneath the electric warmers. We walked back to the high school and sat and ate on the steps. The muffin was tough and chewy and tasted about how I'd imagine the rubber from a tire would taste.

The kid tore through his haul like he'd never tasted the pleasure of sugar before. After some Skittles, a Twix bar and a Ho-Ho, the kid crumpled his empty wrappers and tossed them aside as if he were disgusted by them, rubbed his hand over his stomach and declared, "I think I'm going to barf."

"Again?"

The kid groaned, drew in some deep breaths and let go of them slowly.

"Okay, I think I'm okay. I hate throwing up."

"You shouldn't eat that crap for breakfast. You gotta get something in you that will stick to your ribs."

"I don't even know what the hell that means."

I forced another bite of muffin into my mouth, chewed on it for a bit, then spit it out and chucked the remainder of the muffin into the dead azaleas.

"You need to control your impulses," I said to the kid. "Not take things to the extreme—eating till you puke, drinking till you puke."

"Yo, I miss something? You my Daddy now?"

"You're too ugly to be my kid."

"Whatever, man," Davey chided. "You so ugly, you can't even get a date off the calendar."

"Almost funny, kid." I finished my coffee and the kid sucked down the rest of his Slushie. "Why aren't you in school?"

"First period is Algebra and the second period is Home Ec," he explained. "That shit is a waste of time. What the hell am I gonna do with proofs and theorems and shit? Or a piece of cinnamon toast? I'll tell you what I'm gonna do: Nada."

"What's third period?"

"Gym."

"I used to skip school. You gotta be smart about that kind of thing though. You can't do it too much. And you gotta get good enough grades that they won't bother you, but not too good because then they take an interest in you and try to get you to apply yourself. In my day all you needed was a doctor's note to get out of going. So I would make up some bogus ailment to go to the doctor's office and I would find a way to swipe four or five sheets of his stationery. Then I'd get somebody to scratch out a bogus note, always claiming something nice and contagious, like head lice, and I was good to go for a couple days. My father wasn't around and my mother had to work a lot so that made it easy. Had the chicken pox four times."

"That's pretty dope."

"How do you get away with it?"

The kid started to tell me, but thought twice about it.

"You ain't gonna tell my moms?"

I put a look on him that made him feel ashamed for the question.

"She always working or going to school so it ain't too hard. I just gotta make sure to get to the mail before she does to get the letters they send. That and I gave them the wrong number for their phone records so they don't have any way to get a hold of her. Every time they call they get some Chinese guy down at Wang's," he laughed.

"What's she go to school for?"

"Nursing."

I stood up from the stairs and stretched my limbs.

"I've gotta feed this cat and get to work, kid. I'm going by your school, you want me to give you a lift?"

"Yeah, all right. What kind of stuff you do when you work? Like spy on people or follow them around, take pictures of them fucking or doing crimes? Shit like that?"

"Some days that's what I do. Today, I'm gonna have a few conversations."

CHAPTER FOURTEEN
A TASTE FOR POISON

My first stop was Norman Hinkle. I didn't find him on the Southside, but the crew from his landscaping company was sprucing up the lawn of one of the fancy houses down by Redding Park. One of them was a black guy shaped like a brick called Pigg. Pigg stopped spreading mulch long enough to tell me Hinkle would be the pudgy dude having breakfast down the road at E.B.'s Diner.

E.B.'s was one of these diners that transported their customers to an earlier era. The place had been a fixture in town for over half a century; opened in the fifties; updated its décor in the seventies; then left well enough alone for forty years. Everything from the tiling to the countertops to the wallpaper was orange, brown, or mustard yellow.

Hinkle was in the corner booth gorging on a plate of pancakes, bacon, sausage, and muffins. I slid into the seat opposite him. Focused on the food, it took him a moment to register my presence. He swallowed down a lump of pancake, swilled some coffee and wiped his mouth.

"What you need?"

He lifted the syrup container and drizzled syrup over the pile of food on his plate. Hinkle had a head like a bowling ball and a beard that looked like someone had taken a magic marker and etched a thin line around the perimeter of his fleshy jaw and up over his lip. He had some ink: a talon stretched out from his collar up the left side of his neck, but no Cash City tattoo across his knuckles. Assessing the sum of his parts, it was difficult to couple him with a beautiful girl like Trisha Cammack.

I explained who I was, what I was there for, and laid out his situation as I saw it. His DNA would be easy enough to collect and match with the sample found inside Trisha Cammack. Once that physical connection was established, his status as a murder witness would upgrade to murder suspect before he could dollop more maple syrup over his pancakes. So if he had anything to tell he better tell it.

The whiff of swagger vanished. Fear snuck subtly in behind his eyes. He was the type whose balls crawled into his stomach at the prospect of trouble. Naturally, Hinkle didn't need to know that the police had no intentions on running that DNA.

"Man, I had nothing but love for that girl."

"Define love."

Hinkle put his palms against the edge of the table and pressed back as if he needed to create some additional space between the two of us.

"You think you know me, don't you? You think you had me dead to rights before you even put eyes on me. Well, you don't have me pegged, no sir. Somebody got in your ear about me. Whatever you heard tell, or think you know about me, it's a lot more complex than that."

"Shock me."

"What've you heard?"

"That's not the way this is gonna work. Look here, I'm not the police. If you tell me what went down and you're straight with me, then I take no issue with you in regards to the dealing or anything else you've got going on. But if you're not straight with me, I'll tee you up for the police, tell them you look good for the murder. I do that and they're on you. And once they're on you there's no getting off."

"It's like that?"

"It's like that."

Hinkle ran a hand over his shorn head. The way he talked reminded me of the way the kid talked, that fake hoodrat shit. A waitress doing the rounds asked me if I was going to order anything. I said no. She filled Hinkle's coffee cup to the brim and left us be. Hinkle dumped in some sugar and cream and lifted the mug. A tremor in his hand sent some of the coffee sloshing over the edge onto his pants.

"Damn waitress." Hinkle blotted the spill with a napkin. "Where do I start?"

"The last time you saw her."

"First let me explain something to you. Her parents and everybody else think I'm the reason Trish turned out as fucked up as she did. That she was all innocent and I'm the one who poisoned her."

"That's not the way it was?"

"Not even a little bit. When I met her I knew she was too pretty, too smart, too everything for a mug like me. Girl had goals, aimed at being a counselor to troubled kids and all that. I wanted that stuff for her, too. She was getting with me so she could say she'd gone and done her bad boy phase or whatever. I knew that, I'm not stupid. But I would have changed for her. I would have dug ditches for that girl. For real, anything. I wanted to get that girl's belly swolled up, you feel me? I wanted to put my babies in her. She knew what I slung. I was always honest with her 'cause I didn't want that shit to come back and bite me. One day she says she wants to try some of the product. I told her no way, she didn't want to do that shit. It whacks you out, you know what I'm saying. I've seen it too many times. That shit changes a person. She told me to give it to her or she was through with me, that I was getting boring anyway. So I gave it to her. I tried to quit giving it to her, I really did, but every time she just threatened to be done with me."

"What did she take?"

He expelled a long, audible breath as if the next bit was painful to verbalize.

"At first just coke and pills and shit like that, shit she could handle well enough. Then she got a taste of H. Not from me. I never even dabbled with that, but once she got that taste, that's all she ever wanted. I even tried to get her back to doing just coke."

"Didn't take?"

"Naw. She wouldn't even come around if I didn't have any H to offer."

"You involved with these guys from Detroit?"

"Wait a second." He gazed at me with something like awe and lowered his voice to a loud whisper. "You're that fool fucked up Tremaine Miller, ain't you? You that crazy motherfucker."

"Word travels fast."

"Fast as fuck round these parts. I heard tell of you, dawg."

The obvious pleasure with which he delivered this irked me.

"Good. Then you know I'm not fucking about. Answers. The Detroit thing, you involved in that?"

"Not any more than I have to be."

"Spell it out."

Hinkle scooted his plate aside and leaned forward on his elbows.

"Them crazy fuckers moved in and took over all the game. I mean all of it. I've always stayed smart about shit, have me a good cover job, keep off the police's radar, play the game with some intelligence, you feel me?"

"Uh-huh."

"I never wanted things to get too big for me to handle. Just make a bit of throwing around money, know what I'm saying. I had a select group of customers. I figured these Detroit homies either didn't know or didn't care nothing about me. But I was fucking wrong about that. They came to me and let me know, in no uncertain terms, that there was no business without them being involved. I explained to them the way I do things and they respected that. Told me keep operating small if that was what I wanted. But there was one caveat, if you will. I had to ditch my suppliers and start getting my stuff from them, at the rates they set. Non-negotiable. That's the way they do business, at least with me."

"Who do you deal with?"

"Directly, just one guy that delivers my shit, Tigga-Man. He's the only one I ever deal with. He has other guys with him, but they don't even speak. He does all the dealing and organizes all the deliveries and pay-offs. Think he's in charge of the smaller game like me."

"What's his real name?"

"Fuck if I know."

"What's he look like?"

"Scary looking homie, dark black motherfucker. Has like seven tear drops filled in on his face."

"What else?"

"Tall, kind of chiseled up. You can tell he lifts those weights plenty. Big bucked rabbit teeth with a split in the middle."

"Why do they call him Tigga-Man?"

"I think 'cause he can't talk right with those teeth. Can't pronounce his R's."

"Nobody else?"

"When they very first set it up, there was this one dude that made the deal. He's the one that laid out the terms. Then he pointed me to Tigga-Man and I ain't seen him since."

"What was his name?"

"Called him Cupcake, I think."

This Cupcake guy kept popping up. Hinkle described him: brown-skinned, big rolly head on a short round body, dresses well, not like a thug, has a diamond for a front tooth.

"How'd he get that name, Cupcake?"

"I heard it was 'cause he's a cupcake short of being a total fat ass, but you ain't hear that shit from me. I don't know. Ain't like I'm asking around about the dude too much. I'm trying to stay out of their shit."

"The last time you saw Trisha Cammack?"

Hinkle cupped one of his hands over his mouth and spoke through his fingers.

"It was that night, the night she was found down by the river."

After that admission, Hinkle was forthcoming about the details of his encounter with Trisha Cammack on the last night of her life. She showed up unannounced at his parents' home a little after nine p.m. His parents were dining at a friend's until well after midnight so they would be unable to verify this. A cab had dropped off Trisha. The driver idled in the driveway until Trisha turned around and waved it away. Hinkle showed her in, supplied her with heroin, helped her cook and shoot it, fucked her twice, once in his parents' basement and a second time against the back of the front door before she left on foot, heading west, a tad before eleven p.m.

"I tried to get her to stay the night, but I had given her the last of my stash. I guess she didn't have no more use for me. Called me a pathetic piece of shit on her way out. Great way to leave things."

"You didn't offer her a ride?"

"Naw, I did. She flipped me the bird," Hinkle scoffed and stared out the window at the traffic sliding by. "I know what you're thinking."

"I doubt it."

"She was so fine. Once you had her, I'm telling you, nobody else would ever do. She's ruined me for other women."

"I'm sorry for your loss."

My condolences must have been dripping with sarcasm because he told me to fuck off.

"By the way, Trisha had a handful of STD's so you might want to get to a doctor before your dick starts to look like a PayDay."

I left Hinkle to his breakfast. He left me piecing together the timeline of Trisha Cammack's final hours. He was too stupid to realize it, but Norman Hinkle had just positioned himself as the last person to see her alive, which means he very well may have been the first person to see her dead. If she overdosed in Mommy and Daddy's house Hinkle would have every reason to flush her body in the river. It also gave a reasonable explanation as to why he would pussy out in the end and leave her along the riverbank: love. Young, irrational love, in all its splendor. I'd save the incriminations for later if and when I needed them.

Back in the Skylark, I phoned the taxi company, told them I was a detective without specifying which kind, and asked if there were any fares on the books for Saturday night going from Clifford Avenue to the Hinkle residence on First Street. The dispatcher found one possibility, a fare that had started at 8:47 p.m. The origin point wasn't Clifford Avenue but near there, the corner of Sixteenth Street and Eighth Avenue. The cabbie, a man named Dennis Maynard, had forgotten to log an out marker on the fare. Maynard's next shift began at seven the coming evening. I assured the dispatcher that Maynard wasn't in trouble but not to let him leave the garage until I had the opportunity to chat with him.

CHAPTER FIFTEEN
THE LAST MAGIC TRICK

Lucca's, the Italian joint that employed Tricky Jackson, had a prime location a block from campus. The small diner was crammed tight with college kids, all getting fat on beer, sandwiches, and privilege. I squeezed between some blubbery fraternity types and flagged down the counterman.

"What can I do you for?" he grumbled.

I put in for a meatball hoagie and asked him if Tricky was working. The mention of Tricky's name drew the guy's full attention. His eyes skimmed me over from head to toe.

"He's on a run. Should be back soon to pick up the next batch of deliveries."

I found a spot in the corner and went to work on the hoagie. A couple minutes later Tricky came in. He bumped fists with a few of the college kids and grinned wide at the young tail in the place. His gaze flit from one young ass to another until his eyes landed on me and he spooked. For a split second I thought he might try to duck and hide or run out on me, but he knew I'd already clocked him. To mask his reaction Tricky went big, feigning like he was delighted to see me.

"Malick, what you doing here?"

"Came to see you, Tricky. See how you've been, what you've been up to," I smiled at him. "So what you been up to?"

"Yo, Trick," the counterman called over. "Got six more deliveries getting cold as we speak."

Tricky made a face and flipped his palms flat up.

"Busy day. Sorry I can't catch up."

He walked around the counter and ducked into the back kitchen. I tossed the scraps of my hoagie into the trash, went outside and stood by Lucca's delivery vehicle. Tricky rounded the corner carrying two large bags of food. As he spotted me he stopped and groaned.

"I can't be doing this right now, Malick."

"You dodging me, Tricky?"

"I ain't dodging you, I swear. I got to work."

"Where you headed, I'll tag along."

Tricky popped the hatch on the vehicle, shoved the bags of food in and slammed the hatch shut.

"Man, I can't be seen in public with you."

"We best take it private then."

Tricky glowered, "Get in."

He climbed in the front and I got in the back behind the driver's seat.

"Why you gotta sit back there?"

"Front seat makes me car sick."

"Bullshit. I ain't no freaking chauffer."

He jammed the key in the ignition and started driving. From my vantage I could see his hands gripping the wheel and the Cash City tattoo etched across his knuckles.

"What's the matter, Tricky? We not friends anymore? If I recall correctly, last time I stopped in on you, you told me that getting arrested when you did was the best thing that could have happened to you. Got you straightened out while the straightening was still good. Isn't that what you told me?"

"Something like that," Tricky admitted. He glared at me in the rearview. "That was a long time ago."

Tricky drove through downtown and turned south toward the Eighth Street viaduct.

"You don't feel that way anymore?"

"Man, why you doing this to me?"

"What am I doing, Trick?"

"Putting me in this jacked up position."

He steered under the viaduct into the Southside and made a left, heading toward the East End of town, cruising around like he had nowhere to be.

"Where's your first drop?" I asked.

"Don't worry about it."

"Why are you driving into the East End, Tricky?"

"Because, man. If something about to go down, it's gonna go down on my turf."

"If something goes down, Tricky, you're not leaving this car without a bullet in your skull. You understand me?"

"So we ain't friends no more?"

Tricky pulled the car over just before we hit Clifford Avenue and shifted into park.

"What have you gotten yourself involved in, Trick?"

"It's not what you think."

"I see that tattoo. I know what it means."

He dropped his hands from the wheel to shield his knuckles from view.

"Hands back up where I can see them," I told him. He obliged. Five or six cars rumbled past us along the street.

"This off the books?" Tricky said.

"What books?"

"I'm serious. I can't be getting caught up with no police right now."

"Talk to me, Tricky."

"This the last time you and me ever conversate, you feel me? If they knew I was with you, after what you pulled with Tremaine, and they knew I didn't take your ass out, they'd kill me, my girl, and my two boys. You feel me?"

"Relax. I feel you."

"Don't tell me to fucking relax. I didn't want this fucking tattoo. Cash City. It feels like a goddamn branding. But if these guys ask you to do something, you do it. If they ask you, 'you want to get a tattoo to show your loyalty', you do it. I'm a survivor, man. I do what I have to do to survive."

"Nothing wrong with that."

"They heard about me, I don't know how, guess I still got a rep. Heard I worked at Lucca's doing deliveries. They saw an opportunity at distribution so they approached me."

"So you got back in the game?"

"These guys don't give you a choice, man. If I didn't get with them they would have taken me out. They knocked off a couple homeboys who tried to keep clear of them, no sweat. I got kids now, Malick, you know this, dog. I'm a survivor."

"You mentioned that. So what? People call up, place an order and you take them the drugs?"

Tricky started to reply, shook his head like that wasn't quite the whole story, then said, "Yeah."

"What's the product?"

"Whatever's going. All the way up and down the ladder from pills to meth to smack."

"Motor Seventy-Five?"

"Yeah. That's big right now."

"People are dying from that, Tricky."

"You think I don't know that, man. I know that shit. What do you want me to do about it?"

"So that's it then? Just drop offs?"

"Naw. They got me doing more than deliveries. Sometimes I'll show up at a house and they'll load the car up with guns. All sorts of shit."

"Where do you take them?"

"You know I can't tell you that. That shit will come right back to me."

"You got some product in the car right now?"

"Man, what you think?"

"What about this Cupcake? Who is he in all this?"

"You know about Cupcake?"

"I know about him and Tigga-Man."

Tricky took some time to arrange his next words.

"I've only seen Cupcake a couple times. He the head guy from Detroit runs things. Gives all the orders, makes all the decisions. You better be careful who you throwing his name around to. That motherfucker is everywhere and nowhere at the same time, like he has an all-seeing eye or some shit. Knows everything that's going on before it goes on. You better watch your ass. He hears his name out your lips, then you gonna meet Tigga-Man and you don't want to meet Tigga-Man."

"So Tigga-Man is the muscle and Cupcake is the boss. He order the hit on Gum Drop?"

Tricky stared at me in the rearview again.

"I ain't privy to none of that."

"Where's he get his information? How did he know Gum Drop talked to me?"

"Man, you talking about stuff way above my pay grade."

Tricky either couldn't or wouldn't tell me anything else and he refused to make any deliveries with me in the car. He drove back to Lucca's. I got out, leaned over and addressed him through the driver's side window.

"I'll see you, Trick."

"No, Malick. From now on, you don't see me. You don't know me. You don't speak my name."

"If that's the way it has to be."

"That's the way it is."

"Say, if this is it for you and I, you got any new tricks?"

That wide smile came back for the first time since he spotted me in the corner at Lucca's.

"Yeah, I got a new one. My kids love it. I do it over and over for them and they never get tired of it. My boy's getting pretty good at tricks himself and even he's stumped by this one." The smile faded from his lips. "But you got to have a deck of cards to perform it and I don't have my cards on me, so—"

"No sweat. Some other time."

"Naw, Malick. Naw."

Tricky shifted his gaze from me to the road in front of him. I rapped on the roof and he pulled off. I watched as the car grew small and disappeared down the avenue.

Big Tom's Grocery was on the far side of downtown, half a mile west from Lucca's. A fresh bag of Meow Mix was the one edible thing I had in my place, sure, but that's not the reason I drove my car down to Big Tom's, parked in the lot, and sat there for some duration watching the sliding doors glide open and shut as people entered and exited. An older lady was having a rough time unloading groceries into the trunk of her car so I hopped out to help her. When she caught sight of me approaching she nearly leapt out of her skin and snapped at me to get the hell away from her. When I offered to lend a hand, she reached into her trunk and brought out a can of mace and an air horn. I slowly backed away. As I headed into the store I passed an employee who was rounding up the stray carts in the lot. He chuckled and said, "Them old ladies is jumpy, ain't they?"

Inside, I grabbed a hand basket, browsed the fruits and vegetables and casually scanned the store. Karla was clerking one of the checkout lanes. Her manner with the customers was courteous, but not overly pleasant, enough to be considered friendly without inviting anyone to strike up a conversation. She seemed resolute to do what she had to do to get through another day with a minimum amount of hassle. Her queue moved twice as fast as the other two open registers.

I forced myself to stop watching her and roamed the aisles, picking out some canned goods and other items that I would eat if they were in my cabinets. When I crammed one too many items in my basket and five others tumbled out, I quit stalling and got in line behind an old man with white hairs spitting out of his ears and a young mother with a screaming baby and coupons for every item in her cart. When she was finally finished, I stepped forward.

Out of habit, Karla said, "How are you today?" Then she recognized me. A quick jolt went through her body and she exclaimed, "Oh."

"I'm fine," I replied. "How are you?"

"Good," she said tersely. She began to scan my items and bag them. "Do you have a Big Tom's discount card or any coupons?" she asked, slipping back into work mode.

"No. Listen."

She stopped the conveyor belt and looked at me. Hers were the type of eyes that betrayed her every emotion. What they showed now, rather plainly, was pure contempt.

"I'm sorry about what I said to you yesterday. I had no business saying those things."

"Nope, you certainly did not."

"I have no idea what kind of mother you are, but I'm sure you're a fine one. And Davey seems like a good enough kid. Who am I to pass any kind of judgment?"

"You're nobody."

"That's right," I agreed, the wind kind of gone out of me the way she said it. "Nobody. Anyway, I apologize."

She totaled my items and I paid.

"See you around."

Her eyebrows arched and she shook her head in astonishment before turning to greet the next person in her queue. "How are you today?"

I tossed my bags into the trunk of the Skylark and moved to get round to the front when I saw her striding through the parking lot right at me. I braced for another smack or tongue-lashing or both. She stopped about five feet away from me and crossed her arms.

"I've got a ten minute break. Can I talk to you for a second?"

"Sure."

We sat on a bench out front of the store. She fit a cigarette between her lips and sparked it. Asked me if I had anything else on her kid that she should know about. I told her no, that I had pretty much cleared the decks yesterday. That for what it was worth, I didn't think her son had ever had a drink before and was just trying to show off a little bit for an audience.

"I worry about him. Do me a favor, will you? If you ever see or hear about him getting into any kind of trouble, will you tell me?"

"Will do. In turn, I'm going to need you to promise that you'll never slap me again."

Karla scrunched up her nose.

"Hmm, I don't know about that. How about, I promise never to slap you for anything you don't deserve to be slapped for. Outside of that, all bets are off."

I laughed a little.

"Deal."

She dropped her cigarette on the pavement and tamped it out, then fixed her gaze on me. I'll be goddamned if those sea-green eyes didn't slice me in two.

"See you on the flip," she said. With that, she stood up and vanished through the sliding glass doors.

CHAPTER SIXTEEN
TRADE AND COMMERCE

"You're the last person on God's green earth I expected to get a call from, Malick."

"Oh yeah?"

"Yeah," Ernie Ciccone guffawed. He sat across from me in his office at the *Cain City Dispatch*, grinning and sizing me up. Ciccone possessed a few bristly strands of hair on top, flat ears, tiny slit eyes, a long jutting nose and half a chin. When he grinned everything on his face receded except the nose, which surged forward accentuating his weasel features.

"It's good to see that you don't have any hard feelings."

"Who says I don't?"

"Oh," Ciccone cocked his head. "My secretary said that you were coming in to share some inside information on last night's homicide."

"All the more reason that I'm a little confused at you keeping me sitting on my hands in the lobby for forty-five minutes. What could be more important than an inside source on a fresh murder? I thought murder was your main racket."

"It is. I apologize, I was in a meeting with my editor and there was a pressing call that I had to make before we met."

"Who to?"

"Excuse me?"

"Did I mumble? Who—To?"

Ciccone didn't have a bright lie ready so I let him stew for a moment before I crafted a lopsided smirk.

"You're joking," he sighed, relieved. "Jesus, I thought you were serious. I was going to say, who I talk to is confidential and none of your business."

"Of course."

"Let's get to it. What do you have for me?"

"Well, I know how much you like to ruin policemen's careers."

Ciccone shook his head and blew some air out of his nose.

"Every word I wrote about you was true."

"I didn't claim otherwise. I'm not here to be vindicated."

"My job is to shine a light on the truth of this town, report the facts as they are. Not as you or anybody else would like them to be. And that's what I did. Whatever fallout that produces," he gave an exaggerated shrug, "it is what it is. If you don't like it, tough shit. You have no one else to blame but yourself, so take it up with you. I take down the people who deserve to be taken down."

"That so?"

"Damn right it's so."

I leaned forward in my chair.

"Then you're gonna eat this one up cause it's a doozy. Picture this headline: Cop pays off press to hide criminal activity in city."

Ciccone's face went sallow. Now he saw how I was coming at him.

"Yeah," I said, revving up. "How about that for a sensational story? Exposing a cop who colludes with the press to keep the nasty bits buried on the back pages or out of the papers and news altogether? You ask me, that's front page above-the-crease type stuff."

"That's a pretty big accusation."

"It is. You might want to jot this down."

Ciccone stared at me hard, then opened a drawer, pulled out a legal pad and selected a pen from a cup of them on his desk.

"I'm ready."

"Get this word for word. The lead crime reporter at this paper," I pointed at him and mouthed the word, *you*, "is taking hush money from the top detective in the Felony Unit of the Police Department to bury stories."

"Get the fuck out of my office," Ciccone seethed.

I kept my tone nonchalant.

"You sure about that? Because once I exit that door the train has left the station. I'll tell your editor, your boss, your secretary, the police—the ones on the level anyway—your neighbors, your wife, your mailman, I'll tell everybody about you. I'll post fucking fliers."

Ciccone's knuckles lost their color from his gripping the pen so tight.

"You come in here seven years later, and after all that time, this is the scheme you concoct to have your retribution on me? You wanna dredge up the past? Go ahead. Tell your tale. No one is going to believe a washed up loser like you over me, not with your history. We're headed in opposite directions my friend."

"Maybe you're right. But for kicks, let's play out that scenario. Word gets out you've been taking hush money, but the claim comes from me, someone who has an obvious vendetta, so they dismiss the allegation out of hand. That's all right, but now it's out there in the back of people's minds, festering, growing. One of them gets curious, maybe your editor; after all, everyone likes to cover their own ass. He looks into it a little bit and the more he looks, the more questions keep coming up. Why was this bust never reported, or that homicide given more space? Why do certain crimes escape even the police blotter? What do you think happens once those questions begin?"

"Nothing happens," Ciccone's mouth drew back wickedly, "because it's not true."

"Okay." I stood up and made for the door. "Could you point me to your editor's office?"

"Lick my ass, Malick."

"I'll find it myself."

I opened the door, walked over to the nearest cubicle where a woman was sitting, and asked for directions to the editor's office. She indicated a door in the back corner of the floor. I started for it. From behind me came a hiss.

"Wait."

I turned to look. Ciccone stepped forward from his doorway.

"There's one more thing I forgot to ask you, Mr. Malick," he said, assuming the overly proper intonation of a bad actor. He extended his palm and I strolled back into his office. He shut the door and brushed past me. "Sit your ass down."

I shrugged and reached for the door again. Ciccone softened his tone, though it obviously pained him to do so, as his next words came through gnashed teeth.

"Sit back down please. As long as it stays between you and me, I'll give you what you want."

I took my hand off the knob, but stayed standing.

"You've got some gall," Ciccone snipped. "What do you want?"

"Not much. Just the who, what, when, where, and why of your arrangement with Hale. All the details."

Ciccone mashed his face up to look revolted, took in a big wheezing breath and let it out.

"How do I know you won't burn me with what I divulge?"

"Despite what you may think, I don't give a fuck about you. Or your journalistic ethics. You give me the information I want, you can write or not write whatever the hell you want."

"You'll go to any length, won't you? It must be nice to not have one goddamn thing to lose."

"It has its advantages." I plopped down in the chair. "Spill it."

Moisture beaded up on the high part of his forehead and started to trickle down his face. He dabbed the sweat with his palms and wiped the palms on the front of his shirt. Then he talked. The deal with Hale started out as a professional courtesy. Hale asked Ciccone to keep a couple stories out of the police blotter. Nothing major, a small pot bust, a bar fight where a guy got stabbed in the lung. The two of them had swapped favors before. Ciccone spiked the stories and in return, Hale acted as a source, letting Ciccone behind the curtain on police procedure and case progress, tipping him off when he could, giving inside information that would otherwise be kept from the public.

The first time money exchanged hands was four months ago. Hale implored Ciccone not to write up a drive-by shooting near Redding Park. For Ciccone, quashing a drive-by that took place in a plush part of town was too much. He planned on going forward with the article until Hale pushed four hundred dollars into his hand and explained that there were reasons the story could not be published, claiming actual lives were at stake. Seeing as none of the shots fired in the drive-by had connected with anything vital, Ciccone rationalized killing the report and accepted the money, telling Hale it was a one-time thing. But Ciccone liked the way that money felt in his hands and he liked the way it spent and he kept accepting it. As the buried stories became larger and more frequent, so did the payments.

Ciccone knew better than to ask questions, but then two months ago he got tipped off on a lawyer who was fired for smoking crack in a courthouse bathroom. Ciccone tracked the lawyer down to see if there was a story there. The lawyer let slip there were some new dealers in town. Following that thread, Ciccone stumbled onto a puzzle that, when the pieces were fitted together, formed the Detroit pipeline, Cash City.

Per their arrangement, Ciccone alerted Hale as to what was going down, confident he was giving law enforcement a big assist. Instead, Hale went berserk, begged him to sit on the story for a day. The next afternoon Hale paid him a lump sum of five thousand dollars to stay quiet.

"It was clear he was taking orders from someone to keep this stuff out of the press, but he never let on who. At first I thought maybe it was somebody like the chief of police, or city council, maybe even the mayor telling him to keep me in check. Someone of that nature. He was always saying that if people found out what was really going on in Cain City, they'd go ape-shit. But then he gave me that five thousand. I didn't want to know where it came from. But I'm sure as hell that it wasn't from the city government. I didn't even want it, but at that point I knew better than to not take it."

"What other stories has he wanted covered up?"

"There's no rhyme or reason to them. Some were big ones: murders, shootings, overdoses, that type of thing. If they were too big to be swept under the rug completely he just asked me to minimize them the best I could, you know, make them seem routine. Others were small things I couldn't figure. Seemed silly he was messing with some of them at all, you know what I'm saying. After that five thousand he stopped paying me. Just told me I had to do it now. I was as culpable as him."

"What kind of small things?"

"Some of them were so off the radar they may or may not have made the paper anyhow. Off the top of my head—" Ciccone rolled his eyes to the ceiling. "One was a drunk and disorderly thing I believe."

"You have records on those?"

The corners of Ciccone's mouth curved downward and he made a dismissive gesture with his hand.

"What do you think, I'm stupid? I'm not going to leave any sort of paper trail."

I stood to leave.

"We done?" asked Ciccone.

"For now."

"What am I supposed to do?"

"Do what you do best. Keep talking out of both sides of your mouth, and if Hale wants you to bury a story, you bury a story. Keep taking the money. Act normal. But when he contacts you, you let me know first thing. I want to know what he's covering up. You tip him off, I'll find out about it and then I will burn you. Got it?"

"Got it." Ciccone gave a bitter thumbs up. "You and I settled?"

"We'll see."

I turned to leave.

Ciccone asked, "How did you know I was on the take?"

"I have a bigger brain than you."

"C'mon, I gotta know. How did you figure it out?"

"You just told me."

Ciccone's jaw dropped wide enough to glimpse the crowns on his molars.

CHAPTER SEVENTEEN
THE BLUE TAIL

When I stepped out of the Dispatch Building the sky had paled and the sun was dipping below the rooftops to the west of downtown. Some of the cars motoring by on the avenue had already flipped on their lights. I had an hour to blow before the meeting with the cabbie, Dennis Maynard. Down the street was an old spaghetti diner. I fed a couple more quarters into the meter and went and had some dinner.

Forty-five minutes later when I flipped on my own lights and pulled away from the curb, a dark blue sedan half a block back did the same. I didn't think anything of it until I made a couple turns and the sedan made them with me. Its front bumper, where the license plate was supposed to go, was bare.

I swung into the Yellow Cab parking lot. The sedan kept going straight, rolling past me without speeding up or slowing down. I tried to steal a fast look at the driver, but by now it was full-on night and its passenger windows were tinted. Dealer plates were attached to the rear window, but it was too dark to read those as well. I watched the sedan's red taillights shrink with distance. Two blocks up it turned south.

I killed the lights and the ignition, got out of the Skylark and hustled across the street to a row of buildings. There I hid in the shadow of a doorframe and for ten minutes waited for the dark blue sedan to circle back round. It didn't. I crossed back over the street and entered the Yellow Cab garage.

Fifteen or twenty cabs were parked end to end in rows along the right wall of the garage. A couple of mechanics were working under the hood of one of them. Otherwise, the place was quiet. I went through a door at the left side of the garage that led to a long hallway. At the end of the hallway was a common room and beyond that the company offices. The common room housed a dozen cubicles along the wall, two of which were occupied by dispatchers taking calls on headsets. At the back corner of the room was a door with the word *MANAGER* stenciled across an opaque window. I rapped on the glass. A gruff voice invited me to come on in.

As I entered the office two men rose from chairs. One of them looked apologetic and the other was plenty angry. The angry one, I assumed, was my man Dennis Maynard. He wore thick eyeglasses, had small teeth, big gums, fat sideburns, and a high splotched forehead.

"There better be a good damn reason for me delaying my shift and losing out on a handful of fares," he threatened, glaring at both me and the night manager. "Or I'm gonna go ape on somebody."

I suggested that we go somewhere private to discuss the matter, but Maynard preferred to have it out and done with.

I said, "Tell me about the fare you picked up on Saturday night at nine p.m. on the corner of Sixteenth Street and Twelfth Avenue."

Maynard's face puckered.

"Bah, shit."

"Somewhere private?"

The night manager directed us back through the common room and down the hallway to a small break room.

A bored dispatcher was in there smoking and eating some chips from the vending machine. The night manager ordered her to clear out, which she took her sweet time doing, and then closed the door, sealing Maynard and me in the cramped room.

Maynard asked, "You mind if I get something to eat?"

The stench of decay emanated from his body and from his breath.

"No."

"You want something?"

"No."

He fished out some quarters, shoved them into the vending machine and punched a few buttons. Some Twinkies dropped. We sat at one of the circular tables and he looked at the Twinkies but didn't open them. The corner of his mouth twisted sideways.

"I wish to God she woulda told me right up front she didn't have any money. I woulda never picked her up."

"I'm not interested in what you would have done. I'm interested in what you did do."

"Do I need a lawyer?"

"Why?"

Maynard picked at a patch of dry skin beneath his chin.

"Got a good thing going here. Been at this job for a long time."

Coddling these assholes and assuring them that I wouldn't tattle to their bosses was getting tiresome.

"The police are going to view you as the last person to see her alive," I lied.

"She's dead?"

"Found her body later that night."

"That's friggin' nuts," he replied, incensed. "No way I was the last person to see her alive. I dropped her off at that house on the Southside. That's who you should be talking to, the guy at that house, not me. I ain't do nothing to that girl."

"I thought she didn't have any money?"

"That's right."

"How did she pay the fare?"

I was sure of the answer, but wanted to make him say it out loud. Maynard's manner turned sheepish. He put his elbow on the table and leaned his face forward into his hand, covering his eyes. He stayed like that as he began to take me through the events of last Saturday night.

Maynard was about halfway to the destination, by Redding Park, when Trisha confessed that she didn't have any money. Having yet to comprehend her meaning, Maynard explained to her that they accepted credit cards as well. She didn't have any of those either.

Maynard jerked the car to the curb, hit the automatic lock on the doors, and told her that he could drive to the bank or to the police station, her choice. A few days before a fare had run from the car to keep from paying and he wasn't fool enough to let that happen twice in the same week. That's when Trisha offered to pay him in another fashion. Maynard's face flushed crimson as he recounted what happened next.

He found a nice dark corner in the park beneath some trees and put the cab there. Trisha slipped into the front seat next to him, unzipped his pants, and sucked him off. He told her not to spit it out in the car. She didn't spit it out at all. Just sat up, wiped her mouth with the back of her hand, then leaned her head against the passenger window and didn't speak for the remainder of the ride. In the driveway at Norman Hinkle's, Maynard thanked her, handed over his business card, and told her she could call him anytime for a ride.

"Never said a word. Just fixed on me with these dead eyes and got out. Kind of freaked me out the way she looked at me, like I wasn't even there. Like I was a ghost or something. Then she walked over and thumped on the door of that house. I waited until that guy, the guy you should be talking to, he answered the door."

"And that was that?"

"That was that, except she called."

"She called?"

"That's what I'm trying to tell you. She called a couple hours later. Wanted me to come and get her, same place I dropped her off. But I couldn't right away because I had a fare going out there to Airport Hill. I told her I could be there in a half an hour, but she said forget it."

Maynard's eyes narrowed like an idea had just come and gone in his head and he was trying to get it back.

"Good thing I didn't pick her up, huh? Guess I mighta been murdered, too."

"Good thing. Did she mention where she wanted you to take her?"

"Didn't get that far."

"You didn't go back and pick her up at the house?"

"Why would I?" Maynard scoffed. "She didn't have no money and, you know, I was all spent with the other thing."

Before I left, I checked the records on Maynard's fares for Saturday night. He had three fares in the two hours between dropping Trisha Cammack at Hinkle's and the time she phoned him at eleven p.m. to pick her up, during his fare out to Airport Hill. After that he had two short fares from eleven to one a.m., the time Trisha Cammack was discovered. Plenty of time in there to dump a body by the river. From one a.m. until four a.m., when the bars closed, he took eight fares.

Before leaving, I took a look at the floor mats in Maynard's cab. No crusted mud from the riverbank and the mats were too dirty to have been recently cleaned. Likewise, there were no signs of involvement in the back seat or in the trunk. The tread on the tires were free of mud as well.

If Trisha tried and failed to get a cab, as Dennis Maynard claimed, that gave credence to Norman Hinkle's assertion that she left his house on foot heading west. And if she left Hinkle's on foot, I needed to put myself where she put herself, step where she stepped, and find out where those steps ended. Trisha Cammack may or may not have been murdered, that truth may never be found out, but somebody dragged her body to that riverbank. I was going to find out who the hell did it.

I drove through downtown toward the viaduct and the Southside. A pair of headlights skimmed across my rearview mirror, drawing my eyes. A red pickup truck was behind me, riding me tight, its lights bouncing and reflecting brightly in my mirror. Three car-lengths behind the truck was a green Lexus and some distance behind the green Lexus was the dark blue sedan.

CHAPTER EIGHTEEN
HONEYSUCKLE LANE

The trio of vehicles followed me under the viaduct past The Red Head and on past the high school. At Eleventh Avenue the pickup truck peeled off to the right, leaving only the Lexus between the sedan and me. I stayed straight. At the northwest corner of Redding Park a traffic light switched from green to yellow. I slowed early and stopped at the red, hoping to lure the spook in close enough to get a look at him. The Lexus flipped its turn signal to go left around the rim of the park. For the full minute we idled in the red glow of the intersection, I kept my head forward but my eyes in the mirror, focused on the silhouetted figure two cars back.

No cross-traffic came through the intersection. When the light clicked over to green I eased forward. The Lexus made its turn and the sedan, after a brief hesitation, accelerated into the slot vacated by the Lexus. Tall lamps illuminated the perimeter of Redding Park enough to give me a quick glimpse at the driver. He was a white man with a thick dark beard wearing a baseball cap that cast a shadow over his eyes and masked any other definition in his face.

Pedal to the floor the Skylark only got going to about eighty-five so there was no outrunning him. I kept her at a steady pace and thought over the best way to flip the tactical advantage. There were plenty of reasons for someone to follow me the way this spook was following me, none of them good. I led him down around the west side of the park and across a small bridge over a creek to where the road forked. To the right the road ran horizontal along the base of the southern hills. To the left the road wound up into the hills, eventually spidering off into a half dozen one-lane residential streets. I chose left.

The sedan lingered at the fork in the road, not quite coming to a stop before it pursued me up the hill. Either he was betting that I hadn't made him yet or he didn't give a shit. We ascended the winding road in tandem. Shining yellow critter eyes, frozen by headlights, glared out from the thicket on either side. Every hundred yards or so we passed a house. The higher we climbed, the bigger the houses. The wealth and the wildlife of Cain City resided on this hill.

Through the trees the lights of the town glittered below us. The outlines of the downtown buildings and the golden dome of the courthouse were visible against the night sky. We passed four of the five streets that branched off to our right. Ahead, beyond a bend in the road was the last chance to turn off the main road, Honeysuckle Lane, a dark one-laner that stretched out over the crest of the hill. I accelerated around the bend and, at the last second, veered onto Honeysuckle. The spook didn't go with me. He kept cruising up the main road, which dead-ended in a quarter of a mile at the Cain City Museum of Art. To get off the hill he had to flip around and come back past Honeysuckle.

I reversed in and out of a long driveway, cut my lights and pulled my car into a black shadow beneath a tree. I killed the engine and rolled down my window to listen for the sedan approaching. Good thing, too, because four minutes later the glint of the sedan flew by and I wouldn't have caught it if I didn't hear it. The spook had his lights off as well. I started the car, kept the lights off and hauled ass down the hill after him.

There was no way I could catch up to him but for the way the road corkscrewed and the fact that he, too, was navigating in the dark. The descent felt like a blind slow-motion chase. I couldn't see shit. Halfway down I nearly coasted smack into the rear of the sedan, unable to see it until I was right upon him. I don't know if the spook couldn't see me or if he was concentrating on the road because he maintained the same speed.

When we reached the bottom of the hill the sedan would leave me in the dust with relative ease. If I was going to make a move, now was the time. I flipped on my high beams, punched the gas and rammed the back of the car. It bucked and fishtailed to the edge of the road, teetered over the side of the hill before correcting its wheels and swerving back into control. The spook switched on his beams and went barreling down the lane. The sedan's crunched-in back bumper scraped the pavement creating a track of sparks.

I stayed on him best I could, but his ride had more power. He opened up a little bit of space between us. At the bottom of the hill the sedan cornered sharply onto the bridge and sideswiped the stone railing. I was going too fast to make the corner and skidded past the bridge. By the time I got back to facing the right direction the sedan was blocks away and receding from view.

I stopped the Skylark in the middle of the bridge and got out. The sedan's exterior had been pretty well ripped up. Jagged pieces of taillight were scattered over the pavement. Dark blue paint streaked the bridge's white railing. Just what I needed, some unknown stalker nipping at my ass. Whoever the fucker was, he knew I was onto him now. Tailing me wouldn't be so easy from here on out. Part of me wished the guy had gone ahead and taken a high-flying aerial off the hill so I wouldn't have to mess with it.

I assessed the Skylark. The front bumper was dented and scratched and the two vehicles had traded some paint, but that was the extent of the damage. I got back behind the wheel and continued to the Hinkles'.

Their neighborhood was dark and peaceful. I parked at the curb in front of the home. Windows were lit in both the second and third floors. A figure moved past the window on the second floor and the light coming from there extinguished. I got out, leaned against the hood and looked toward the West End. The night was cold and the temperature was still diving. I hugged my jacket around my body, tugged my cap tighter over my head.

Where did Trisha Cammack walk to on that last fateful night of her life? When she left here did she have a destination in mind or did she set out aimlessly? The way the city was laid out, like a grid, made for an infinite amount of possibilities. Whether she kept going west or reversed course to the east, at any point she could have veered right, left, or doubled back. She could have been picked up on the street by someone she knew or by a total stranger. She may have gone anywhere, with anyone. A girl in her condition, pumped full of a lethal quantity of drugs, could not have gotten too far on her own. I needed to find out if she had any friends or flames that lived nearby.

I climbed back into the Skylark and, with the Hinkle house as a starting point, drove different routes in an attempt to find anything that made one route more plausible than another. One pass I followed the best-lit streets from the Southside into the West End. The next pass I went straight down the avenue west, which eventually merged with the avenue running along the creek. Next I turned right and drove north until the street came to an end at the train tracks. Then I alternated turns: right, left, right, left.

I kept this up for a couple of hours, roaming every street and tracing every possible route within a mile radius of Hinkle's, hoping for some piece of luck to jump out at me. Nothing did. It was all fruitless.

A crummy little bar called Rummies stood on the First Street divide between the Southside and the West End. I went in and flashed the picture of Trisha around the place. The bartender, a skinny gray woman missing her two middle teeth on the bottom recognized Trisha, claimed she had not patronized the bar for months and was most definitely not in there the previous Saturday. "I'd remember that face in here," she said.

That left me out of plays for the night. My skull throbbed; my eyes throbbed. I was starved for a drink and six more after that one.

"You got Maker's?" I said to the woman.

"Nope, got Old Crow."

"Give it to me."

I sat down at the bar and she served one up. As I lifted the glass to my lips, a wild idea came to me that was so clear and simple that I cursed myself aloud for not having thought of it before I'd wasted the last two hours of my life burning gasoline and paying for the shitty drink in front of me. I left the drink and drove back to the Hinkle home. From there I drove the most direct route into the West End and to the Cammack house. The distance between the two dwellings was six blocks; two blocks north and four blocks west. She would have only had to make one turn. Six short blocks. It was the type of epiphany that was so simple it would surprise me if it didn't turn out to be true.

Trisha Cammack had walked home.

CHAPTER NINETEEN
FAT CHANCE

The Red Head, for a Monday night, had a few more customers than usual milling about. A dollar beer special was on. I found a slot at the bar.

Tadpole fixed me a drink and performed his latest joke.

"This blonde is flying from New York to Houston and she plops down in a first class seat, even though her ticket is for coach. So the flight attendant informs her she's in the wrong seat. The blonde replies, 'I'm blonde, I'm beautiful, I'm sitting right here and I'm flying to Houston.' The flight attendant asks her very sweetly to please move, but the blonde gives her the exact same response, 'I'm blonde, I'm beautiful, I'm sitting right here and I'm flying to Houston.' The flight attendant is at a loss now, so she notifies the pilot of the situation. The pilot says, 'Let me talk to her. My ex is a blonde. I speak the language.' So he saunters back there and asks if he may see her ticket. The blonde hands it over. The pilot takes a look at it, sees that it's for coach, and tells her she is in the wrong seat. To which the blonde responds, 'I'm blonde, I'm beautiful, I'm sitting right here and I'm flying to Houston.' So the pilot, unfazed, leans over and whispers something in her ear. Immediately the blonde jumps up like her ass is on fire and zips right back to coach. Can't get there fast enough. The flight attendant is awestruck, understandably. She has to know what the pilot said to her. The pilot shrugs, 'I told her she was sitting in first class, and first class isn't flying to Houston.'"

Tadpole slapped the countertop with his bar rag. Normally, no one got a bigger kick out of Tadpole's jokes than Tadpole, but somebody next to me was gut-laughing, so much so that Tadpole stopped his laughing. He seemed insulted by the amount of gusto the guy was putting into it, like he was mocking him or something. I glanced at the offender. It was the same silly drunk who talked me dull the night before. His laughter wound down and he shook a finger at Tadpole. "You know how to tell them." He sighed audibly, elbowed my arm like he wanted me to validate this assessment. I nodded along, a mistake, because then the lush honed in on me with his riff about the ills of technology and all the same shit he always yapped about.

Tadpole fixed me another drink and as soon as I got it in my hand I walked away from the chittering dimwit in the middle of one of his sentences.

"Where you going?" he slurred.

"To get away from you ear-raping me."

That hurt his feelings. He muttered that he was on the verge of making his point.

I found an open booth in the back corner of the place and sat there. My phone buzzed—Willis Hively. I let it go to voice mail. From the booth I could see the whole bar and everybody who came and went. In she came. She was no longer dressed in the plain grocery uniform. She wore a loose pair of jeans slung low on her hips. A thin white t-shirt clung softly to her figure and stopped short of her waist, revealing a sliver of skin when she moved. Her hair was down. A black purse was strapped across her chest. She stood just inside the doorway, eyes roving over the place. A man and woman entered behind her and she stepped aside to let them through.

She scanned across everyone sitting at the bar and playing shuffleboard and then she looked at the people sitting in booths until finally her eyes landed on me and she stopped looking. She walked over to me.

"What are you having?"

"Maker's Mark."

"Straight?"

"Straight."

Karla went to the bar and ordered up two bourbons, came back, put one of the drinks in front of me and slid into the opposite side of the booth. Before anybody said anything she started laughing.

"Where's the comedy?"

"It's nothing." Her laugh dwindled out and she lifted her glass. "Cheers."

I hoisted mine up and we drank.

"Whew!" she exulted, her eyes going red and filling up with water. "Oh my God, that'll clear your senses. Tastes like fire."

"At first."

She tilted her head to indicate the bar and everyone in it.

"So this is where you bring thirteen year old boys to get them liquored up?"

"Only the fun ones."

"Ah, I see."

"You come here to apologize?"

"Ha, fat chance. I'm just trying to gauge how big of a lush you are."

"Sizable. I prefer to think of it as marking time."

"Until what? Time runs out?"

"Something like that. Besides that it helps me sleep."

"Right."

The hair on the right side of her face fell loose and she tucked it back behind that ear. Her demeanor became stern.

"I want to get one thing clear with you before anything else happens. I'm a good mother."

"Okay."

"No, don't just nod along and brush it off like it's some trivial statement. Like it's something I say to fool myself. I need you to hear me when I say that to you."

"I hear you."

"Do you have kids?"

I shook my head no.

"Well, if you ever do then you will see. It's not so simple. Everybody has a plan for how they are gonna raise their kids and have them grow up to be all perfect. They're gonna read to them and not stick them in front of the TV, and teach them to play a musical instrument, speak a foreign language. And then they have a kid and all that shit they were gonna do to make their kids better than everybody else's goes right out the window. You know what I'm saying?"

"I heard this thing once that some boxer said about the people that he fought. This is when he was at his peak. He said everybody had a plan when they stepped into the ring with him and they meant to follow through with that plan right up until the moment they got hit in the mouth."

"Wow, you're so deep," she teased. "If getting hit in the mouth is meant to be a metaphor for parenting—"

"It is."

"Then that sounds about right."

"So what's your master plan?"

That amused her. She relaxed into her seat, rooted through her purse and brought out a cigarette.

"Do you mind?" she said, sparking it before I gave an answer.

"It's against the law to smoke in here now."

"Funny they have the ashtrays out then."

She blew a column of smoke out of the side of her mouth and sipped her bourbon. A flake of tobacco or something stuck to her tongue. She picked it off, examined it on her fingers, and dusted it onto the floor.

"I'm going to school at night getting my pre-requisites for nursing. I want to give my son more opportunities than I had, yadda yadda yadda. Make enough money to put him through college hopefully, if I can get him through middle school first. The grocery store has a shit health plan, but at least they have a health plan, and they give you a discount on food if you work there. So that's what I'm doing."

I must have had a funny grin on my face because she said, "Is that funny?"

"Not at all. Sounds good to me."

"It's a plan," she said, taking another drag.

"I've never seen you in here."

"I used to come in here when I was younger."

"How much younger?"

"Before I was old enough to come in here. The bartender used to be this old redneck, had this mustache that grew all the way down past his bottom lip. Kept it immaculate. I always wondered how he ate."

"Everything else the same?"

"Jukebox is new. The people are different. But they're the same."

I looked around at the inhabitants of the bar, took a drink and settled my gaze back on her.

"What brings you here now?"

The back of the booth had a soft padding. She rested her head against it. Her eyes didn't come off me.

"Because for one night, I don't want to think about the future. I don't want to think about the past. Or all the ways I'm fucking up. I don't want to think about anything. I just want to forget my life for a little bit."

"Thought I'd be a good companion for that?"

She took another drag off her cigarette and stuffed it out in a tray.

"Was I wrong?"

"Probably."

"Why did you come to the store today?"

"Needed some fruit."

"Yeah? I've never seen you in there before."

"I do all my shopping at Big Tom's. Maybe you don't remember me."

She gave me a whimsical little look.

"I think I would remember you."

Beside us a roar erupted as somebody won in shuffleboard. The victors scooped their dollars off the score box and celebrated with a clumsy little choreographed dance move, waving the money in the air.

Karla said, "Looks fun."

"You should play."

"Maybe another night."

"Can I ask you a serious question?"

"How serious?"

"World serious."

She considered me for a moment.

"Why not?"

I lifted my glass.

"'Nother round?"

"Sure," she said, hiking up her eyebrows. "It's your turn to buy. Throw a little Coke in mine."

I poured the bourbon left in my glass down my throat and carried our empties over to the bar. As I waited for Tadpole to finish regaling some patrons with that same blonde joke, I looked back at Karla sitting there in the booth. She took a deep weary breath that she slowly let go of, once again leaned her head back against the padding, closed her eyes and kept them shut for a good while until a sudden whoop from one of the men playing shuffleboard jolted her alert. She looked at them and then on past to me at the bar. I smiled. She smiled back, wanly.

I delivered her drink and sat down.

"Where's the kid tonight?"

"At home in bed, I hope. That's where I left him anyway."

"Are you tired?"

"No, I'm fine. Cheers."

She slurped the top off her fresh bourbon and Coke. A wave of people who were all together came into the bar. The volume of the place went up and made talking more difficult.

"It's getting crowded in here."

I leaned forward over the table.

"They've got a dollar beer special going."

She nodded. "So what's your story?"

"No story."

"Everybody's got a story."

"No future, no past. Just here, right now, with you. Remember?"

"Passing time?"

"Passing time."

"Just how I like them. Ever been married?"

"Yeah. You?"

"No, never made it that far. What happened?"

"You get down to it, don't you?"

She shrugged. "You don't have to tell me."

"She left me," I admitted. "She's from here. Still in town, remarried to a guy named Tom. He's a doctor."

"Oh, she's moving up in the world."

"Indeed. What about you? Is the boy's father around?"

"He's in Alabama, last I heard. Working some kind of offshore construction job, but that was a while ago. Who knows really?"

"Too bad for the kid."

"I was fifteen when I had Davey. Ronnie was nineteen. He stuck around for all of six months before he split. Since then, I can count the times he's seen Davey on one hand and the amount of times he's called him on the other. Ronnie's mother lives over in the West End. Blames me for his staying gone. I know that every boy needs a father and all that, but Davey's better off without him, even if he doesn't know it. Lesser of two evils. Ronnie is a piece of shit really."

"That kid is lucky to have you."

She tossed her head back and cackled.

"Try telling him that."

"He knows it. Even if he pretends not to, he knows down deep how lucky he is to have a mom that cares about him like you care about him, enough to go give some stranger a good tongue-lashing and whack across the face anyway."

"When are you going to get over that? It wasn't even that hard."

"My jaw still clicks when I open it."

"You must have a glass jaw."

My drink was finished and she was close to done with hers.

"How about I get us another round?"

"It's my turn."

"I got it." I stood up.

"Hey," she called out to stop me walking away. Her green eyes were heavy-lidded from the two drinks. Her voice was a little tipsy and she was looser in her body.

"Nope, I got it."

She reached out and clutched my forearm. "Why did you come to the store today?"

The way she gazed up at me, expectant, vulnerable, carnal, cast a spell over me that paralyzed my body and tongue. She let go of my wrist, but her arm didn't drop. It stayed suspended in the air between us like some discontinued bridge. I stood there not moving or speaking, fixated on her.

A drunk passing between our booth and the shuffleboard table banged into my back and nearly knocked me on top of her, disrupting the spell. I whipped around and must have looked plenty angry because the guy apologized first thing, declared that he wasn't looking for trouble. I warned him to watch where he was going and then turned back to Karla, who was waiting for an answer.

"To see you," I confessed.

The words came out in a whisper, impossible to hear above the din of sound that enveloped us, but she heard me.

She set her unfinished drink on the table, stood up and said, "Let's go."

Outside it had started to mist. By the time we reached the high school we were both damp with rain. I led her through my office and into my studio and switched on the lamp. She kicked off her shoes and appraised my sparse, shitty little living quarters with neither approval nor disapproval. The cat was on the bed, tail curling and slapping silently onto the sheet, apathetic to our presence. Everything was quiet except for the rain tapping the windows.

"Lay down," she instructed.

I batted the cat off the bed and shooed her into the other room, then did as I was told and laid there. Karla faced away from me taking off her clothes. She peeled her shirt up over her head and draped it across the lampshade, diffusing the light. She unlatched her cream-colored bra and hunched forward to let it fall off her arms, exposing the full under-curve of her breast. She unbuttoned her jeans, shimmied them to her ankles and stepped out of them. Hooked her thumbs inside the band of her yellow panties and slipped them down her legs. Then she turned and faced me and let me see the whole thing.

She was bigger out of clothes than she was in them, but it isn't the size of a woman I admire; it's the shape, and she had plenty of shape. The backlight from the lamp cast a silhouette over the contours of her body. Her skin was perfectly pale, and it felt like, if I gazed hard enough, I would be able to see sheer through her. As a whole, she was one of the dazzling visions of my life. She slunk onto the end of the bed and crawled on top of me.

And I had all of her.

After, we lay there breathless and panting, not talking as the sweat on our bodies cooled and dried. Her head lay snug in the crook of my arm. My heart thumped against her temple. The glow of the moon through the rain-streaked windows made distorted shadows on our bodies.

"I didn't picture you with a cat," she said, running the backs of her fingers along my chin and jaw.

"I inherited her."

"Your face is rough."

"Is that your subtle way of telling me to shave?"

"No."

"Already trying to change me?"

"No," she smiled. "I like it. Your face is rough, your hands are rough, your lips are rough—you're rough." The tips of her fingers followed her words as she traced the palm of my hand and then my face and lips. "And I like it all."

I craned my head down and kissed her mouth. Her hand crept down my chest on past my navel and she took hold of me. When I started to get riled up again she squeezed me hard, once, and then let go.

"Mmm, I have to leave."

"Okay."

She rolled off the bed and got dressed. Her hair was thick and wild. She ran her fingers through the tangles and shook it loose. "I want to see you again."

"Okay."

After she left, I lay there in the dark for a long time, perfectly still, aching all over, replaying the night from the moment she walked into the bar to the moment she walked out of the bedroom, and every moment in between. Her body, the symmetry of her ass, was like a visual feast I couldn't get out of my head. Just what I fucking needed, I thought. After a while the cat crept back into the room and hopped onto the bed and we lay there together, slayed.

CHAPTER TWENTY
IN DEATH A SAINT

The funeral service for Trisha Cammack was held at two-thirty p.m. at the First Baptist Church downtown, an immense red-stoned building with four pillars at the entrance and a pair of bell towers on the front corners of the roof. Light streamed into the vast sanctuary from large, stained glass windows. Each window depicted a different scene from the Bible. Three in particular pulled my attention.

They were side by side over the west balcony. The image on the left window was of a genial Abraham leading Isaac up the mountain to be sacrificed. The middle window was the traditional image of Jesus nailed to the cross, and the glass on the right portrayed a large crowd of people with their arms extended skyward to a glowing sun. The way I read it, if God and Abraham had the conviction to sacrifice their own children, what is it for the common man or woman to fork over a good chunk of their hard earned cash? After all, as the last window illustrated, the meek shall inherit the earth. Had to hand it to Jesus, that shit had worked on people for thousands of years; the longest running racket of all time.

A grand total of eleven mourners showed up to pay their respects. Norman Hinkle was not among them. Nor were any co-workers from the Midnight Run or, far as I could tell, any of her boyfriends. Everyone in attendance seemed to have some relation to the Cammacks. Joe's family shared his dark complexion and ruddy Irish traits distinguished Katherine's relations. No one snuck any furtive glances my way or exhibited any behavior that could be labeled as suspicious, but I made a mental note to ask Joe Cammack if any of them lived within walking distance of his house.

The preacher, a portly fella, stood at the pulpit above the casket. Above him were an empty choir pit and a massive window depicting a giant Jesus with his arms outstretched as if to embrace the flock. The preacher spoke as though he were addressing a full congregation rather than the eleven people clustered into two pews. He hit all the high notes necessary for a funeral: Trisha Cammack was a precocious child, unable to stay quiet for the duration of a sermon or sometimes even the duration of a prayer, often blurting out just how boring she found the lessons or readings to be. She was a beautiful child, the preacher testified, who became an even more beautiful adult.

To this point, Katherine Cammack's crying had been silent. Now she wept aloud. The sound of it hollow and lonely in the expanse of the sanctuary.

The preacher marched on. A bright future was lost when Trisha was taken from us, tragically before her time; God's plans were sometimes beyond our comprehension; Trisha was in a better place now, looking down on her loved ones from the prosperous heavens above.

He described these heavens and speculated on the wonder God must have felt when his newest angel appeared in front of him. Listening to him made me queasy. The families nodded along and sighed and sniffled, dabbed the corners of their eyes with tissues and wiped their noses. They didn't mind the preacher's performance the way I did. They needed it. Death had transformed Trisha Cammack into a saint. Miraculous.

When it was over and everyone had hugged one another and shuffled up the aisles and out of the sanctuary, Joe Cammack caught up with me by one of the pillars out front and took me aside. He asked me to come to the cemetery, saying the burial shouldn't take long. He and his wife were the only ones going, and he wanted a progress update on the case.

The cemetery was on the outskirts of town, beyond the East End. I stood in the shade of an oak tree on a knoll across the lane from where they lowered Trisha Cammack into the earth. The day was pleasant and warm, serene. A steady breeze rustled the leaves in the branches above me. Thick clouds moved imperceptibly across the sky. Somewhere far off was the sawing of a lawnmower.

When the burial was complete, Joe Cammack put his wife in their car, crossed the lane and climbed the knoll to join me under the tree. We stood there for some duration listening to the breeze, gazing down upon his daughter's gravesite. Cammack loosened his tie and undid the top button on his shirt.

"I think she got a good spot, don't you?"

"Yeah, it's nice."

"Good little plot. Good place for her mother to come visit her. Pretty. Peaceful. I wonder if she would have liked it."

Joe looked away from the gravesite, off beyond the rolling hills of the cemetery.

"Ain't nobody should have to go through what I went through today. Ain't nobody should ever have to put their baby in the ground. It ain't the natural way of things."

"No, it's not."

"You know, we wanted to have more kids. Wanted to have a bunch more. Katherine wanted me to have a boy.

I wanted a boy, too—and more girls. Katherine was very pretty when she was younger. Still is, don't get me wrong, but she was really something when she was younger. I wanted a bunch of girls that looked like her. Could you imagine? A bunch of beautiful little Cammack girls. We tried. It just never happened. Just Trish. She was enough though. She was enough and she was too much."

The last couple words caught in his throat. He cleared it out and hocked some loose phlegm onto the grass.

"Thanks for sticking around."

"No problem."

"It's a beautiful day," Cammack said. "A beautiful goddamn day." He sighed and made a small, pained noise. "When Carl Turnbull told me you was the man I ought to see, he told me that you had a son who got killed. That true?"

"Yeah, that's true."

At the mention of my son my chest got tight, my jaw clamped shut, my vision narrowed, but I tried not to show it.

Having noticed no outward change in me, Cammack asked, "No getting over something like that, is there?"

My ears felt clogged up, as if the sound of the world had been unplugged, replaced by blood screaming through my skull. Air went thickly in and out of my nose. After a delay, I answered him.

"Some people maybe can. You go on living, one way or another."

"I imagine one day down the road, who knows when, I'll wake up and it won't be the first thing that comes to my mind. I'll sit up and get out of bed and make my coffee and then it'll hit me that I hadn't thought of it all that time until then. Maybe I'll even feel bad about forgetting her for that tiny bit. Maybe it will be a relief, who knows. But my wife, you know women, she'll think about it every second of every day. She'll be a raw nerve for the rest of her life."

He turned and faced me now for the first time since he had climbed the knoll. Beneath his bloodshot eyes, dark pouches sagged halfway down his face.

"How old was your boy?"

"I don't talk about my son."

"Oh, okay. I'm sorry."

"It's not personal. When other people talk about it—makes it feel cheap."

"I understand. Did they ever catch the fella who did it at least?"

"Not yet."

"I just want to catch the people who did this to my baby. You can understand that. That's all I want is to catch those bastards and watch them burn."

"About that," I leaned against the tree, "I need to ask you, do any of the people who were at the funeral today live close to you down there on the West End?"

"No," he shook his head. "Wait."

He rocked back on his heels and tilted his head back to where it seemed like he was peering up through the branches of the tree.

"No, my cousin Janet used to live a couple blocks away, but she moved to the East End last year. The rest of my family is all still down in Kentucky and Katherine's side is all over there across the river in Ohio. Why?"

"I've tracked your daughter's movements on the night she was found up to a point. She was back in the neighborhood. I believe she may have been trying to get home. Now, either I'm wrong and she wasn't going home, or something occurred to where she never made it. Someone picked her up or she stopped somewhere else, I don't know."

"Where was she walking from?"

"A boyfriend's house."

Cammack twitched.

"That's who you should be checkin' out, that boyfriend of hers. That's who got her into this business."

"She had a few boyfriends, Joe."

Cammack raised a palm in the air.

"I don't want to hear no more."

"She had been a few places that night."

"I don't want to hear no more," he yelled at me.

One final question gnawed at my gut. I didn't particularly want to ask it, nor have it answered, but I couldn't avoid it any longer so I put it to him.

"Did Trisha make it home that night, Joe?"

Joe looked down once more to the gravesite of the only child born to him, then over to the tiny figure of his wife in the passenger seat of their car. Her face was cupped in her hands, shoulders visibly convulsing.

He slipped a hand into his inner breast pocket and removed a flask, unscrewed the lid, took a long tug and sighed, "Yes, she made it home." With his voice flat and absent of emotion, as if he had detached from the proceedings and was simply relating the details of some mundane memory, some trivial matter, Joe Cammack related his account of the night his daughter died.

"It was late. I couldn't sleep and I was tossin' and turnin' all over the place, so I figured I would let Katherine get some sleep because she hasn't slept well since Trish disappeared and she had fell to sleep that night, for a change. I was in the kitchen, sitting at the table. Had a drink in front of me but I wasn't really drinkin' it. Just sippin'. Didn't hear Trish come in. She just kind of appeared at the doorway. She could have been there for a long time, I don't know. I looked up and she was just standing there, starin' at me. I could tell she was fucked up. Her eyes were all glazed like. But I was so excited to see her I didn't care.

I got up and went over to her. I remember I was saying, 'Thank God, thank God, thank God you're alright.' Then I hugged her and she didn't hug me back, which I didn't care about. I was just so happy she was back.

"I couldn't wait to tell Katherine. Finally, all her worrying herself sick could be over, you know. I was about to go wake her up and I pulled back from Trish and she was still just staring right through me. I told her that I loved her and everything was gonna be good now. But then she said something that made me kinda step back. She said, 'You love me, huh? Why don't you show me how much you love me?' I asked her what she meant by that and she asked me if I had any of the Motor. I didn't know what she was talking about. Then she grabbed me, she grabbed me between my legs and said, 'C'mon, I know you want me. Give me some of that Motor and you can have me any way you want me. You can have me all night.' I pushed her away but then she kept coming at me, trying to kiss me and clawing at me. I didn't know what to do. I kept fighting her off and pleading with her.

"She started to get belligerent then, saying all kinds of nasty things, callin' me nasty names. Sayin' I wasn't man enough for her. Trish would never talk to me like that. I knew she was out of her head, but I couldn't stop her. She just kept comin' for me. I started trying to get her to be quiet, shushing her, so she wouldn't wake up Katherine. That's when she started undressing. She took off her clothes and started touching herself and saying that she had what I needed. She said I could do whatever I wanted to her. Said I'd never felt anything 'til I'd felt her. I shouldn't have had to see that.

"I told her I wanted her to put her clothes back on and sit down. She gave me this look, scary, and her eyes—I swear they was red. Not just the whites, even the colored part. She said, 'Why you lookin' at me like that bitch.'

Them was the last words she ever uttered. Her mouth started to foam up and her eyes fluttered, rolled back in her head and she flopped down to the ground and started convulsing, shaking all over the floor."

Cammack shuddered at the memory.

"I didn't know what to do. I was trying not to wake up Katherine. I didn't want her to see what was happening. I tried to give Trish some water and I got down there with her and I was cradling her in my arms and soothing her and I thought she might be comin' out of it. She stopped shaking and the gunk stopped leaking out of her mouth, but then she looked at me with this disappointed face, like she couldn't believe I would let this happen to her. And she went all limp. I thought maybe she was all right for a second, but she was dead."

The pleasant breeze that blew through the leaves of the trees had quit, leaving the air thick and sticky. Sweat trickled down my back.

"She didn't know who you were, Joe. It was like you said. She was out of her head. Her getting to your house was on instinct. That wasn't really her. Joe?"

Cammack was no longer present; he was off reliving that night.

"You took her to the river."

He nodded.

"I knew where I could take her where she wouldn't be found. If I put her in down there by the shallows, I thought maybe that would be better. If Katherine believed Trish might still be alive, out there somewhere in the world, having fun, making something of herself. At least Katherine would have hope, you know. Something to live for. That'd be better than the truth. Better than this shit.

"So I wrapped my baby in a blanket, put her in the back seat of my car and drove her down there to the river.

But I couldn't do it. I couldn't put her in that water. I just ran away. I ran away."

A few days before, standing in my office, Joe Cammack had been an imposing presence. Now he looked a foot shorter. He was a brittle, irreparable old man, never to be whole again.

"I just wanted the person who made her into what she became to pay."

"There's nobody to blame here, Joe. She put herself where she was."

"Perhaps." Joe shook his head slowly and chewed the front of his lower lip. "When did you know it was me?"

"I didn't know. It crossed my mind last night that she might have been heading home. That she might have made it there, I had to entertain the possibility. You know the river, worked it for years. Whoever took her down there knew where to put her in. The day you came to hire me you had fresh mud on your shoes, size thirteen shoes I'm assuming, that looked similar to mud by the river. Now, that didn't mean anything because you hadn't put her there yet. But it got my mind working. I'd hoped I was wrong, that it wasn't you."

"I wish it wasn't me either, friend. I wish—"

He tipped the flask back.

"You should know what you set in motion. A woman died because of this business. Her five kids no longer have a mother. They're getting split up as we speak, shipped off in all different directions to live with strangers. I was shot at and could have been killed."

"Yeah," Joe winced. "I wish I was sorrier about it, but to be honest with you, Mr. Malick, I am sorry you got shot at and I'm sorry about that lady's kids and all, but really I don't give a goddamn no more. You can turn me in to the authorities if you want to. It don't matter."

Off to our right a column of cars, all with bereavement flags on their hoods, snaked their way down the lane and disappeared over the hill.

"Somebody else getting buried."

"I don't see any point in turning you over. You've had enough. Take care of yourself, Joe."

I left him on the knoll and walked down the lane past his wife sitting in their car. She never looked up from her hands. Her shoulders were still shaking from her crying. When I drove out of there Cammack hadn't moved from beneath the tree.

CHAPTER TWENTY-ONE

IN THE TANK

I drove to the nearest ATM and withdrew a hundred dollars from my bank account. The remaining balance: a whopping two hundred seventeen dollars and fifty-three cents. Some business needed to be drummed up and drummed up quick, but that would have to wait until tomorrow because on this day I was getting drunk.

At The Red Head, I deposited sixty dollars' worth of Maker's Mark into my belly in less than two hours and was feeling great about it when that belligerent drunk that haunted the place sidled up next to me.

"This seat taken?" he asked, chipper as a fucking bluebird.

"Yeah."

He laughed as if I were funny, squeezed my shoulder and planted himself on the stool.

"And how is your day coming along, sir?"

"Worse, now."

The chatterbox ordered a beer from Tadpole, who kept an eye on me as he pulled the beer from the cooler, twisted off the top and served it to the guy. The guy was long and loose-limbed. His thin fingers looked like they were strangling the bottle as he lifted it to his mouth and took loud swishing gulps.

He set the bottle on the bar, opened his mouth wide and made some satisfied vowel sounds.

"My name's Teddy," Teddy the drunk said, engaging me. "Haven't seen you in here before. You from around here?"

"Are you fucking serious?"

He squinted and leaned closer to scrutinize my face.

"Have we met?"

"You gotta be kidding me," I said sourly. "I've seen you in here a hundred times. Last night and the night before you ear-banged me so hard I wished I was deaf."

"That doesn't sound like me," Teddy the drunk said. A perplexed expression made his face droopy and stupid.

"It was you."

"Doesn't sound like me. I don't remember you and I'm not a talker."

"Listen, it was you. Don't try to tell me it wasn't you when you know goddamn well you get so fucked you can't see straight or even form a goddamn sentence."

Teddy the drunk huffed, affording me a whiff of his rot breath. I fluttered my hand in front of my face to shoo away the smell.

"Don't talk to me that way taking the Lord's name in vain. I've never seen you and I think you're plum crazy. I don't know what's got you so rankled, but I won't stand for nobody talking to me like that."

"Fine, I'm the crazy. Just don't talk to me, not about the ills of technology or any other bullshit."

When I mentioned the technology thing, a faint recognition came into Teddy's face, but left just as quickly. Even if he realized that he'd chatted me up before, pride prevented him from backing down now. The black whiskers at the corners of his mouth twitched.

"I'm not going to sit and take this horseshit from you."

I motioned across the bar.

"There are fifty other seats in here. Choose one."

"You're an asshole."

He hocked a loogie onto the floor.

Tadpole chimed in.

"Take it easy, Teddy."

"I'm just trying to converse while I wet my whistle a little. Just a little conversation to pass the time. And this fuckbucket," he jerked a thumb my way, "decides to be a cantankerous son of a bitch. Someone needs to learn him a lesson."

I said, "It's not gonna be you."

"The hell it ain't. I'm not scared of you."

"Take it easy, fellas," Tadpole said.

"C'mon you asshole," Teddy taunted. He grabbed his beer bottle by the neck, stood up from the stool and cocked the bottle up by his shoulder. Beer spilled from the bottle onto his shoulder and feet and he cursed at himself.

Tadpole hollered, "What the fuck, Teddy? Take it outside."

I took a sip of my Maker's, placed it on the bar and swiveled around to face the guy. He was crouched down with that beer bottle still raised and his left elbow sticking out to act as a shield. His eyes were bugging out of his head.

I said, "You want a piece of me?"

"I want some fucking all of it."

"Why don't you put that bottle down and fight like a man?"

Teddy bristled, indignant at my calling out his masculinity, and promptly set the bottle down on the bar. As soon as he did I picked it up and smacked it across his face. Teddy the drunk yelped and covered his face with his hands. Blood spurted through his fingers as he collapsed to the floor.

"My eye, my eye, I cain't see! I cain't see!"

While Teddy lay there bleeding and screaming, I sat back down and picked up where I left off with my drink. A couple of people got up from the booths to tend to Teddy. Tadpole came around the bar with a towel and a cold compress. He shot me a disgusted look.

"You saw him," I said. "I've always been cordial."

One or two people had gotten on their cell phones right after the altercation. A cruiser must have been in the vicinity because a pair of uni's arrived before I even finished my drink. Upon their entrance, everyone in the bar pointed their fingers at me. A unanimous vote. The officers wrenched my arms back, snapped on the cuffs and marched me out of there. At the station, they processed me and tossed me in the drunk tank.

A metal bench ran the length of the three cinderblock walls. In the corner was a metal toilet. There were two other guys in there. One, a fat sweaty mouth-breather sitting with his elbows on his knees, stared at me like I was familiar. I didn't recognize him. The other guy was propped against the toilet, half-conscious, dried puke all down his front. He kept nodding off until his head smacked the toilet, wherein he would sit back up to do it all again.

I sat on the empty bench along the far wall. The sweaty one, nose wheezing with every fat breath, aimed a wooly finger at me and declared, "You're that pig busted me for stealing copper from those wires."

I said, "Wasn't me, not a cop," then lay down on the cold bench and shut my eyes.

I woke up with two thick hands wrapped tight around my throat. I punched and slapped at the bends of his elbows but the fat fucker didn't budge. He had gravity and a few hundred pounds working for him. There must have been a security camera in there because four guards came hustling in and tasered him in the middle of his back. His whole body went rigid and he released my neck and fell to the floor like a sack. I flung myself upright, sucking for air and clutching at my windpipe to make sure it was still intact.

It took a minute for the air to get going in and out properly. The guards gave me a cursory once over to make sure I was going to live. Then each guard took hold of one of the fat guy's limbs to haul him out of there, but he was too heavy to lift. They had to drag him by the ankles into another cell. The guy covered in puke slept through the whole ordeal.

My throat hurt like hell. For the next few hours I tried not to swallow. In that time, two more guys got thrown in the tank, nobody I knew. Around nine p.m. one of the guards opened the cell and bellowed my name. Willis Hively had already visited the property clerk and was waiting in the holding room with my possessions.

"Rumor going around somebody tried to murder you in here, too."

"It's all the rage."

He tossed me my wallet and looked at the marks on my neck, let out a little whistle.

"Jesus."

"My money better be in here."

"Don't worry. I didn't take your forty bucks."

So he'd sifted through my wallet. I stuck it in my back pocket, strapped on my gun and put on the flat cap. Hive held up my phone.

"You have four missed calls from me. You planning on returning one ever?"

I snatched my phone out of his hand.

"You want to come search my place too or have you already done that while you had me pinned in here."

"I'm not searching anything. What are you doing getting into a bar fight?"

"He started it."

"Enough witnesses from The Red Head agree with you. Else you'd be staying put in here. Tadpole said you didn't need to hit him with the bottle though."

I shrugged.

"C'mon," Hive said. "We can talk while I drive you home."

Outside the night was warm and the town was still. Hive drove us into the Southside.

"You find Tricky Jackson?"

"I found him."

"Get anything out of him?"

"Tricky's scared shitless. Way he tells it they didn't give him an option not to join up. They tell him to drop something off he drops something off. They tell him to pick something up he picks something up."

"He know anything about Aisha Bryant?"

"Claimed not to. I think he's keeping his head down, does what he has to do and tries to steer clear of these guys best he can."

"Maybe we can use him."

"He seems pretty set on not sticking his neck out to cross them. Told me to be careful about the one called Cupcake. Says he's got eyes and ears everywhere."

"How the hell do you get a street name like Cupcake?"

"Maybe it's like a Johnny Cash 'Boy Named Sue' thing. They give him that name and he has to get tough or die."

"Or maybe he's got a sweet tooth."

"Or maybe he shits sugar. Anything new on your end?"

Hive pushed his lower lip overtop his upper one, tilted his head to the side thoughtfully.

"Ballistics on the bullets extracted from Aisha's body were a match for a Browning .22 used in a robbery five years ago. Never found the .22. Suspect in the robbery was Chad Fowler, but we could never pin it on him."

"Fowler? Fowler didn't kill Aisha Bryant."

"His gun might have. If we can find Fowler, maybe he can lead us somewhere. Getting anywhere with the Cammack case?"

"It's over."

Hive's eyes cut sidewise at me.

"What do you mean, it's over?"

"It's all dead ends with that girl. Doesn't matter who took her to the river. She was going to die no matter what happened. All she did all night was go around scoring junk from everywhere she could think of. Whoever took her down there was probably just the last one that had her when she croaked."

"It wasn't Tremaine Miller?"

"He was her first stop, not her last."

"Damn. So that's that?"

"That's that."

Hive wheeled the car into the high school parking lot and shifted into park.

I put my hand on the door handle.

"Somebody was following me last night. You know anything about that?"

"I warned you that they might come after you the way you worked Tremaine over."

"The guy following me was a white guy."

"White?"

"With a big beard."

Hively shifted in his seat and sat up straighter.

"Any ideas on who it could be?"

"No. He was driving a dark blue sedan. Chrysler. Dealer plates."

"Let me look into it."

"Do that." I opened the door and set my feet flat on the ground. "Thanks for the ride."

Hive said, "You being straight with me?"

I twisted back at him.

"You being straight with me?"

"Of course," he frowned.

"All right then. See you around, Hive."

I got out and watched Hive's Chevy Malibu roll down the street. When his taillights dwindled out of sight I stepped between two cars and checked my Beretta to make sure all the bullets were in there and it hadn't been fucked with or jammed up in any way. It was fine.

I tucked the gun away and turned to head into the high school. A slight figure standing by the trunks of the cars startled me. I went for my gun, but then the figure started cackling with delight. The goddamned kid. He held his belly and doubled over in hysterics, a big shit-eating grin plastered across his face.

"Jesus Christ, you're a sneaky little son of a bitch," I said, sliding my gun back into the holster.

The kid thrust his arms in the air.

"Don't shoot!"

"What the hell are you doing out here?"

"Yo, you should have seen your face. You damn near lost your shoes from jumping out of them."

"All right, all right. It wasn't that funny. Sneaking up on a guy with a gun isn't the smartest thing in the world."

"I didn't sneak up on nobody. I saw you getting out of that car and I walked over here. That ain't sneakin'. What am I supposed to do, walk like an elephant?"

"Where's your mom?"

"Class."

"You hungry?"

His laughing died out suddenly.

"Hells yeah, I could eat."

CHAPTER TWENTY-TWO
DEAD NESTER

The kid and I sat at the picnic table outside the hot dog stand. The place was lit up by a string of Christmas lights draped along the awning and a couple of tiki torches spiked in the ground. The kid had already wolfed down two dogs and was halfway through a third. My throat was raw and swollen and I had to stretch my neck out like a baby bird to swallow a little nibble. But I was famished so I kept nibbling. I said, "How come I never see you pal around with anybody your own age?"

The kid lifted his shoulders and flipped his palms, talked through a mouthful of food.

"Them kids at school are stupid. They think they all cool and shit. I'm not into it."

"It's weird, a kid with no friends."

"Look who's talking. You the one said friends are overrated. I ain't never seen you hanging out with nobody accept those ass-clowns who come in there looking for you to spy for them or whatever."

"It's different when you get older. When I was your age I hung out with all kinds of people."

"Yeah, right. What's different?"

"Well—" I forced another bite down.

"Something wrong with you?"

"My throat's sore."

"You sick?"

"No."

"Whatever man, don't be breathing your skeevy shit this way."

"When you get older things get more complicated. Having friends isn't the same. They think they know you, think they know what's best for you more than you know what's best for yourself, but nobody knows that kind of thing about somebody else. Anybody that thinks they do is a jackass. Know what I'm saying?"

"Not really. When you're old sounds about the same as when you're young to me."

"When you're a kid, nobody ever tells you that life doesn't get easier. When you're young you think you will grow up, figure shit out and then everything will be neat and perfect. But let me save you the grief, it doesn't work that way. Shit just gets more muddied up. You never figure anything out. Hell, there might not be anything to figure out. That might be the problem. Life isn't short. Life is a long, hard slog."

"That's your big wisdom? Life is hard? So you're saying I'd be better off living fast, dying young and making a pretty corpse?"

"No, not—forget it. Anyway, you gotta be pretty to make a pretty corpse."

"Whatever. I'm pretty as hell. And I already know all that bullshit," the kid mocked. "Life is hard. No shit. Real pearls of wisdom."

The kid polished off his last hot dog, sucked down the remainder of his soda and we set out for home. As we passed the gas station and crossed the street, the kid picked up the thread of conversation.

"I used to hang out with this one dude, Mike-Mike. This one time he asked me what I was scared of. I thought we was tight so I told him I was scared of snakes and he told me that

I was gonna die someday from a snake bite. That he could just feel it that that shit was going to happen to me. Like he could see my future or some garbage and that was what was going to happen. What kind of fucked up shit is that? I told him it wasn't cool to say that kind of voodoo shit 'cause I really am scared of snakes, but that just made him laugh and he would taunt me with it. Pretend to be a snake and sneak up on me, trying to scare me in front of everyone. Then he went and told everybody at school that he made me cry."

"What did you do?"

The kid looked at me like I was dense.

"What do you mean, what did I do? I fucked that boy up, son."

Approaching the high school I noticed a silhouetted figure skulking in the shadows of the strip mall across the road, nearly imperceptible against the wall. Every atom in my body prickled up. The lot over there was empty of cars and the shops were long-closed for the night. The man in the shadows lit a cigarette and feigned like he wasn't watching us, which was what gave him away. Him, me, and the kid were alone on the street. Nobody at the gas station or outside the high school, no cars driving by. You see two other people on an empty street, you're gonna check them out, at least nominally. This guy's head never tilted our way. But his eyes tracked us, ever so slightly, across his frame of vision, like the fucking Mona Lisa.

The kid kicked at some crabgrass sprouting from the cracks in the pavement.

"What's up with you and my moms?"

I kept my eyes glued to the lurker in the shadows.

"Did she say something?"

"No."

"Then nothing's up."

The lurker's right hand disappeared into his pocket. The kid made a smacking sound with his lips.

"Man, you straight up lying to my face. I saw you with her last night. I saw you and her come out of the bar and go to your apartment."

"Where were you?"

"Over in that little nook on the landing."

"You are a sneaky little fucker. Don't worry about it. Nothing's going on. I was just walking her home. She came over for another drink."

"I don't want her to get hurt, that's all."

The kid kicked at the sidewalk some more and didn't look up at me. At the portico I hustled the kid up the stairs. Glancing back, I saw the shadow lurker draw a phone from his pocket, punch in a number and lift it to his ear.

Inside, I hurried down the hall. The kid had to almost trot to keep up with me.

"Listen, Davey, I can't hurt your mother. She doesn't care about me enough for me to hurt her. The only person that can hurt your mother is you. So if you don't want to see her hurt, be a good kid don't do anything stupid. You hear me?"

"I hear you," he said, peering over. "But she does care about you."

"Did she say something?"

"No, she ain't say nothing. She just doesn't hang out with dudes much."

"No?"

"Naw."

At the stairwell I said a quick goodbye and pretended to head off to my apartment, but then doubled back and listened to Davey's footfalls as they ascended to the third floor. I waited until I heard the doors swing open and slam shut before I drew my Beretta and skirted down the hallway along the lockers. No one was lying in wait for me. I reached my door without incident.

The lock on my office door didn't look to have been tampered with, but looks don't mean anything. I twisted the knob carefully as to not make noise. It rotated halfway and caught. Still locked. If someone had jimmied it open, it meant they had re-locked it from the inside, which meant I was walking into an ambush. One way to find out. I scanned the hallway once more, then slipped the key in the lock and rotated it clockwise, ever so gently, until I heard the tiny click of the bolt unlatching. Gun at the ready, I burst into the office. The cat, perturbed at being startled, hissed at me. But she was the only living thing in the place.

I shut and bolted the door. Keeping the lights off, I did a quick sweep of the apartment, found nothing amiss, hurried over to the window and peered outside. The man was no longer in the shadows. The whole street was empty. I scanned the trees and the parked cars and everywhere that could hide a person. I didn't see anything.

Then, from the hallway, soft footsteps approached. I moved away from the window and crouched low beside the door. The footsteps came to a halt. The slit of light coming from beneath the door darkened with the shadow of two legs standing on the other side. Then a knock. I didn't move. Another knock.

"C'mon, man, I know you're in there."

The kid. I didn't answer.

He said, "I know your ass ain't sleeping already."

I yanked the door open. The kid saw the look on my face and the gun in my hand and froze stiff.

"What are you doing here, Davey?"

"I wanted to say thanks for dinner. I forgot to say thanks for my dinner."

"No problem, get out of here."

Whoever was outside must have been waiting for the next sign of life from within the office. The naked bulb shining in from the hallway gave it to them. A torrent of gunfire ripped through the windows, spitting glass all over. Bullets plugged into the walls all around us. I tackled the kid to the floor, made sure he wasn't hit with any bullets, and yelled for him to stay put. He curled into a ball with his hands over his ears and his arms covering his face. Splinters of wall rained down on him. I crawled over the shards of glass and took cover beneath the windows. The bullets kept coming. Sounded like a symphony of destruction above my head.

After a minute there was a lull in the barrage. My ears were ringing like someone had struck a tuning fork inside my skull. I peered over the sill and clocked at least six of them on the street. They were reloading. One of them pointed at the school and barked some orders. The others fanned out. One, wielding a shotgun, bolted for the entrance of the school. I popped a couple of shots in his direction that missed him wide. That kicked off another round of strafing. A second attacker made for the entrance. I couldn't get clear of the window to take a shot. I crawled back over to the kid.

"Davey," I grabbed him by the shoulders and shook him. His eyes snapped open. They were big and white and wild with fear. "Across the hall there is a locker, one-twenty-one. It's open. Crawl out of here, shut yourself inside that locker and don't come out until I come get you. Don't come out. You understand me?" He nodded. "One-twenty-one," I repeated. "Go."

Davey scurried out of there on his hands and knees and I followed behind him. He found the locker in the hall and squeezed into it. I got clear of the door, got to my feet and ran down the corridor, took a right down one passage, a left down another and stopped short at the intersection of the main entrance hall. At the far end of the hallway across the intersection was the stairwell that led up to the residences. I wasn't going up there. On my left was a set of double doors that opened to an auditorium.

Twenty feet past that another set of double doors opened to a gymnasium.

The firing outside ceased. I poked my head around the corner. Empty. Silent. They hadn't made it that far yet. On the opposite side of the hallway a long glass trophy case that displayed all the old school trophies lined the wall. From behind the case I could maybe get a bead on them, see them coming before they saw me. I made a break for it.

From my right came the concussion of the shotgun. Spray thudded into the wall behind me. I dove past the trophy case and scrambled to get my back against the wall. More bullets zipped past, ricocheting off the floor and walls and shattering the trophy case. I threw a handful of blind shots around the corner and then crouched low to take a peek down the hall. The wall beside my face exploded and I jumped back.

They opened up on me. The shooting built to a deafening crescendo and then stopped abruptly. The echoes from the sharp cracks of gunfire bounced around the confined hallway. When the echoes faded, I heard the careful footfalls of the two men advancing up the hallway, getting close. I threw a couple more bullets at them and made for the doors leading to the gym. As I plunged through the door, the one with the shotgun got me. The impact of it knocked me off my feet and into the gymnasium.

My momentum through the door caused it to bounce hard off the wall and fling shut. A snap of pain seared my elbow and radiated down my arm. But as fast as the pain came it went, leaving the arm limp and numb. I got to my knees and, with the arm that worked, pushed off the ground and then sprinted the length of the court. There were exit doors at each end of the gym. The exit to the right led to an old weight room. To the left were the locker rooms and a passage that linked to the backstage of the auditorium. I chose left. As I ducked into the passageway, behind me the two gunmen kicked in the doors of the gym. Bursts of gunfire rang out. They were shooting just to shoot now.

I hurried down that passage past the locker rooms. Blood sluiced down my arm and off my fingers to the floor, leaving a neat trail for them to follow. But there was no time to stem the bleeding or cover my tracks. I had to keep moving. I emerged from the passageway into the backstage of the auditorium. The area was stuffed full of all kinds of junk. I stumbled over a drum kit and sent a cymbal clanging across the floor. At the far end of the stage a door opened to a stairwell that led down to the boiler room. Didn't want to get cornered down there.

I parted the curtain, ran out over the stage and leapt down to the floor, then ran up the center isle of the auditorium to the entry doors. I peered through the tiny square windows of the doors out into the hallway. All was quiet. I felt something drip onto my shoe and looked down. I had been standing there for no more than ten seconds, but a significant pool of blood had already collected on the floor below my arm. When I lifted my head again my vision blurred for a moment before coming back into focus.

In the hallway, a figure brandishing an automatic rifle floated past the window, moving in the direction of the gym. He neglected to look in the auditorium windows so he didn't spot me. I stuck my Beretta in its holster, gripped the handle of the door, took in a deep breath and exhaled. Then I threw the door open, stepped into the hall and drew my gun. The man spun around, but before he was able to level the rifle, I squeezed off two rounds that thwacked into his chest. His arms and legs flailed out from his body and he toppled backwards onto the ground. The rifle clattered across the floor.

I kicked the rifle against the wall and put another round into him to make certain he was done. Then I squatted down on my haunches and, with my good arm, dragged the thick fucker over to the wall. There I sat and braced myself, leaned him back onto me, and readied for his two comrades.

They had to come from the gym or the auditorium. I was positioned to cover both. They came from the gym. As they stepped through the doors I unloaded on them. The first one out got a bullet to the throat. The second one popped two quick shots in my direction, the first of which thwacked into the stomach of the dead guy on top of me. The second exploded the wall over my head. I fired into him and he flopped backwards into the gym. When the shots stopped resonating off the walls, everything was still save for the second gunmen's legs twitching. They were jutting out from the gym door keeping it propped open.

I sat there for a minute, waiting for more of them, but no more came. Soon the wail of sirens approached. I tugged the big dead guy to the side and got out from under him. I struggled to one knee and tried to stand but my head whirled and my legs buckled and I stumbled onto my ass. The floor was slick with blood.

I reached over and rifled through the pockets of the big dead guy, found his wallet and removed his ID. He came from Detroit, no shocker there, and had seven teardrops inked on his face, all of which were filled-in. This was Tigga-Man. His real name was Nester Treadway. Dead Nester Treadway. I dropped the wallet and ID and scooted sideways across the bloody floor to where the other man, the one I'd shot through the gullet, was splayed on the ground. He was still alive, but the seconds he had remaining were numbered. Blood spurt from his neck like somebody had shaken a bottle and popped the cork. It spilled into his mouth and all around him.

"What the fuck, Tricky?"

Tricky Jackson could not speak nor move his body. The bullet had gone through his larynx and probably severed his spinal column. A gurgling sound rose from his throat. The fear of death, the knowledge of it coming, was present in his yellow eyes that fixed on me now. Yesterday, Tricky had told me that he was a survivor, and that was what he was doing, keeping his head down, doing what he had to do, and surviving. So much for that. He hedged his bets and played the odds. Couldn't blame him really.

The blood gushing from his neck slowed to a dribble and his eyes went calm and glassy. As he expired, I wondered what that magic trick was that he refused to show me—the one his kids loved. Tricky's last trick.

My head began to feel heavy, like some gravitational force compelled it downward. Waves of black cut my vision. Then, without knowing how I came to be there, I found myself prone on the ground beside Tricky. Dead Tricky. There was no longer any feeling in my arms, or my chest, or my face, nowhere, only the hard wet floor against the back of me and the blood leaving my body with each successive beat of my heart.

Then the kid's face hovered above me. He was shaking me, much like I'd shaken him in the office not ten minutes ago—by the shoulders. But he seemed far away now, rapidly receding at the deep end of a long tunnel.

In the next moment the kid was gone and in his place was a canopy of faces. Heads, arms, lips flapping, hands moving all over me as I slipped further and further down the tunnel that now caved inward; sounds coming from mouths, the words dissolving before they reached my ears, the volume of the world dialed down to zero. I was surprised at how warm the muteness felt. As if all along I had been waiting for this to fill the absence. The tunnel, which now seemed infinite, constricted to a tiny speck that burned bright orange, and then, as if taking a gentle step into the abyss, flamed out.

Holy shit, I thought as I lapsed into blackness. Me too? Dead Nicky?

Then, black.

All black.

CHAPTER TWENTY-THREE

THE ONE-ARMED MAN

I awoke in a dark hospital room, IV's stuck in my veins, tubes jammed up my nose. My fucked-up arm was swathed in some sort of sling, throbbing. The curtains were drawn over the windows. A sliver of daylight slipped in around the curtains' edges. The wall clock read three forty-eight.

I was still here.

My head was groggy and my body was all stoved up, to move or even blink was positively excruciating, but I was still here. I attempted to sit up, quickly realized the futility of the effort, and laid my head back down. I tugged the oxygen tubes out of my nose and tried to call for a nurse, but only a soft expulsion of air leaked out. My mouth was dry and burning. I worked my tongue around to create some spit and loosen up my throat. The effort was sufficient enough to produce a couple of croaks. A policeman stuck his head in to investigate the noise. I extended my middle finger and he went back out and shut the door. I heard him get on his walkie to tell somebody I was awake.

Moments later a dumpy nurse barged into my room, introduced herself as Frances, shone a light in my eyes and ears, and asked me a series of questions.

"What's your full name?"

"Nicholas George Malick."

"How old are you?"

"Thirty-eight."

"Where are you?"

"Cain City, West Virginia."

"How many fingers am I holding up?"

"Two and a thumb."

"What month is it?"

I had to think about that one.

"How long have I been in here?"

"Two days."

"April."

Nurse Frances scribbled something on the chart.

"Did I pass?"

"Barely."

"How 'bout some water?"

She stepped to the sink and filled a paper cup with water, came back and pressed the button that inclined the bed. When I had been raised to a satisfactory angle, she tipped the cup to my lips.

I said, "I can do it."

She fit the cup in my hand and squeezed my fingers around it. I gulped the water down, wiped my chin on the back of my hand and told her to fill it again. She served me another, then showed me how to recline and incline the bed and where the call button was located on the bed frame. As she went out the door the doctor came in.

Nurse Frances handed the chart to the doctor, they whispered a few things to each other, and she left the room. The doctor fitted on a pair of plastic gloves and strode over to my bedside.

I addressed my ex-missus.

"Dr. Malick."

"That has not been my name in quite a while. What have you gotten yourself into this time?"

"Sorry, Dr. Orvietto. You do this to me?"

"If you're referring to the surgery, I did."

"I'm shocked that I'm still alive."

"Can't say I didn't think about offing you while I had the chance."

"Should've. You're still my beneficiary. Would have gotten all my money and earthly possessions."

"Which amounts to?"

"Rough estimate—two hundred dollars and a stray cat."

Her lips got tight and thin and she bobbed her head as if she were mulling over the moral implications.

"Yip, you're right, I should have done it."

Joanna Orvietto, formerly Joanna Malick, originally Joanna Newsome, had her hair stretched back into a crisp ponytail. Matching gray streaks arrowed back from each temple. Her makeup was minimal, enough to look professional. Creases spidered out from the grooves at her eyes and her mouth, but they didn't detract from her beauty. Far from it. Joanna was one of those women who possessed a natural elegance and grace; something about the way her face was shaped and her jaw was set. She would always be beautiful, as she was at twenty when I met her, now, at thirty-seven, when she reached sixty, always.

Joanna brought out a thin metal rod that resembled a knitting needle, and with it, poked each fingertip on the hand that was attached to my dead arm. I felt dull tingles on two out of the five, but lied and told her I felt all of them. She jammed a thermometer under my tongue and straightened out my good arm to take my blood pressure. Doing this, Joanna gave me the medical rundown of my injuries.

The shotgun blast had shattered my humerus, radius, and ulna bones around the elbow, lacerated my radial nerve and my brachial artery. I was minutes away from bleeding out when the paramedics arrived at the high school. They staunched the bleeding enough to transport me to the hospital where she performed emergency surgery. A stent was placed in the artery and the nerve was re-attached. Two small rods were inserted into my radius and ulna bones to stabilize the lower part of my arm and there were eleven pins in there holding all the loose bits around the elbow together. They put a couple pints of blood in me to give me the strength to last the surgery. Joanna had remembered my blood type, A-positive.

After the review, she removed the bandages from my arm to examine the wounds, prod and clean them, and apply fresh bandages. She told me it was probable I would lose some feeling or dexterity, but that I should regain some use of the limb if I monitored and rehabbed properly. They were keeping me in the hospital until certain I was out of the woods and showed no signs of infection. She asked me if I had any questions.

"You look good."

"Yeah, well, you look like shit," she quipped, peeling off the plastic gloves.

"I didn't have time to spiff up."

"Nearly eating a bullet will do that to you. Oh, here is a bedpan for you if you need it." She reached into one of the low cabinets to get it and placed the bedpan by my legs.

"A woman came to see you. A woman with a boy."

"Neighbors maybe."

"That's it? Just neighbors?"

"Just neighbors."

Joanna nodded.

"How bad of trouble are you in?"

"Hell if I know."

"You don't know why you have to have a policeman standing guard outside your door?"

"Tell him to leave. I don't care. Can't do any good anyway. This town's gone insane."

"If Cain City is so bad then why do you stay here?"

"You know why I stay here. Of all the people to ask me that fucking question, you know why I stay here."

She walked over to the window and spread the curtains wide. Hot afternoon sun flooded the room. I shielded my eyes.

"Don't get touchy. I didn't mean anything by it. I just don't understand why you don't leave this town. If I were you, no anchor to hold me here, then I would get as far away as I could, that's all."

She came back over to my bedside hugging the clipboard to her chest.

"If you want out of town so bad, then why don't you just pick up and go? It's not that hard."

"My family's here. My job's here."

"Your family will always be here. You can find a job anywhere."

"It's not so simple."

"How is Tommy?"

She frowned at me; a sad, pitying frown.

"His name is Tom."

"Pardon me. How's Tom?"

"He's fine."

"You and him hunky-dory? Do they ever get confused here with two Dr. Orviettos'?"

"Nick."

"What?"

"Don't start."

"I'm making polite conversation. I'm interested in what's been going on with you. "

She shook her head.

"Nothing."

"I want to know if you and him are hunky-dory. What's wrong with that?"

Joanna looked down to the floor.

"Nothing."

"The two of you still living up on Honeysuckle?"

"Yes."

"Well, that must be swell, living the lush life. Your mom must be so proud she could burst into a thousand tiny hearts."

"Don't be mean."

"How was that mean?"

She looked up to me now.

"I'm pregnant," she said.

Two little words that shut my fucking mouth and stopped me breathing.

"Thought you might have heard."

"I hadn't."

"I wanted to tell you myself."

"You've told me."

"Yeah."

I looked at her belly to see if she was showing, to see if I'd missed it, but you couldn't tell. Not even a pooch.

"Do you know what it is?"

"No. Not yet. We'll find out soon, next week."

"Good for you."

"Nick—"

"I hope it's a boy."

"I'm rooting for a girl."

"Yeah, that would be good, too. Either way, congratulations."

It took every fiber in my being to muster up a smile, but I did it.

"Are you hungry?" she asked.

"Not really."

"You need to try and eat. I'll send someone with some food and then a nurse will come in and help you walk around, get your blood moving, take your catheter out if you want her to."

"I've got a catheter in?"

"You do. I'll check in on you in a little while."

The meal they carted in was a turkey plate with soggy vegetables, clumped mashed potatoes, cold gravy, a watery cup of applesauce, and a box of orange juice that didn't come from any kind of orange I ever tasted. I forked up every last morsel. Nurse Frances came back in, got me out of bed, and guided me and my IV stand up and down the hallway. Two other patients were also being dragged around by nurses. One was a slack-jawed old man with liver spots covering his face and neck, a glob of drool dangling from the corner of his mouth, eyes fixed dead ahead. The other was a young guy hobbling around on a cane. In the spirit of wounded solidarity, he winked or saluted me each time we circled one another. I acknowledged him the first time, but ignored him after that.

Nurse Frances cooed encouragement at me like I was a child, but ten minutes of glacial hallway laps got me clammy so she led me to the bathroom and stood outside the door while I did my business, and then put me back in bed. I flipped on the TV and must have dozed off because the next thing I knew Willis Hively was nudging me awake.

"You've always been ugly, but this is a new low."

"Rinse my bedpan out, would you?"

I pushed the button and inclined my mattress. Hively grabbed a chair and dragged it over beside me.

"How you feeling?"

"Like I got eaten by a mountain lion and shit over a cliff."

"I told you to watch out."

"Yeah, you told me all right."

"You want to tell me how it went down?"

"You collecting my statement?"

"Somebody has to."

"Jesus Christ, get me some water."

In broad strokes, I recounted the events of that night, from the time Hive dropped me off in the parking lot until the moment I blacked out in a lake of blood. In turn, he filled me in on what had transpired over the past two days in town. Of the group that stormed the high school, the three that didn't die fled the scene and led the police on a car chase into the East End where they took a corner too hot and wrapped their vehicle around a tree. A shootout ensued and two of them were killed. The third, a banger named Dante Short, was wounded and presently resided on the third floor of the very hospital in which we sat.

With Tricky Jackson killed and four Detroit bodies laid fresh, the police department braced for retaliatory action. The reprisal began in the form of a letter that arrived yesterday to the *Cain City Dispatch*, declaring war on Cain City law enforcement. The Detroit gang also found a way to hack into the police database and obtain the names and addresses of every police officer on the force. Early this morning, there were two drive-by shootings at officers' homes on the Southside.

"The doors are blown off this thing," Hive said. "The mayor is talking about calling in the National Guard."

"It's in the papers?"

"Can't keep this quiet, too big. They're trying to keep the story from breaking nationally because it'll kill the college and then the town with it. Ciccone's going for the goddamn Pulitzer all of a sudden. Can't write enough words about the shit. You're famous, two stories in the same paper. Front page for getting shot, back page for busting a bottle on that poor bastard's face."

Hive chuckled, but cut his laughter short when he noticed I wasn't in a laughing mood. "People are terrified. Kids are leaving college before their final exams, just throwing away the semester. You started yourself a fucking doozy here."

"I didn't start anything."

"You sure helped fan the flames."

"All over one missing junkie."

Hively nodded his head and then shrugged.

"Probably would've happened anyway, eventually."

"Where's Bruce?"

"Hunkered down like the rest of us. Trying to figure out how we can take the fight to them. Feds came up from Charleston this morning. There's two outside waiting to talk to you now, when I'm through."

"You through?"

"What can you tell me about the attack at the old high school?"

"It was excessive."

"That it?"

"That's it. Send them in. Get it over with."

"Okay. There's one more thing."

Hive opened a folder that was resting on his lap, thumbed through the paperwork inside and pulled out a sheet of paper. He grit his teeth and spoke through them.

"I'm not supposed to share this information with you so this can't blow back my way, you understand me? But it doesn't sit right keeping it from you."

Something about the way he said it twisted my insides and jerked my stomach north of my throat.

"Out with it."

"This is a list of the people who were in The Red Head when you broke that bottle over that guy Teddy something or other's face. If you can recall, it was the eyewitness accounts that got you off the hook and backed your saying it was self defense."

"I remember."

Hively handed over the sheet of paper. Fifteen names were listed.

"Number seven," he said.

I scanned down the page. The name beside number seven was typed in the same font and looked as innocuous as the other fourteen names, but those names didn't make my heart sputter. This one did: *Kincaid, Randall.* I stared at the letters as if they were an anagram, as if they were written in Russian. I kept my voice even, didn't look up from the page.

"Is this another Randall Kincaid?"

"Not in this town."

"He's not due out for a year."

"He was released two weeks ago. Good behavior. Overcrowding. We were instructed not to tell you."

"By who?"

"Everybody involved."

"Bruce?"

"Everybody. All the way up. Kincaid informed his parole officer that he wasn't going to come back to Cain City. Said he was moving to Columbus. Evidently, that was a lie. When you told me someone was following you, I had an inkling—"

"Was it him?"

"Maybe. He leased a dark blue Chrysler sedan three days after he got out."

"It was him."

"I tried to track him down. He hasn't used a credit card or written a check since he leased the car. His mother had a little money squirreled away that she left him when she passed, uh—"

"Three years ago."

"Yeah. He withdrew four thousand dollars from Chambers Bank the day after he got out. Her house is vacant and doesn't seem to have been touched. It's overgrown and crumbling. I don't think he's there, but who knows. Technically, he owns the place. Here's his statement from The Red Head."

Hively passed me a second sheet of paper and waited while I read the transcript of Kincaid's statement:

Kincaid: I was in the back booth drinking a tonic water and reading the newspaper when the melee began. I heard the tall skinny man threaten the man in the coat sitting next to him and I looked over.

Officer: You say the tall skinny guy verbally threatened the assailant?

Kincaid: Oh yes, most definitely. The man in the coat responded by saying something to the effect of 'get away from me,' but the skinny man became even more enraged and held a beer bottle above his head as if to hit the man.

Officer: It was the skinny man who brandished the bottle?

Kincaid: Correct.

Officer: How then did it come to be that the assailant ended up with the bottle and hitting the skinny man in the face?

Kincaid: The skinny man moved to strike and somehow the other man managed to get the bottle from him and defended himself accordingly.

Officer: You say he was defending himself?

Kincaid: Oh, without question.

Officer: How did the whole thing begin?

Kincaid: That I do not know. The first thing I heard was the loud threat from the skinny man.

Officer: You didn't hear anything before that?

Kincaid: Not a single thing.

I gave the transcript back to Hively. He said, "I thought you should know. That how it went down?"

"For the most part."

"Thing is, Nick, there were other statements claiming the guy instigated it, but every single one of those statements also claimed that you were spoiling for a fight. And when you got it, you finished it. Kincaid's statement is what tilted it in your favor, got you turned loose. His was the lone voice saying you didn't provoke the situation, that you were defending yourself, unequivocally. Million dollar question is why would he help you out like that?"

"Beats me."

Hive kneaded the pet rock in his hand. He took a big breath in through his mouth and expelled it from his nose.

"I can't guess what he's up to, but he might have plans for you."

"What a coincidence. I've got plans for him too."

"Don't make me regret telling you this, Nick. I told you because you have a right to know. But don't go doing anything stupid."

I gestured toward my lame arm and my surroundings. "Where am I going to go?"

Hive stood up and made for the door.

"Stay put. Get better. Let us handle this."

"Sure. You handle it."

Hive grimaced, "I'll send in the Feds."

"Fantastic."

As the door shut behind him I heard Hive talking under his breath to the guard, warning him not to let me out of his sight. The two Feds came in.

CHAPTER TWENTY-FOUR
THE NIGHT DOCTOR

When the federal agents were through with me I pressed the buzzer for Nurse Frances and asked her to send in the lady doctor. Ten minutes later Joanna came through the door with a concerned look on her face, asking if everything was all right.

"I need you to do me a favor."

"What kind of favor?" she asked, perturbed.

"I gotta get out of here and I need you to help me do it."

"This is what you summoned me for?"

"Yes."

"I can't do that. Jesus, you don't change."

"You can do whatever you want."

"No," Joanna stated flatly. "I can't. And even if I could I wouldn't because, in case you've forgotten, you almost died a few days ago. You aren't even out of the woods yet, not to mention an armed guard is planted outside your door twenty-four hours a day because some gang wants to murder you. You are a danger to yourself and in no shape, physically, and most certainly mentally, to be anywhere other than right where you are. So no, there is no way in hell that you are going anywhere."

"If you're done I'll have my turn."

"No. I'm leaving. I have to prep for surgery. And I'm not going to let you kill yourself you selfish son of a bitch."

She turned for the door.

"I'm not killing myself."

"Not all at once, you're not."

"Joanna."

"What kind of doctor do you think I am?" she said, wheeling back round. Her voice quivered with anger. "That I would let you stroll out of here as what, a personal favor? Like I owe you something. Are you nuts?"

"Joanna—"

"You've just always thought you could do whatever the hell you want, haven't you? With no regard for yourself or anyone around you—"

"Joanna—"

"What?"

"I've found him."

She became still.

"Who?"

"Him."

Joanna blanched.

"I've heard that before. So many times before."

"It's for real this time."

She turned to the window and looked out onto the lovely day. She stood there like that for some time where I could see the back of her but not her face.

"What if you're wrong again?" she said. "You're so possessed by this—this thing. How long are you going to keep chasing ghosts?"

"I'm not wrong."

"How do you know?"

I told her then about the letter I had sent Randall Kincaid and four other child molesters who lived in or around Cain City and were incarcerated in the six months after our son's murder. In the letter I notified each of them that I was going to be waiting for them when they got out of prison and that, if they were in fact responsible for the death of our son, I was going to kill them. Four of five responded. Three of them vehemently denied their guilt. A fourth one didn't give a shit. I'm told he trashed the letter. Kincaid, on the other hand, responded in kind with a letter of his own. It consisted of a simple sentence: 'I look forward to seeing you.'

I told her about his being released early for good behavior without my knowledge; his tailing me around in his car and being in the bar when I got arrested. I told her about the boy that Kincaid was convicted of molesting; the method used to lure the boy into his house; how the boy escaped by jumping through a closed second story window and, naked and bleeding, ran into the middle of the nearest intersection to stop traffic and was hit by a car. The boy survived the accident. Last year, at age fifteen, he jumped from the balcony of his parent's house with a bungee cord tied around his neck.

I told her that Kincaid was arrested exactly one month after our son's warped, mutilated body came bobbing to the surface amongst the flotsam of the Ohio River. The third such body to be found this way over a four-month period.

"No more boys were found after this man went to prison?"

"Not a one."

Joanna, still facing away from me, stepped backwards, reached her hand behind her to find the foot of the bed and sat down.

"A letter saying he looks forward to meeting you is hardly evidentiary proof."

"That's why I gotta find out the truth."

"But you think it's him?"

"Yeah."

Her back began to heave in and out with her breath.

"And if it is? What will you do?"

"I'll make sure that he gets punished to the full extent of the law."

"The law? So you won't do anything stupid? You'll keep it legal?"

"Yeah, legal."

Her whole back shuddered. "Okay," she whispered, turning to me. Sheets of tears, blackened from mascara, slid down the length of her face and dripped off her chin. Her hands and lips were shaking.

"Come here," I said. She scooted up the bed. I wiped her wet cheeks with my hand and she sank into my chest and I wrapped my arm around her.

After a bit she stopped crying, got out from my arm and put some distance between us on the bed.

"I know you're lying," she said, looking me in the eye.

"You could always read me well," I confessed.

Her face scrunched tight to ward off more tears.

"The sad thing is, I still want to stop you, but there's no way I can do that, is there?"

"No."

"You're going to kill him?"

"Yes."

Joanna shook her head rapidly.

"I cannot be complicit in this."

"I'm not asking you to."

"Yes you are. By helping you escape this hospital that's exactly what you're asking me to do."

"I tried to lie to you," I said, shucking the blame.

"You're a shitty liar. And I can't let you go in your condition. You're too weak now. You've got to get your strength up."

"I'll manage. I just need you to get me some clothes and get me past this guard."

Joanna emitted a low groan. Her face contorted with the internal debate taking place in her head.

"You've got to make me a promise."

"What's that?"

"Make sure it's him. Before you do anything, please make sure."

I agreed. Joanna stood to leave. I said, "I might need one other thing."

"Why does that not shock me?"

Before I skipped out, I needed to pay a little visit to Dante Short on the third floor. Problem was, I had a guard who was under strict orders not to let me out of his sight, and Short had a guard under strict orders not to let anyone near him, specifically me.

After I explained to Joanna the necessity of speaking to Short, she sat back down and started nibbling her fingernails, a tic that arose when she got to problem solving. Then she stopped and looked up at me with a lively expression.

"He falls asleep."

"Who?"

"Your guard. Not this one. Your night guard. Once you've gone to sleep he gets lazy and drifts off."

"Some protection. What about Dante Short's guard?"

"Let me think."

She got back to work on the fingernails and paced back and forth at the foot of the bed. Abruptly, her head shot up like a bright idea had come to her. She turned to the mirror and assessed her reflection.

"I'm a mess. I'll be back."

"Where are you going?"

She went out without answering. A little over an hour later she returned. The guard clocked her ass as she walked in. "How are we feeling, Nick?" she said, in her most mannered, professional voice.

As soon as the door clicked shut Joanna produced a pair of khaki pants, a belt, and a plaid button-up shirt from under her medical jacket. She tossed them to me. I held up the shirt and inspected it.

"Tommy's clothes?"

"Shut up. Put them on."

"Easier said than done," I said, wagging my fucked arm. "Bad fin."

Joanna took hold of my legs and swung them over the side of the bed, grabbed my good arm and pulled me up to standing. She unhooked my IV, turned me around, ripped the Velcro apart and tugged the gown off me.

"If you wanted to see me naked—"

"Dream on."

Joanna knelt down, instructed me to lift my feet and slipped the khakis on me one leg at a time, nimbly avoiding even the slightest glance at my dick. The jeans were at least six sizes too big.

"Jesus, how fat is this husband of yours?"

"Shut up."

Joanna slid a belt through the loops on the pants and yanked it tight to cinch the pants and buckle it. After helping me into my shirt, she fitted my hospital gown over the clothes and situated me back in the bed. She removed a travel-size canister of shaving cream and a disposable razor from the pocket of her lab coat and set them on the counter.

"Shave your face. He checks on you around eleven o'clock. Pretend like you're asleep. As soon as his chin hits his chest I'm coming to get you."

"What's the plan?"

"Shave your face."

"What's the plan?"

"Be ready," she said. "Trust me."

Like I had a multitude of other options. Joanna hurried out, leaving me with a few long hours to kill. I flicked on the TV. The lead story on the six o'clock news was about the FBI assisting with the investigation into the increased drug trade and violent crime in the city. To combat the Cash City threat, police had SWAT snipers placed on strategic rooftops surrounding the police station. They broadcast images of the snipers, concealed beneath helmets and Kevlar, carrying assault rifles. The whole thing looked like some surreal circus, like some police state you would see on the other side of the world.

The news segment concluded with a recap: the shootout at the old high school, the subsequent chase, the retaliatory drive-by's, how both the police and FBI were frustrated with the lack of leads in the investigation and urged anybody with pertinent information to call a police hotline. I hollered for the guard to fetch me a newspaper. I wanted to see what Ciccone had been up to.

His latest column headlined the front page: *POLICE TO BLAME FOR ORGY OF VIOLENCE*. He conjured a hell of an image, I'll give him that. In the piece, Ciccone advocated for a crackdown on any gang or individual connected to the rampant violence, citing a lack of civic vigilance on the part of law enforcement as the primary reason Cain City was on the verge of an epidemic. Ciccone warned that if the tide of crime was not soon reversed, Cain City would become synonymous with depravity and bedlam. Irreparable damage would be done to both the community at large and the college. In closing, Ciccone professed that the only way to restore the city to its former glory was to eradicate what he termed a 'plague of lawlessness.'

Seven hundred and fifty words of fancy bullshit. Easy enough to write. Two months ago, a month ago, while he was lining his pockets with hush money, a column like that could have woken this town up. Maybe made a difference. But not now. Now Ciccone was spitting in the wind with this garbage. He made it sound like we were living in the Wild West. Hell, maybe we were.

I finished the paper. Nurse Frances came in with dinner and after that I watched a couple of re-runs of *Everybody Loves Raymond.* Then I shuffled into the bathroom with the shaving cream and the disposable razor and scraped my face smooth. The shave rejuvenated me a little, made me feel fresh and vital, but when I splashed my mug with water and assessed my appearance, the reflection in the mirror caused me to flinch. Thick crags lined my face like a jagged roadmap. Sallow, gray pockets of flesh bloated out from under my eyes. My cheeks were concave. Not that I had ever been some great beauty, but presently I looked like I'd been exhumed from the grave.

I got back into bed. As the eleventh hour approached I feigned sleep and waited for the guard's nightly look-in. At a quarter past, he peeked his head through the door, saw what he thought was me sleeping, and was sweet enough to flip the lights and the television off. Twenty minutes after that Joanna slunk into the room with a pair of men's loafers and a spare lab coat.

"He's down," she said, moving to the bedside to help me to my feet. "Put these on," she said, handing over the lab coat and loafers. "Hide your arm under there good."

I removed my gown, slipped on the loafers, put the lab coat on and fiddled with the sleeve until my rotten arm was mostly hidden. We opened the door and snuck past the night guard, whose head was tipped back against the wall, mouth hanging agape, snoring away. Some guard. The loafers Joanna provided were too large. They flopped when I stepped so I had to lift my heels and walk on my toes. At the reception desk Joanna snagged a medical chart and we boarded the elevator. She pressed the button for the third floor.

When the doors slid shut and the elevator began its ascent, Joanna exhaled as if she'd been holding her breath from the time we left my room. She cleared her throat and asked, "How are you feeling?"

"Good."

"If you start to feel weak or dizzy, let me know."

"I'm fine."

"Are you going to hurt Dante Short?"

"Not much. What about his guard?"

"Take this."

She handed me the medical chart and clipped a hospital ID onto my coat pocket.

"The guard is expecting an orthopedic surgeon named Jerry Wilson to consult with Dante Short about his injuries."

"At eleven-thirty at night? That's your plan? I don't want to get you in trouble."

"Just follow my lead, Dr. Wilson."

Joanna quickly detailed the injuries Dante Short sustained in the car accident. His leg was shattered, he had three broken ribs, one of which punctured a lung, a severe concussion and a chest contusion. Since he had been in the hospital he had received one visitor every day, the same one, a woman in her mid-thirties claiming to be his girlfriend.

The elevator doors split open. At the far end of the hall, a lone guard was posted outside of Dante Short's room. He was perusing a magazine. Joanna walked in front of me to shield my absent arm. She whispered through her teeth, "Do you recognize him?"

The guard was a young, beefy guy with a round face and a butt-chin. I'd never laid eyes on him. No doubt a rookie drawing the shit detail.

"Who are you?" the beefy guard said, peering over the gossip mag.

Joanna straightened her posture and began her pitch.

"I'm Dr. Orvietto, this is Dr. Wilson. We are scheduled to examine and consult with the patient this evening. We should be on your list."

Her delivery was over-rehearsed and too proper, but the young guard wasn't in the mood to be bothered. All he wanted was to go back to reading about how movie stars are just like us. He yawned and gave a cursory glance at our ID badges, failed to notice the bulk of my arm under the lab coat, and swatted a lazy paw at Dante's door. Police vigilance exemplified.

I feigned that I had forgotten a stethoscope and sent Joanna to retrieve one for me. The last thing I wanted was for Dante Short to set eyes on her and be able to link us in any capacity. When Joanna was safely down the hall and out of sight, I entered the room.

CHAPTER TWENTY-FIVE
FAT MAN'S CLOTHES

The room was dark but Dante Short was not asleep. His right wrist was handcuffed to the metal railing of the bed. His left arm lay flat at his side above the covers. The moment I entered the room his steely gaze locked in on me and never came off. He was a slight man with a small head, large ears, and a beaked nose. His hair was braided in four fat cornrows. Three teardrops were etched on his cheek, two of which were filled in.

I flipped on the light, set the medical chart aside and stood over him. Dante Short did not blink nor move, but the muscles in his jaw bulged from his cheeks they were clenched so tight.

I said, "Do you know who I am?"

"You the walking talking dead man."

"Well, that's not exactly accurate now, is it?"

"You dead soon, bitch."

"Not if they send you after me again. They send you after me again, you're gonna be the one on the slab just like the rest of your buddies."

"Fuck you," Dante Short hissed. "You wanna finish me? Then finish me. Don't matter, you gonna be put to sleep soon enough. You see this empty teardrop?" He pointed to his cheekbone. "That's for you, motherfucker."

"I'd love to help you take your last breath. And hopefully one day your dumb ass will give me the chance. But right now, I need you to deliver a message to your boss."

"I ain't got no boss."

"Cupcake."

Dante Short averted his eyes from me for the first time since I had walked in the room.

"I can't get no message to nobody."

"C'mon, don't kid a kidder."

"Man, they don't let me call nobody or nothing from up in here."

"You're a smart guy. Find a way. Your girlfriend comes to visit you, have her pass it on. I don't care how you do it. But I'm certain that if you don't give it to him, he's going to be a lot more upset than if you do."

Dante ran his tongue over his gold-capped front teeth.

"What's the message?"

"I'm out of this thing. I don't give a shit what he wants to do to this town, to the police department, I don't care, I'm out. I've got one thing left to do in Cain City and then I'm done with the place. He can have it for all I care. Until then, he stays away from me, I'll stay away from him."

Dante laughed, a protracted, hysterical laugh that made him clutch his ribs in pain, but he nonetheless embellished his hooting to prove a point.

"You dumb motherfucker. Cupcake don't make no deals."

"I'll offer this once. If he comes at me again then he better get me, 'cause if I even catch a whiff, if one of you walks by me on the street by accident, I'll kill all of you. I'll start with you for a warm-up. I'll walk back into this hospital, put a gun in your mouth and blow those gold teeth out the back of your head. And I won't stop until he's dead. You can tell him that."

Dante's mouth curled into a maniacal little sneer. He was enjoying this now.

"He is gonna fuck your shit up."

"Which ribs are broken?"

"Huh?"

I dropped my fist down like a hammer on his ribcage. Dante Short lurched up from the bed and shrieked like a hurt dog. I grabbed his throat and squeezed.

"Deliver the message."

The guard burst into the room.

"What the hell's going on?"

"Allergic reaction," I said, brushing past him.

Joanna was sitting behind the desk in her office, waiting for me. She looked exhausted. Her hair, no longer in a ponytail, fell loose over her shoulders. I lowered myself into a chair across from her. My wallet, keys, and phone, which she had retrieved from storage, were on the desk. I packed my wallet away. The phone was dead. The crevices in the keys were crusted with blood. The other possession I had on me when I was admitted to the hospital, my subcompact Beretta, was now locked away in an evidence locker down at the police station.

Joanna asked, "Did you get what you were looking for?"

"Maybe. How come you don't have any pictures in here?"

"I don't know. Never got around to it I guess."

"You used to have lots of pictures in your office."

"I did. Of you and Jake. Maybe when the baby comes I'll put a picture up."

"When that baby comes you put its picture up all over the place."

A wisp of a smile crossed her lips. "Okay." She pressed her fingertips to her temples and massaged her scalp. "Do you need anything?"

"You've done enough. Unless Tommy has a gun that he doesn't mind me using to commit a felony."

Joanna tilted her head to the side and chuckled despite herself.

"No, Tom does not own a gun."

"He the bat under the bed type?"

"He's more the alarm system, panic room type. So what now?"

"Now," I flipped my palm up. "Now I go home and change out of these fat man clothes."

"He's not that fat."

"I'm sure there's lots of muscle underneath."

"Listen," Joanna said, dismissing that line of dialogue. "If you start to feel faint or nauseous or anything, you call me immediately. A number of things could go wrong with you right now. Don't get your arm wet. If you get an infection that penetrates into the bone, it's possible you could lose it or get sepsis or worse. If you get it wet, call me immediately. If your arm has some kind of physical trauma, you could start bleeding internally and not even know it until it's too late. In three days, you will come in and let me run some tests, check on your arm. Doctor's orders, non-negotiable."

"Sure, Doc. I'll put it in my calendar. If I'm not a carcass in three days, I'll come in for a check-up."

"Don't talk that way," she scolded me. Joanna tossed a pill bottle across the desk. "Twice a day with food."

CHAPTER TWENTY-SIX
YOU HAVE THREE MESSAGES

Joanna offered to give me a lift to my place. I told her again that she'd done enough and to go home, get some rest, and not worry about me. This elicited a scoff, but she didn't press the matter further. I found a phone in the foyer and dialed up the taxi company, gave my name, and asked them to send me Dennis Maynard.

The night was pleasantly cold and clean. I stood out on the curb in front of the hospital watching my breath purl out in front of me. Fifteen minutes later Maynard showed up. I lowered myself into the backseat. The inside of the cab possessed that same rotted meat smell its owner had.

"Where you been?" I asked.

"Had a fare. Jesus," Maynard whistled, scanning me over. "What the fuck happened to you, man?"

"You should see the other guys."

"They dead?" Maynard snorted. I didn't answer. He chauffeured me to the old high school. I had him circle the block twice before giving him the okay to drop me at the front.

"This one's on me. Free of charge."

"You don't say."

"No blow jobs or nothing," Maynard grinned, showing off those grubby teeth and diseased gums.

"Next time I call you, I want you there straight away, understand. I don't care if you have a fare. Drop them off." Maynard lost the magnanimous grin. "Comprende?"

"Yeah, I got it," he muttered. I got out of the cab and shut the door. Maynard jerked the cab away from the curb and hooked a right at the corner by the gas station. The street was empty and still, no signs of life. The distant ruckus of The Red Head, usually an alluring beacon, held no appeal in my current state. I trudged up the stairs and into the school.

The building was quieter than the street. Tommy's scuffling loafers and the low hum of electricity running through the place were the only sounds. The walls in the vestibule and along the corridor were pockmarked with bullet holes. As I passed the gym and the auditorium I glanced down to where all the bodies, including mine, had been sprawled out like bloody snow angels. The floor and walls had been scrubbed clean save for a few spots around the edges of the gym doors where flecks of dark, dried blood remained. And there were spatters of blood all over the ceiling; the cleaners always forgot to look up.

A strand of yellow crime scene tape lay crumpled on the ground in front of my office. A thousand bullets from automatic weapons had shred the door pretty good. It swung freely within the frame, no longer clicking shut. I stepped inside. A cold draft flowed from the shot-out windows through to the busted door. The light switches weren't working, but the glow from the streetlamps was bright enough to see around.

My hat and coat were on the counter, as if I'd just laid them there. The rest of the place looked like it had been gutted by a tornado. The refrigerator door was hanging open. Something inside it was rotted and stinking. The floor was blanketed with glass from the windows along with chunks of wood from the cabinets and walls. Glass crunched underfoot as I stepped across the room to my desk. Somebody, maybe the police, maybe not, had rummaged through the drawers. My files were strewn across the floor and the desk, but nothing seemed to be missing.

I sifted through the files and found the one marked Randall Kincaid. Inside was his booking photo. I lifted it from the folder, laid it on the desk and stared at it for the thousandth time. There was no beard, just a couple bushy eyebrows above a drooped left eyelid. His round, plain face lacked any expression. No person walking down the street would look at that man and realize he was a monster. They may even think him pleasant, seek eye contact, smile and nod hello, afford him a 'how ya doing?' like he's anybody else. No one would guess that he raped and mutilated children. I placed the picture back in the file and closed it.

Perched on the shelf along the wall was a bottle of Maker's, unharmed. If ever there was a sign from God, I thought. I fished out the pill bottle, popped one of the prescribed antibiotics in my mouth and took a nip from the bottle to wash it down. Then I toured the rest of my apartment.

The bedroom was pretty much intact, though the police had ransacked the place and left the drawers open and the sheets off the bed. I shut the drawers and checked the latch on the bedroom door. It worked so I latched it, took my time getting out of Tommy's oversized clothes, laid down in the tub and let the shower pummel me for a long while, careful to keep my bad fin propped outside the curtain away from the water.

Out of the shower and in my own wardrobe, I went back into my office and plugged my phone into the charger. The electrical sockets were working and the phone came buzzing to life. Three messages were waiting for me. The first, from a potential client, I deleted. The second was from my mother in Chicago. In a wandering three-minute message she covered a spectrum of topics such as the local weather (poor), the number of people from her church that had been diagnosed with cancer since last time we had spoken (two), the latest family gossip (one distant cousin had broken it off with his wife; another was mooching off his mother's social security payment), and her new favorite shows on television that she was sure I would like (all police procedurals). Delete.

The third and final message came from a blocked caller. "Call this number," a man's voice ordered, "597-3409." My palms went slick and I stared at the phone in disbelief. One of two possibilities were on the table. Either Dante Short was more capable than I had given him credit for and had already conveyed my message to Cupcake, or, I had just heard the voice of the man that, for seven long years, I had lived to kill; a spectral voice rearing up from my own private circle of hell, the voice of Randall Kincaid. I replayed the message a few times over, once to memorize the number, again to hear the voice, and another time after that to steel myself before I returned the call.

On the third ring the call was picked up. The same deep voice from the message said, "Who this?"

Hip-hop music and a woman's voice murmured in the background. I couldn't make out what she was saying, but I heard the words, 'cheeseburger,' and 'true love.' The rest of her speech was muffled like they were being spoken underwater. The man on the phone must have signaled for the woman to be quiet because all at once she stopped speaking and the music ceased. So, I thought, Dante Short moved quick. My heartbeat gradually slowed to its normal tempo.

"Who this," the voice said again.

I said, "You called me."

There was a pause. Then, "We need to meet."

"As much as I'd love to make your acquaintance, whoever you are, I think I'll pass."

"Don't be clowning. You know who this is. I got your message." Cupcake paused as if waiting for me to respond. "You think I'm just gonna kick back and let some mug who has spilled so much of our blood traipse the fuck away, like it ain't no thing?"

"Why not? Way I see it, you've got two choices. You can take your chances, keep sending wave after wave of pawns and hope one of them can take me out. Or, you can leave me be and you'll never have to worry about me again. You want this town, you can have it. I've got no rooting interest either way."

Cupcake's voice dropped an octave; his words came very measured.

"You're smart enough to know that I can't allow you to live."

"You'd be surprised, I'm pretty dense. Listen, maybe you'll get me. Good on you if you do. But if you don't, and I keep knocking those pawns of yours down, you're smart enough to know that before long, you're going to have to send in the king. Because if you want a job done right you have to do it yourself. I don't see that being beneficial for either of us."

The line went silent. I checked the display to make sure the call was still active.

Cupcake piped up.

"You've got twenty-four hours."

"For what?"

"To kill the sick bitch that did that to your kid. I'll hold my guns off you for twenty-four hours. After that, you still here, your eyes close for good. You feel me?"

My body went cold.

"How the hell do you know that? How do you know about my kid?"

"Doesn't matter. What does is that we understand each other. Do we understand each other?"

I suppressed the urge to scream into the phone.

"You tell me right now how you know about my kid."

"Twenty-four hours."

The line went dead. I set the phone down and walked over to the gaping void in the wall where windows used to be. The cold air streaming in and out of my lungs made me feel alive, made the muscles in my body taut. I stood there in the dark and plotted my next move.

It was doubtful that my hunting of Randall Kincaid would be so simple as to be accomplished in twenty-four hours. But a day with the Detroit thugs off my back was better than a day with them all up in my shit. I'd take the time allotted, and when that time was up, Cupcake could come at me with everything he had. I wasn't going anywhere as long as Randall Kincaid still drew breath on this earth.

The disconcerting piece of information brought to light during the phone call was that Cupcake was aware of Kincaid, aware of his significance, aware that I was after him. Only a few people were planted on the inside of that information and all of them owned a badge. Cupcake had a man in the department, someone close to me, there was no question of that anymore.

Flip a coin: Bruce Hale or Willis Hively? Hale had been working over the press, greasing who knows how many palms to keep a large amount of criminal activity hidden. Hively grew up in the projects with Tremaine Miller and a dozen other criminals who were still in the game. And if Hively wanted to get me off the Cash City beat, the best way to do it would be exactly what he did—put me on to Randall Kincaid. Who knows, it could be both of them, or neither. I didn't give a fuck anymore. What mattered was that I had a one day head start to track down Randall Kincaid.

As I stood at the busted windows, gazing out into the frigid night, absorbed in these machinations, I failed to see the figure standing in my doorway.

CHAPTER TWENTY-SEVEN
BOX OF BULLETS

The kid, silhouetted by the light in the hall, was standing there watching me. I didn't startle. By now I was accustomed to Davey creeping up on me like a perfect little thief.

"How long you been there?"

"Who was you talking to?"

I brushed some glass off the edge of my desk and leaned against it.

"Nobody. It's three o'clock in the morning. Go to bed."

The kid took a long look around assessing the wreckage of my office.

"Man, your joint is hella-messed up."

"You don't like what I've done with the place?"

"It smells like somebody died in here."

"Not in here. That was down the hall."

The kid tip-toed into the room as if he were avoiding landmines. No longer backlit from the bulb in the hallway, I could see the fright plainly in his face. He was looking past me to the windows as if the bullets may start flying again at any moment.

"You okay?"

"I'm cool. You okay?"

"Fantastic."

"You look like dookie."

"Wait 'til you're my age. We'll see how you look."

The kid leaned against the desk beside me.

"We've got your cat. I've been feeding her and stuff. You want me to go get her?"

"How 'bout you keep her with you for a while, if you don't mind. This place isn't exactly pet friendly."

"Okay."

Davey took his ball cap off, scratched his scalp and replaced the cap.

"I didn't tell my mom."

"Didn't tell her what?"

"You know, that I was with you that night. I didn't tell her."

"No?"

Davey shrugged.

"She would've been crazy pissed, for real."

"At me or you?"

"Both. It would've been ugly. You've seen her when she gets all fired up."

"I've seen her."

"Anyway, she was really worried about you. They wouldn't let us see you at the hospital. They told her you were touch and go or some shit like that. We thought you were a goner."

"Yeah, well, I'm still here. You can tell her I'm fine."

"Tell her yourself."

Some sort of primal moan that sounded like a cat in heat came from below the missing windows. I peered over the sill.

"That's not Lucifer. She's upstairs with my mom."

"Listen, Davey, I need you to do me a favor. Keep an eye out for me around here. Let me know if you see anything strange."

"What do you mean?"

"You see anybody hanging around you haven't seen before, anybody scoping out my office or car, or somebody who strikes you funny, anything different, you let me know. Sound good?"

"Sure, yeah. I can do that."

"Anything peculiar since I've been gone?"

Davey pondered his answer.

"Not really. A bunch of police coming and going, shit like that. The yogurt shop across the way bit the dust." He used his thumb to make a throat slitting motion across his neck. "Dunzo."

"Never tried it."

"Me neither. Who wants yogurt? Hook a brother up with some ice cream, know what I'm saying. Anyway, everything else has been same old same old."

I took another tug on the bourbon and asked Davey if he wanted a drink. He kidded that he gave up the sauce cold turkey. His mouth stretched into a big oval yawn. I told him to get to bed.

"What are you gonna do?"

"I have some things to take care of."

"Those guys gonna come after you again?" he asked softly.

"Probably."

"How you gonna fend them off with one arm?"

"Fuck if I know, kid. I didn't do very well with two. Listen—" I wrapped my arm around the kid, then flinched at my own show of affection.

"What's wrong?" he asked.

"Nothing."

But an odd sensation came over me. I withdrew my arm and patted Davey's shoulder clumsily. He knew this second gesture was pretend but he allowed me to keep patting him.

"It's dangerous to be around me right now. You have to keep away, both you and your mom. I need you to help me there. Smooth it over with her. Let her know I'm okay and I'm sorry, but I'm not going to be able to see her again."

The kid twisted his shoulder out of my grip and stared at the tops of his sneakers.

"You mean like, ever?"

"For a while, kid. A good while."

After the kid got out of there, I eased my jacket over my shoulders and fit my cap on and was all set to hit the door when suddenly my head went dizzy and my whole body started to tingle. I slurped some cold water from the faucet and splashed some of it on my face but it didn't shake the queasy feeling. I sat down on the corner of my mattress to take in a few breaths and rest for a minute.

When I woke it was five past eight.

The morning sun shone through the east-facing windows cooking the place. My hair was sweaty beneath my cap, still in place on my head. Before collapsing, my last intention was to begin the pursuit of Randall Kincaid. Five hours of vacant, dreamless sleep revived me enough to get moving, so that's what I did. I got moving. I was already dressed and ready for the day. By Cupcake's accord, I had nineteen hours.

In the middle of downtown across the street from the old movie theater was a pawnshop known for trafficking black market guns. Their hours of operation, per the stencil on their glass door, were nine a.m. to six p.m., so I had a few minutes to kill. The Mexican cantina next door was open for breakfast. I went in there, picked through some soppy eggs and waited for nine o'clock to roll around.

At five past the hour the pawnshop opened for business. The door jingled as I walked in. Junk was crammed into every nook of the place and stacked high on the walls. A stout old woman was perched on a stool behind the glass counter. She set aside her crossword puzzle, stuck her pencil into the headband that secured her gaudy, red-dyed permanent, and tilted her head back to look down her nose at me.

"Well, if it ain't the big swinging dick," she said, voice full of gravel.

"Hello, Vada."

"What the hell happened to you?"

"Fell in the shower."

"My ass," she said, craning her neck forward to examine me closer, as if that could ferret out the truth. Her bloated head made all of her features looked like they had been cinched into the middle of her face. "If you're looking for Lionel you can turn your little pecker ass right back round and get off my property. I haven't seen him for damn near a year and you can tell that ex-wife of his to go straight to hell on a magic carpet."

"I'm not here about your boy."

"Well, good, 'cause I don't know where he is. What can I do you for?"

"I'm looking for some protection. Something short and heavy."

Vada's shrewd little mouth cinched in tighter.

"You're not back with them coppers, are you?"

"No."

"'Cause if you were, you would have to tell me. Them's the rules. You can't deny it and trick me into doing nothing. That's trapping."

"I'm not with the cops, but didn't you hear, there are no rules anymore."

"Yeah, well, our code words ain't short and heavy no more neither. Been for a long spell since they been used. And I got a good sniffer for horseshit. Only undercovers come in here using them words anymore, trying to trip us up. Nothing gets my gourd more."

"I haven't been a cop for seven years, Vada, you know that. Now, I need a gun and I'm not leaving here without one. So tell me whatever words I need to use and I'll use them."

I stuck my hand into my jacket pocket. Vada recoiled at the action, but then broke into a large grin when my hand came out with a wad of money. I thumbed out five twenty-dollar bills and dropped them on the counter.

"Show me what you've got."

"You can't put that money out there like that if you're a copper. You know what that is. That's trapping," she said curtly.

"You're right. This proves I'm not trapping you. Now, are you going to take my money or do I need to go somewhere else."

"It spends, don't it?"

She scooped up the money and hopped off her stool, beckoning me with a gnarled old finger to move with her to the end of the counter.

"Quick and dirty," she said. "Those are the code words."

"Fine. Show me something quick and dirty."

At the edge of the counter Vada bent over and brought out a ring with some forty keys on it. Behind her was a tall cabinet and she tried about twelve keys in the lock before finding the one that fit. Vada opened the cabinet and stood aside so that I could see the display. A number of handguns were hanging on nails tacked to the back of the cabinet. Boxes of ammunition were stacked on its floor.

"See anything you want?"

"Let me see that snub-nose."

Vada handed me the .38. The metal was scuffed up and the serial number was partially filed off, as if someone had gotten bored and quit halfway through the job, but the action worked well enough and the piece fit well in my hand and in my pocket. I turned my attention to the selection of knives on the bottom shelf of the glass counter.

"Throw in a box of bullets and that switchblade and it's a deal."

"Which one?" Vada grumbled.

I pointed out the knife I meant and she gave it over. I made sure the blade wasn't too dull and slipped it in my pocket. Then I held up the gun.

"If this doesn't shoot straight I'm coming back for my money."

"That ain't the way this works. You walk outta here with that gun and you ain't getting nothing back. Test it in the basement if you want to."

I wanted to. Vada bolted the front door and hung a 'Back in 5' sign. She led me into the back of the shop and down a rickety flight of wood stairs. The basement was damp and moldy. Water dripped from exposed piping into half a dozen buckets. But the room was padded for sound. An old target, already riddled with holes, was tacked onto the far wall.

I opened the chamber of the .38 and held it out to Vada.

"You mind?"

She shook three bullets out of the box and loaded them in for me. I flicked the chamber shut and took aim. The gun worked fine.

Back upstairs, Vada unbolted the door and removed the 'Back in 5' sign. I asked her if she had any dealings with the Detroit pipeline, Cash City. She harrumphed.

"You plum out your head if you think I'm doing dealings with anybody 'cept for God-fearing people."

I took her at her word, whatever the hell her words meant. Before I left, Vada was kind enough to load all six chambers.

CHAPTER TWENTY-EIGHT
SHADOW OF A SHADOW

The house Randall Kincaid's mother bequeathed him upon her passing was a one-story prefab on a tiny lot on Fourteenth Street in the West End, less than a half mile from the Cammack home. I had driven past it while canvassing the area for markers on Trisha. A chain link fence marked the perimeter of the front lawn, which measured roughly thirty feet wide and ten deep. Adjacent to the house was the West End Baptist Church and down the street was a Little League baseball diamond.

I cruised the gravel alley behind the house, circled around the next block and parked the Skylark in front of a house two doors down on the opposite side of the street. There I sat and watched. The dark blue sedan was neither on the street nor in the alley and there were no hints of life from inside the Kincaid residence; no lights on, no garbage in the trash cans, no newspaper waiting to be picked up on the front walk, not so much as a lawn chair on the front porch. The lawn hadn't been cut in months.

I switched the radio on and rolled through the AM dial, found the local news and stopped to listen. The droll broadcaster reported that after a relentless three-day crime spree targeting police and inciting a citywide panic, the violence had stalled in the last twenty-four hours. Police had made a couple of minor, unrelated arrests in the last day, but that was the extent of the action. The mayor released a statement saying that while he knew everyone was disturbed by the seemingly overnight appearance of gangs on our streets, he was optimistic that our stellar police force had control of the situation and the worst was over.

The news ended, an old bluegrass song came on, and I switched the radio off. Maybe Cupcake and company were taking the day off. Maybe Hale or Hively or whoever was playing both sides had convinced everyone to pump the brakes for a hot minute.

It was Saturday so there were some people out and about in the neighborhood. Some function was going on at the church. Kids carrying sleeping bags and camping gear were being dropped off by their parents and loading into a couple of blue vans. Down at the ball field a game was starting.

Directly across the street from me two little girls came tearing out of their front door screaming their heads off. They started turning cartwheels and doing handstands in their yard. What a perfect little pocket of the world for Randall Kincaid to reside. Children every which way you looked.

I rolled down my window. I could hear the announcer down at the ball field calling the game over the loudspeaker. After a couple of innings and not a hint of activity from the Kincaid house, I got out of the car and crossed the street. The little girls were spinning in circles, making themselves dizzy and falling on the ground. They stood up wobbly and giggling, but when they noticed me approaching them they stopped their fun.

"Who are you?" the taller one blurted.

"Can I ask you guys a question?"

They eyed me suspiciously.

"Depends on the question."

"I came here to surprise my brother. I haven't seen him in a long time." I gestured at the Kincaid house. "He lives in that house, but nobody's answering the door and

I don't know if he's there or if he's on vacation or if he's moved. Have you guys seen him around?"

"That house?" the little one pointed.

"That's the one."

"No one lives in that house. That old lady croaked a long time ago."

She clutched her throat and pretended to choke for air while desperately yanking her head around. In a dramatic little flourish, she spun around and dropped to the ground and played dead.

The taller one laughed.

"Yeah, she croaked. She was an evil old bat."

I said, "Bet she was."

"She wasn't your momma, was she?"

"No, she wasn't my mother."

The little one came back to life and hopped to her feet.

"We watched her get rolled out of there on the cart. Her bony old arm slipped out of the blanket and was just dangling like one of them skeletons you see at the doctor. Nobody noticed it but us. They packed her up with her arm sticking out and everything. It was creepy."

"And you haven't seen anyone else coming or going into the house since then?"

"Nope," they said in unison.

The tall one whispered into the little one's ear and the little one giggled.

"What happened to your arm?"

"Fell off a unicorn."

"Did not."

The girls stood gawking at me as I strolled down the street to the Kincaid house. The hinges on the front gate were rusted and stiff. As I forced the gate open, the bottom raked the pavement and the hinges screamed with resistance. If there was anyone inside the house, unless they were hard of hearing, I had announced myself.

The wood beams on the porch sagged in the middle. A window to the left of the front door had drapes clamped tight, blocking any view into the place. I knocked on the door. It was thin and hollow and rattled loose in its frame. I stepped back and got the .38 ready in my pocket. Nobody answered. The drapes didn't flutter.

Two doors down the girls were still spying me. I took my hand out of my pocket and waved at them, came down from the porch and walked outside the gate and around to the side of the house. A thin tract of mulch and dirt ran between the Kincaid house and the house next door. Hip-hop music reverberated from within the neighbor's house.

On my toes I was just high enough to peer into the two windows that were back there, but drapes obstructed both those as well. I slipped the blade of my knife under the windows and attempted to pry them open, to no avail. After that I ventured past a shed and around back. There I found what I was looking for.

The lock on the back door was a cheap knob lock. I stuck the tip of the blade into the keyhole and popped it loose. The door swung lightly inward. As I stepped into the kitchen a rush of air swirled past my face, as if the house was letting out its breath. I shut the door quietly and stood still for a good while, listening. The thumping music from next door and the loudspeaker from the ball field were muted, but still audible. Somewhere outside a lawnmower churned to life, but inside the house not a creature was stirring.

The closed drapes kept the rooms of the house dim. It had been a long time since the house had seen any natural light. The bottoms of the drapes were all mildewed. The kitchen had a circular wooden table and two chairs in the middle of the room, a counter and sink to the left, and to the right an empty cubby where a washer and dryer used to be. Opposite the table was a refrigerator with its door ajar. A thin layer of soot covered the surfaces in the room.

The kitchen door led to a narrow hallway. Across the hall was a bedroom. In there was a queen size mattress that had been stripped of sheets and flung into a corner. A large brown stain graced the center of the mattress. Beside the mattress was a table and lamp. There was also a dresser with an old analog TV perched on top of it. A sheet and a quilt were wadded up in the corner of the room. The wallpaper on the back wall had come loose at the top and curled halfway to the floor. In an attached bathroom was a toilet with no seat and a shower with no curtain.

Down the hall in another half-bathroom, a toilet had been ripped up from the floor. A closet in the hallway was crammed with dusty coats and luggage. The end of the hall opened into a bare living room. The middle of the living room floor was rotted out where water had dripped down from a leak in the ceiling. Off to the side of the living room was a second bedroom furnished with a mattress and a desk, no chair. There were no items of note in the desk, nothing to suggest Randall Kincaid had set foot in the house in the past hour or year or decade. The only evidence that he ever existed in the house was a 1973 comic book of *The Shadow* that I found in the bottom drawer.

I tried the light switches in every room. None worked. The faucets didn't yield any water nor did the gas on the stove turn on. The kitchen cupboards had some old jars of beans in them, an empty box of pasta and clusters of rat turds, but that was it. The whole house smelled stale and lifeless.

I sat down at the kitchen table and flipped through the comic book. It was almost noon.

I checked my phone; one missed message from Willis Hively, sounding fried.

"I'm at the hospital right now. Looks like you made your great escape. For the love of God, don't do anything stupid."

CHAPTER TWENTY-NINE

ALL THE LITTLE SOCIOPATHS

The Livingston Chrysler dealership was located downtown across the street from the football stadium and catty-corner to the basketball arena. On game days George Livingston, the owner, cleared his lot and charged tailgaters three hundred and fifty bucks a season for a parking space. But the first football game was four months out so I was a little surprised to see the lot empty on this Saturday.

The front entrance was locked. I could hear the heavy clanking sounds of metalwork coming from the garage behind the dealership. I cupped my hands against the tinted window and peered in. A stout little janitor, as wide as he was tall, was aimlessly shoving a mop near the back of the showroom. I thumped on the door. The janitor looked up and saw me, made a shooing motion with his hand, and kept on with the mop. I banged on the door again.

"We're closed," the janitor groused, turning his back to me. I pounded the door harder. He whipped around scowling. "Can you understand the words that are coming out of my mouth? We—Are—Closed."

"No shit." I pressed my investigator credentials against the glass. "Police. Open up."

The janitor frowned, dropped the mop where he stood, looked for a route around the freshly glossed floor and, deciding there was none, moseyed straight across it.

He took his time sifting through a loop of keys, jammed the right one in the bolt and cracked open the door far enough to poke his head out, no further. He eyeballed me with a bitter countenance that gave the impression he'd just tasted his own piss.

"Now I got to go over these spots again."

I improvised a story about a hit and run involving a child and a dark blue Chrysler sedan. The tale took the pucker out of the janitor's face.

He shook his head vigorously.

"People ain't got no brains."

"The car had dealer plates. Is there anyone here that I could speak with about recent sales?"

"Manager just took off to lunch. He's a big eater, takes plenty long lunches, but you're welcome to wait for him if you want to."

"I want to."

The janitor stepped aside reluctantly and swung his arm toward the interior of the dealership.

"Might as well wait in here. Floor's already ruined."

I stepped in and looked around the showroom. It was a vast bright room with a white floor, a high white ceiling, white chairs, white door handles, and white pots for the fake trees in the corners. Tall windows spanned the length of three of the four walls. The only visible blemishes in the room were the janitor's dirty footprints tracked across the floor.

"Where are the cars?" I asked.

"C.C. High rented out the Civic Center for their prom so St. Linus ain't have nowhere to have theirs. Bad scheduling if you ask me. You can't pick up the phone, see when the other school's gonna have their prom? Shit." He shook his head in irritation. "Well, St. Linus, that's Mr. Livingston's daughter's school, so he offered to let them have their prom here, so now I've got to get this place spotless. Already painted them damn flower pots. Long, long day," he sighed.

"Nice enough place to have a prom."

"Oh, yeah, we have Heritage Junction coming in here to cater the food and everything. Should be a real nice time for those young people."

"I'm sure they'll think they're in heaven."

"You know, I hope so all the elbow grease they got me putting into this place. But the kids of this generation."

He put a fist over his mouth and cleared some mucus from his throat.

"Back in my day going to the prom was a big deal. Nowadays it just seems like kids don't give a shit about nothing. All they care about is not caring. I see kids brought in here by their parents for their sixteenth birthdays and the parents buy them brand-spanking-new cars. Kids couldn't give a shit half the time; it's not the right color, not the right model. Sad, really. They're all little sociopaths if you ask me. No reality, smoking drugs, glued to them phones and computers."

He made the sour face again and swatted the air in front of him.

"Eh, I don't know nothing. What do I know?"

He pointed to a row of white chairs along the front windows.

"You can have a seat there if you want. I can bring you a magazine or a donut or something."

"I heard some action going on back in the garage," I said affably. "I need to have a chat with one of the mechanics, too."

"Only got one back there. Everybody else got the day off with the event coming in."

The janitor escorted me back through a small passage

that led to a waiting room. At the back was a glass door that opened to the garage. A half a dozen cars were back there in various states of disrepair. Jutting out from beneath one of them was a shirtless torso on top of some knobby legs.

"Charlie," the janitor called. "Somebody here needs a word."

"Fuck's sake Vernon, I'm workin' here."

Charlie pushed out from under the car, sat up, held his wrench out at arms-length and dropped it to show us he was peeved.

"This here's a detective needs to ask you some questions."

Charlie looked quickly from Vernon to me and back to Vernon.

"What's this about?"

"He'll tell you," Vernon said. "You ain't the only one with work to do around here, hell."

Vernon shambled back into the dealership.

Charlie got off the ground. His jaw hung down off his skull like it was free of its hinges and his body looked like a suit of loose skin draped over a thin set of bones. He stood tall and lengthened his neck to measure himself against me. He was only an inch or so shorter than I was, which he seemed satisfied by. I asked if any vehicles fitting the description of the dark blue sedan had been in for repairs or body work.

"This about my cousin?"

"Depends. Your cousin's name Randall Kincaid?"

"Nope. My cousin named Bobby Mounts. He's a good kid. Hasn't figured out how to get straight yet, but he'll be just fine if people just leave him be out and stop trying to force him one way or the other."

I assured Charlie that I had never heard of his cousin Bobby Mounts and fed him the same hit and run story I had given the janitor. Charlie scratched at an open sore on his concave chest and worked that low-hanging jaw from side to side. "You know what?" He turned his back to me and walked through to the rear of the garage, halted by a red pickup and pointed behind it. "This the vehicle you talking about?"

I stepped beyond the pickup to see the car in question—and there it was. The dark blue Chrysler sedan, headlight busted out, side doors gashed and streaked with white paint from the railing of the bridge. Every pore on my body prickled up.

"You okay, man? You looking a little peaked."

"I'm fine. How long has this car been here?"

"Couple days."

"When is it supposed to be ready?"

"Couple days."

I walked around to the driver's side. The door was locked but the window was open. I reached in, unlocked the door and climbed behind the wheel. The inside of the car looked and smelled brand new. There was no dust on the dashboard, no personal trinket dangling from the rearview mirror, no smudge to indicate it had ever been adjusted. On the driver's side floor mat there was a collection of shoe imprints. No imprints on the passenger mat or the mats in the back. The gas tank was a third full. The odometer indicated that the car had traveled a mere eighty-seven miles. There was nothing in the glove box or in the middle console except the owner's manual.

I searched between and beneath the seats, in the pockets attached to the back of the seats, under the mats, everywhere. In the trunk there was a small toolkit that came with the car. It contained a spare lug nut, a gas cap and a small wrench. Nothing that alluded to the car being owned by a depraved child rapist and murderer.

"Excuse me," a high-pitched voice exclaimed from behind me.

I closed the trunk. A fat man dressed in a tie and khakis stood at the front of the car scowling at me. The janitor stood next to him with a sheepish expression.

"May I ask what the hell you're doing?"

"Ask away."

"You better have a search warrant or you are about to have some serious problems."

"Do you know who this car belongs to?"

I stepped over to the fat man.

"It belongs to one of our valued customers," he stammered. "We have a reputation that we take a great deal of pride in and I am not about to let it be sullied. Now, if you have a search warrant, that's one thing. If you don't, I suggest you high-tail it out of here before I call the authorities."

"I told him what you told me about the kid and the car," the janitor mumbled apologetically.

"Vernon, shut up," the fat man yelled.

I said, "He told you, did he?"

"Yes, Vernon and Charlie informed me of the story you used to dupe them into allowing you to search this vehicle."

"You want me to go and get a search warrant?"

"Congratulations. Now you are putting two and two together."

"All right, I can get your warrant. But let me tell you how this is going to play out. First off, that wasn't a story you smarmy fucker. You have a reputation to protect? How about this for your reputation? I'll go get that warrant and I'll come back here and I'll turn over every piece of junk you've got in the middle of the floor just in time for prom night, good luck explaining that to your owner, but before I get two steps out your door, I'm going to call my good friend Ernie Ciccone at the *Cain City Dispatch* and I'm going to tell him we had a great lead at catching a child killer, but our investigation was hampered by the manager—insert your name here—of Livingston Chrysler, who thwarted our efforts to apprehend the assailant and gave them invaluable time in which to disappear. Authorities are now uncertain if the suspect is still in the area and cannot afford the resources necessary to conduct a nationwide manhunt."

The manager's face reddened and his jowls quivered so hard they nearly slapped beneath his chin. Sweat circles bloomed in the pits of his dress shirt.

"This is how you conduct your business?"

"If need be."

"I'll have you know, sir, that I will not be bullied by flat-out threats and I believe what goes around comes around. You are not the only person who has friends in high places whom you can call for favors. What goes around comes around."

I brought out my cell.

"I'll call mine now."

On the fifth ring, Ernie Ciccone picked up the line.

"Hey, Ciccone. Hold on a second." I passed the phone to the manager. "Tell him your name, will you? Make sure he gets the spelling right."

The manager grabbed the phone, cleared his throat and attempted to sound dignified.

"With whom am I speaking? Ah, I've got a detective here who says he will feed you a story to write in the paper if I do not do precisely what he says—I see—I see—Thank you for the advice."

The manager handed the phone back.

"Vernon, Charlie, back to it," he commanded. He waited for them to get out of earshot before fixing his eyes back on me. "You are a nasty piece of work, aren't you?"

I followed him to his office and we sat down across from each other. He plucked a handful of tissues from a box and dabbed at the wetness on his face. The nameplate on his desk read 'Howard Hockensmith.'

"What do you want?" Howard said.

"The file on your valued customer. How he paid for the car. If it was credit, I want the card number. The address he listed. His phone number. What he looked like."

"I didn't sell him the car."

"Then call up whoever did sell him the car and ask him. And if a car was loaned to him, I want to know what kind of car it was and the license plate number."

The revulsion Howard Hockensmith felt toward me showed plainly on his face.

"Snap to it, Howard."

"Don't you tell me to snap to it."

Howard booted up his computer and banged on the keys. A printer in the corner chugged to life and spit out a sheet of paper. Howard rolled his chair across to the printer, retrieved the printout, rolled back over and shoved the paper across the desk.

The credit card number Kincaid used to purchase the sedan was at the top of the page. Below that were his mother's address and a phone number. The car loaned to him for the interim of repairs was a red Chrysler Pacifica. I racked my brain to remember whether I had noticed any red cars flashing in my rearview. Came up blank.

When I looked up from the page Howard Hockensmith was hanging up his office phone.

"My salesman is not picking up. No doubt because he does not want to be pestered by his employer on his day off. Now, if you will be so kind as to please get the hell off this property."

"Where's the fire? I need you to call this number here and tell Randall Kincaid his car is ready to be picked up."

"The work on the car is not scheduled to be completed until Tuesday."

"A pleasant surprise for everybody then. Like that," I snapped my fingers, "your dealership has become the model of efficiency."

"I cannot be expected to invite a criminal to these premises. If something goes awry I could lose my job."

I picked up the phone and held it out to him.

"If you don't make the call, you lose your job for sure."

"You have some nerve," he snarled. "I just about believe that you would ruin an honest career for your own selfish purposes."

"Well, you're dumber than most."

"I cannot abide this. A choice between two blunders is not much of a choice."

"Nope."

Howard snatched the phone from my hand and dialed the number. When the line was answered he sat up straighter.

"This is Howard Hockensmith at Livingston Chrysler.—How are you?—Yes, sir, I have good news. Your car is ready a few days early—No, we aren't officially open today, but I'll be here all afternoon so if you are available to pick it up today, you may come by anytime—Otherwise—"

I mouthed the word, 'today.' Howard shrugged to indicate he had no influence over the direction of the conversation.

"Yes, of course, if you can't come by today then you can retrieve the vehicle on Monday."

I leaned forward to grab Howard's attention and mouthed "today" again, more emphatically. Howard extended a finger to shush me as he listened intently to the man on the other end of that call, to Randall Kincaid. I could hear the tinny sound of his voice through the earpiece of the receiver. Blood thumped through every blue vein in my body.

Confusion waved over Howard's face. He held the

phone away from his ear and stared at the receiver as if he were riveted by it, then handed it to me.

"He asked to speak with you."

"What?"

"He told me to give the phone to Mr. Malick."

I took the phone and put it to my ear. The line was quiet; I began to wonder if the call had been disconnected. Then came the voice I had never heard, but recognized instantly as Randall Kincaid's.

"Is that you?" he asked. For the past seven years I had lived with the sole purpose of murdering this man. And here he was.

"It's me."

The line went quiet again.

"I wonder," he spoke, voice light and nasal, "how you saw this vendetta you hold for me playing out. If you thought it would be so simple as my walking into a car dealership and you would what—interrogate me? Ask me if I was the one who killed your son? Or would you forego any proof or plea for my life and simply put a bullet in my skull?"

"Why don't you come on down here and find out?"

He laughed. A gleeful squeal that set my teeth on edge.

"Your former colleagues, they warned me about you. They said that they were unable to protect me. They said that when someone wants to hurt someone as badly as you wish to hurt me, no one can protect them. So they released me secretly, ahead of schedule in the dead of night, and advised me to get as far away from Cain City as humanly possible, as far as the map would take me."

"That was nice of them. Too bad you're not much of a human."

That laugh again.

"You have been such a curiosity. I thought the stories of your desire for vengeance were exaggerations. Surely after all this time you had come to your senses; this torch you held for me had dimmed. But they impressed upon me how relentless you were, how righteous. They said you were—how did they put it?—'the most bull-headed son-of-a-bitch you will ever meet in your lifetime.' That's a quote. So I decided to follow you. To see for myself. To hear for myself."

"Not much of a spook though, are you?"

"Oh, I wouldn't say that. I watched you every day for weeks before you finally spotted me in your rearview mirror that night. I imagine that if you did not catch the case of that addict girl I would still be following you now, invisible, amused at your pathetic existence, your enduring obsession, you still duly unaware. I have to say, I've found the whole affair quite addictive. You cannot imagine the thrill it gave me to watch you chatting with those two little girls down the street from my mother's house. You bumbling around trying to get in. I loved the rush, the danger of possibly being discovered. It was different with children. That part was easy. That danger was not there."

"I'm going to kill you."

"Oh, I have no doubt as to your intentions. But I'm not too keen on dying."

"Then you shouldn't have been born."

"That's why I'm going to heed your colleague's advice. I see now that you will never stop, that you will never listen to reason, so, I must take my leave of this sorry town and—"

As tenderly as possible, I placed the phone on the desk, stood up, and ran flat out from the office to the front of the dealership. The showroom floor was still slick from the mop. As my feet touched the surface my legs flew out from under me and my head cracked hard against the tile.

"Fuck!"

I grabbed my head, rolled to my knees. The janitor scurried over, took hold of my good arm and helped me to my feet. I jerked out of his grasp and flailed the rest of the way across the wet floor, smashing to a stop at the glass doors. Outside, across the street in plain view, sat the red Pacifica. Randall Kincaid, no longer disguised behind a beard, still had the phone pressed against his ear. And he was still talking.

I yanked the handle of the door, but it was locked.

"Unlock the doors," I screamed at the janitor. He nervously sorted through his loop of keys and fumbled them onto the floor. Randall Kincaid noticed me then. He lowered the phone from his ear and gazed straight into my eyes. A smug, bemused look came into his face. I took the gun out of my jacket, stepped back, and fired four times into the door. The glass splintered and I kicked the pane out.

As I barged through the shattered door, Randall Kincaid waved, nonchalantly, as if he were acknowledging a neighbor, and punched the gas pedal. The Pacifica zoomed away down the avenue. I fired the remaining two bullets at his fleeing vehicle. They both missed. Kincaid turned the corner past the stadium and vanished. I hopped a couple steps that way in hopes of seeing which direction he went, if he turned or kept straight. But he was gone.

I stood in the middle of the avenue, paralyzed as to what to do next, four words looping in my ears:

He was right there—he was right there—he was right there.

That motherfucker was right there.

My head was doing somersaults. My legs faltered and I slumped down to the curb, where I situated the .38 on my lap and pried open the empty cylinder. I rummaged through my jacket pocket for the box of bullets, found it and started loading the chambers. My hand was shaky. I fumbled twice as many bullets into the street as I thumbed into the pistol.

Behind me, a crunch of glass. I slammed the half-empty

cylinder shut and whirled around. The janitor and manager were standing just outside the busted door. Their hands shot up above their heads. Both of them looked scared shitless. The faint wail of a siren became audible.

"I've called the police," the manager murmured.

I got to my feet and tried to walk away from them, but my head was wrecked. I started listing sideways. The janitor stepped through the door and caught me beneath my arms as I collapsed down to all fours and vomited.

"You okay, Mr. Malick? Your head is bleeding."

The approaching sirens were like bombs detonating in my ears. I slipped the .38 in my pocket and signaled the janitor to get me up. He dragged me to my feet and I staggered across the street to the Skylark. The tires on the left side were slashed. I slapped the roof of the car and scouted the street for the nearest escape route. The skinny mechanic stepped through the busted door and joined the janitor and the manager gawking at me.

A cold sweat dampened my entire body. Blood gushed from the split in my head down my neck and back. The closest alley ran between a row of fast food joints and the near side of the stadium. I put my head down and went for it. Walking a straight line proved difficult. My legs were sluggish. They didn't seem to like the orders my brain was giving them. Once I got deep enough into the alley where the spectators could no longer clock me, I brought out my phone and dialed the number for my favorite cabbie, Dennis Maynard.

"Yup," he answered, hocking something up from his gullet. "Maynard here."

"Wake up, Dennis. You need to pick me up."

"You gotta be kidding me? Now?"

"Right fucking now."

CHAPTER THIRTY

ONE MAN HUNT

Maynard found me out back of the Speedway gas station, retching my guts out behind the icebox. He reached back and swung his rear door open. I crawled across the sidewalk and into the backseat. After wolfing in gas fumes for the past fifteen minutes, the stench of his cab was nearly too much to bear.

"Drive," I said.

"Don't be getting no blood on the seat now. If you got to puke you tell me and I'll pull over."

Maynard swung the car onto the avenue.

"Where am I going?"

"Honeysuckle Lane."

He pointed the cab toward the southern hills. A police car sped past us, heading to the dealership. The siren pierced my skull and made my eyeballs feel as if they were going to spring from their sockets.

"That for you?" Maynard asked, adjusting the mirror to look down on me sprawled across the seat.

"Yeah."

Every lurch of the cab, screech of the breaks, bump, or curve of the road as we wound up the side of the hill was excruciating. I closed my eyes to settle my head and didn't open them until we came to a stop at the top of the lane.

"This it?" Maynard asked.

I pushed myself up to a sitting position.

"This is it."

My ex-wife was waiting for me on the steps of her house, a three-story behemoth that overlooked the span of the city. That's what two doctors' salaries got you: lots of rooms. She hurried toward the cab.

Maynard got out and opened my door and helped me to my feet. Joanna took hold of me by the elbow.

"Do I need to pay the fare?" she asked Maynard.

"I've got a running tab," I told her. "Wait for me," I said to Maynard.

"For how long?"

"Until I come out."

"Well, hell."

Maynard shuffled off toward the cab.

Joanna secured me by the elbow and guided me up the walk.

"God, you're worse off than you let on. What happened?"

"I slipped on a wet floor."

"I wish you wouldn't lie to me."

"I wish I was lying."

As we started up the steps the front door swung open. An oafish man shaped like a bowling pin came out.

"You must be Tom," I said.

"That's right. And you must be 'that self-destructive idiot' that used to be married to my wife."

I looked at Joanna.

"That's accurate."

Tommy and Joanna led me through the foyer down the hall to the kitchen and sat me down at the table. Tommy produced a penlight, shined it into my eyes and had me follow his finger while Joanna parted the bloody hair on the back of my head and examined the gash.

"You have a concussion," Tommy said.

"No shit."

"Lean forward," Joanna said. She poured some peroxide on the wound that stung like a motherfucker. "You need stitches."

"Stitch it up then."

Tommy peered over my head and I could see him using his eyeballs to communicate with Joanna.

"I'm not going to the hospital. If you want to stitch it up, stitch it up here."

Tommy sucked a breath in through his teeth.

"You need to recuperate properly. The concussion isn't severe, but it's not minor either. The amount of trauma you've suffered, take another shot to the head, even a light one, and you could be in for some serious impairment."

"I think your wife will tell you the damage has already been done there."

Tommy smiled politely but he did not laugh.

"Listen Tom, you know what's going on right now—she's told you?"

"Yes. She's told me."

"Okay. Then you should know that I'm not stopping, now or ever, until I see Randall Kincaid suffer what will hopefully be a slow and fucking torturous death."

"How do you know you can find him?" Joanna asked. "Or do anything about it when you do, in this condition?"

"I'll manage. I was twenty yards away from him today. Twenty fucking yards."

"You found him."

"In a manner of speaking."

Tommy fetched me some bread and water while I summarized the morning's events for them. After I ate the bread and washed it down, my head stopped whirling and I stopped sweating. Joanna stitched my scalp together and redressed my arm.

Tommy excused himself to another wing of the house and Joanna escorted me to the door.

"Have you taken your antibiotics?"

"Yeah."

"It's important."

"I'm taking 'em."

At the door Joanna turned and faced me.

"What if he *is* gone, Nick? What if he's already fled? He could go anywhere. It's a big world."

"I'll find him. If it's the last thing I do on this planet, I'll find him."

"Nick." She placed her hand on my chest. "If there is any part of you that is doing this for me, then you should know that I don't want you to do it. If I could choose between you being in the world or this man being out of it, I choose you being here. So if you are doing this with me in mind at all, please don't."

I put my hand atop hers on my chest. Tears welled in her eyes. She nodded her head and smiled.

"If you do leave town, please let me know first." Her voice wavered. "Keep me updated. And I'll need to keep assessing that arm."

"Sure."

"I so much want to say, 'be careful,' but saying that won't really mean anything or change anything that's going to happen, will it?"

"Afraid not."

I pulled her hand away from my chest and guided it down to her side, kissed her forehead and walked out of the house.

Maynard was sitting on the hood of his cab, looking across the expanse of the city.

"Hell of a vista, ain't it?"

"It's something."

"Where to?"

"Downtown."

I checked my phone. Two new messages. The first was from Bruce Hale. He informed me that I would be arrested on sight for impersonating an officer of the law, amongst other things, and he would see to it personally that I got locked up for a good long while. The next message was from Willis Hively, advising me to stay out of sight.

The rest of the day, Maynard shuttled me to every hotel and motel in town, as well as the motels outside city limits and across the river. I flashed the booking photo of Kincaid to all the desk clerks, doormen, bellhops, lodgers I happened across, meth-heads out front of the shady motels, maids, handymen, anyone who may have come into contact with Randall Kincaid. If a restaurant was attached to a place, I checked with the wait staff and the hostesses. Not a one of them recalled seeing Kincaid. I asked them to envision the man in the picture with a thick beard.

Nada.

The sun was a long way gone, replaced by a dull moon and a bone-chilling cold, when I emerged from a motel on the Ohio side of the river called Shut Eye's and slumped into the back of the taxi. I laid my head against the fogged window and shut my eyes. My crippled arm was stinging from the cold air.

"That's the last of the motels I know of," Maynard said. "I'm sorry you ain't found your guy, but my boss thinks I'm out here taking fares and if I don't get to taking them real soon I ain't gonna be able to fudge it any more than I already have. I know I owe you my job or whatever, but he's up my ass already after your visit last week and hell, if I don't got no job to owe you then that ain't too good for you neither."

"It's okay," I said, not opening my eyes. "Take me to the high school."

Kincaid's gone, I thought to myself. A snap of the fingers, and he was gone.

On the sidewalk out front of the high school I bid Maynard adieu, turned and looked up at the hundreds of bullet holes pocked around the shattered windows of my office. If Kincaid blew town I had one chance of tracking him—the credit card receipt from the rental car. That is, if he didn't slice it up the moment he saw me stroll into the dealership. If he never used it again I had no idea how the hell I was going to find him.

I dialed up Willis Hively and got his voicemail, asked him to call me back at his earliest convenience, then decided there was nothing left to do except drink large quantities of bourbon.

The Red Head was busy with the college rabble. Made the air thick with a smell like untreated chlamydia. I bellied up to the bar and watched Tadpole divvy out a dozen light beers before he made his way to me.

"What's a guy gotta do to get a bourbon around here?" I kidded him. He didn't seem amused. "C'mon, let me hear the latest blonde joke."

"No jokes. I can't serve you, Malick. You got to go."

"My money spends like anyone else's."

"Ain't up to me. Word came down from Marvin."

"Marvin? You tell him the cops cleared me for self-defense?"

"I told him what I saw."

I tossed a fiver on the bar.

"Haven't I earned a couple a chips here?"

"Whatever chips you earned you played out. I'm sorry."

"You're not fucking sorry. At least give me one to go."

Tadpole threw some Maker's and ice into a styrofoam cup.

"Keep your money. Just stay away for a little while. We can't have shit like that going down in here. People will stop coming."

"People are never going to stop drinking."

"Get gone, Malick."

"Shouldn't be a problem."

I tipped the cup his way, lifted it above my head to part the college kids, and went back out into the night.

Nowhere to go, no lead to follow, I braced against the cold and trudged back to the high school, swept the shards of glass and case files off my desk and laid there flat with the styrofoam cup of bourbon sitting on my chest, watching my breath plume out and dissipate a foot from my face.

As I sipped the drink, a not-so-unpleasant thought breezed into my head. Maybe I would never get up from this slab of desk. Maybe I would lie there until the bourbon was gone and then maybe after it vanished I could vanish. Maybe life would simply drain from me, and my soul would sail away on one last cold breath with me being none the wiser.

Just gone.

The phone jangled against my thigh. I placed the bourbon aside, fished the phone out of my pocket and answered it.

"Something's happened," Willis Hively said. "Where are you?"

"You're not going to haul me in that easy, Hive."

"I don't give a shit about what happened at the car dealership. And after what's gone down tonight, nobody else will either. Where are you?"

"My office."

"I'm three blocks away. Meet me out front."

"Now?"

"Yeah, now."

Willis Hively's Malibu was idling at the curb when I exited the high school. I eased into his passenger seat.

"Where's the fire?"

"Southside."

CHAPTER THIRTY-ONE
A SPLASH OF MURDER

Willis Hively swung the car into a gravel alley off Seventh Street between Eleventh and Twelfth Avenues, a Southside residential block.

"Where the fuck you taking me?"

"You'll see soon enough," Hively warned. "This is two blocks from my house."

"Yeah, I know where you live."

In the middle of the alley he shut off the car, got out and led me through a gate into the backyard of a duplex. Two patrolmen were posted at the patio door on the left. Hive acknowledged them and they stood aside to let us pass.

We stepped into the back room of the unit. The stench of weed filled my nostrils. The room was furnished with a cheap wooden table, an old couch, and a giant hi-def television mounted on the wall. The television, muted, was on a music video channel. Presently, a bunch of girls in bikinis were shaking their asses on a yacht. A pillow was stuffed into the corner of the couch. On the floor beside the table was a matching pillow that still had an ass-print in it. Some pills were laid out on the table, half-crushed. Next to the pills was a green bowtie. On the floor between the table and the couch was a large bong that had been snapped in two. Some of the bud had fallen out if it onto the floor.

Hively said, "We think one or more of our perps came in from the back door here, surprised the victims who were sitting on the couch or the floor, doing whatever they were doing."

"How many victims?"

"Four."

Hively motioned for me to follow him down a hallway past a small kitchen, a stairwell, and a dining room. We sidestepped a framed R.I.P. poster of Tupac and Biggie that had been knocked off the wall and stomped through.

"Seems like they were flushed this way toward the front door where someone else must have been waiting for them."

The front door was wide open. We stepped out onto the stoop. Floodlights cast a fuzzy pall across the property. Their glare sent jolts of pain slithering through my head. I shielded my eyes and surveyed the scene. Lots of visual commotion in the yard and on the perimeter; news vans, cops and techs sternly going about the tasks at hand, snapping photographs, collecting evidence. Onlookers crowded the yellow tape. Jerome Kipling and Red Lewis were working their way down the line, asking each person if they saw or heard anything. Every window in the neighborhood was lit up, children with their noses smooshed against the glass, gawking at the morbid sight.

An eerie hush lay heavy over the whole business. No one moved too fast or spoke too loudly or looked one another in the eye, as if an acknowledgement of the living might offend the dead.

The dead were still on the lawn. Four bodies, all of them face down and lined up side-by-side execution style, a single bullet to the backs of their heads.

"Christ," I said. "This is what you wanted to show me?"

"This is it."

The lawn sloped forward. Blood sluiced from the victim's heads down through the grass and onto the sidewalk where it united into one pool, like tributaries feeding into a great red lake.

"You gonna tell me why you brought me here?"

"Take a look at the girl."

"Why?"

"Take a look."

We walked across the lawn to the bodies. The girl was young and white, her dark hair in a matted tangle where the bullet pierced her skull. She was wearing a long, green sequined dress. A flower corsage was wrapped around her wrist. The guy next to her, also white, donned a black tux minus the bowtie. The two guys on either side of them, both black, were dressed regular.

"The one on the right is Freddy Brown, petty dealer, rented the duplex, dropped out of C.C. High last year. No ID yet for the one on the left. The two in the middle, as you might have guessed, attended the St. Linus prom earlier tonight."

"At the car dealership?"

"Yeah."

"So what, wrong place wrong time?"

"Maybe. Recognize the girl?"

"No."

I stepped around to the other side of her and squatted to see her face.

"Holy shit."

I did recognize the girl. The last time I saw her she was a pudgy fourteen year old who knew all the words to the three shit pop songs the local radio station played on a loop. She had lost the pudge, but the face was unmistakable. Before tonight, she was set to give the valedictorian's speech at her graduation and attend a college of her choosing. Charity Hale, daughter of Bruce Hale, was now eighteen years old and dead at my feet.

Hively glanced around to make sure no one was within earshot.

"Awful big coincidence she happens to be hanging out here when someone comes for the dealer. If that's what this was."

"Awful big. Does Hale know?"

"He showed up. Took four guys to restrain him. Fucking brutal. I don't know the move here, Nick."

"Where is he now?"

"I took him home right before I called you."

I stood up.

"Take me over there."

Somebody from behind the tape whistled and called my name. Ernie Ciccone, downright feverish with excitement, beckoned me over to him.

"What the hell is going on in this town?" he said, as I ducked under the tape and motioned him away from the cluster of watchers.

"You tell me," I said. "From what I've heard tell, you're the expert on the subject."

Ciccone cracked a grin.

"News is news. I just report it."

"Uh-huh. Hale been in contact with you?"

"Not a peep since you and I last chatted."

"What about after you started writing about this stuff? He hasn't tried to blunt the impact?"

"Not a word, cross my heart. I'm as surprised as you are. Thought for sure he would be at me pretty quick to keep a lock on something. Sorry about your arm by the way."

"I'm sure you enjoyed penning that story."

"That hurts my feelings, Malick. You're a goddamn inspiration in my book, a real-life hero."

I scowled.

"Don't butter me up."

"I'm on the level here. This shit has gotten out of hand. Drugs, gangs, guns, throw in a splash of murder and you got yourself a potent little Molotov cocktail."

"Save the hype for your cockamamie stories."

"I saw the high school," Ciccone said, letting out a long whistle. "I don't know how you got out of that shit alive, man."

"You the one went through my office?"

"You know, despite what you might think, I do have some ethics."

"Right."

Ciccone flicked his hand to indicate the scene behind me.

"What can you tell me about this carnage? Who do we have over there?"

I bent down to get level with his ratty eyes.

"You're going to find out soon enough so I'm going to tell you, but you report the names and that's it, not one more thing. You understand me?"

Ciccone shrugged, "Yeah," and readied his pencil.

"You understand me?"

"I understand you."

"The dead girl is Hale's daughter."

Ciccone nearly choked on his spit.

"His daughter?"

"Keep your stupid voice down. Stick to the basics. Nothing accusatory or speculative about Hale, you got me. You write anything other than his name and occupation and you'll be dealing with me and I'm not just talking about your job, got it?"

"I got it, I got it."

Ciccone whistled and ran a hand over his bald pate.

"This confuses me though. I thought you were moving against Hale."

"I am against him."

"Then why the sudden concern?"

"I've seen how you deal in these situations before. I'd like to think maybe you learned something since then, but I'm not going to hold my breath. The man just lost his daughter. Have a little tact."

"At least give me an idea of the big picture here, some piece of the puzzle to make sense on what the devil's going on in this town."

"That's what I'm trying to find out."

CHAPTER THIRTY-TWO
SONS OF BITCHES

Hively dropped me off in front of Hale's house. I told him not to wait for me, climbed the stairs and rapped on the door a couple times. No one answered and nothing stirred inside. I jostled the knob and the door creaked open. I announced my presence, got no response but the bounce of my voice off the walls, and entered the house. A lamp shone from inside the study. I walked over and peered around the door.

Hale sat slumped in a leather armchair, staring dead-eyed into a false fireplace. In one of his hands was a bottle of vodka. The other held a Glock 9.

"Come on in," he said.

"You mind setting that gun aside?"

"What, this?"

Hale held the gun up and looked it over as if it were some foreign object he had never handled before, then set it on the side table. I entered the room and took a seat in the other armchair. Hale hoisted the vodka bottle my way.

"No, thanks."

"Well look at that," he chided. "You turned down a drink. I've seen it all now. Don't look at me like that. Don't you fucking look at me with the smug little smirk you son of a bitch."

"I don't drink vodka, Bruce. And I'm too tired to give you any kind of look."

"Yeah, well, I know what you're thinking," he jabbed a finger into his temple. "I know why you came here. To fucking gloat. To tell me I got exactly what I deserved, now I know what it feels like. To throw it all in my face. I know why you're here."

His big belly and chest heaved up and down and he looked away from me back toward the fireplace.

"She was so good, Nick. Going to be the valedictorian, go to college somewhere far away from this piece of fuck town, get married, have kids, all of that life ahead of her. She was so good I couldn't believe I made her. Did I tell you she was going to be the valedictorian?"

"You told me."

"My baby girl," he whispered.

"I know, Bruce. I'm sorry."

"You know what she asked me the other day? She asked me, 'Are you proud of me Daddy?' Am I proud of her she asks. I should have told her she's the best thing that ever happened to me. That she's the one thing in my piece of shit existence that I've ever been proud of. You know what I did say?"

"What?"

"'Sure I am, sweetheart.' That's all I said. Pathetic."

Hale flung the vodka bottle at the fireplace, shattering it into a hundred pieces. A chunk of glass ricocheted off the floor and landed back by his feet. He stomped on it until the pieces were too small to break down further and he was too winded to continue. He capped the tirade by screaming at nothing and then sinking back into the chair.

"Why are you here?" he said, once he'd caught his breath.

"I gotta know, Bruce. I got to know why they killed her and what you had to do with it."

Hale stared at the broken glass scattered across the floor.

"Maybe they killed her because they declared war on the Cain City police department and she was the daughter of the lead detective. Maybe she was there to get high with her boyfriend after prom and she got caught in a bad situation. Maybe they killed her because the earth is round. How the hell am I supposed to know?"

"I know you were involved with this Detroit crew. You impeded my investigations any time I even whiffed them. I know you were paying money, good money, to keep the stories with links to them out of the news."

That I knew this information didn't surprise him. He turned his head and focused his eyes on me. Started slow clapping.

"You want a pat on the back? What are you going to do, turn me in? I don't give a shit," he laughed, desperately. "Hell, turn me in. I don't care."

"The other night, did you know that they were coming to kill me?"

Hale's eyes hardened.

"Yeah, I knew. I couldn't stop them from it."

"You could have warned me."

"I thought maybe if they killed you I might be able to get them back under control. Back to where I had them before all this shit happened. Then you went and killed all of them you crazy bastard. Good on you."

"Is Hively involved?"

Hale swiped a dismissive hand through the air.

"Hive is too good an egg. Hasn't been in the jungle long enough. Still thinks he can make a difference. Maybe if this job had worn down his decency, made him start to wonder if he didn't deserve a little something better. Maybe then I could approach him with this. I probably would have brought it to you if you were still around."

Hale's eyes probed mine. I don't know if he was trying to equate him and me in some manner, insinuate that I would be corrupt now too if I had stayed on the force, or if he simply wanted to be saved from the responsibility of this night. Maybe he feared the direction this conversation had to go. Whatever the reason he dangled that big worm on a little hook, I wasn't going to swim anywhere near it.

"Did they kill Charity because of a vendetta with you?"

Hale nodded slowly.

"They shot Charity because she's my daughter. Because they knew it was the best way to slice me through to my fucking soul. It's my fault that she's dead. Those other kids, they probably got killed because they were with her, no other reason. Does that satisfy you to hear that? Does it make you feel good, you piece of shit?"

Hale wiped some spittle onto the back of his hand, looked at it, then balled the hand into a fist and hit himself on the side of his head twice, hard.

We sat there quiet for a minute.

"Why didn't they just kill me?" he wondered. "Hell, maybe they still will."

"I'm not going to turn you in. This is punishment enough for a lifetime. But you gotta tell me what you were into them for."

"I do get it now, Nick. I get why you went off the rails when Jake died. I thought I was helping you out by telling you to pull your shit together. I thought, you know, I could see the bigger picture that you couldn't see. You still had a wife, still had something to salvage, something to live for. I knew if you kept on the way you were going you'd lose the job, not to mention the wife. Not to mention I'd be losing you as a partner. Now, I know why you didn't give a fuck about the job anymore, or the wife, or anything. You lose a child, nothing else matters. There's no way to get your shit together ever again. I should have done more for you besides telling you to move on. What an asshole, huh? Maybe I do deserve this."

"Nobody deserves what we got, Bruce. But if you are so inclined, there's something you can do to make it up to me."

"Randall Kincaid."

"Randall Kincaid. He might have blown town. Don't know where he's going, but I've got a credit card number. I need it tracked in as close to real time as possible so I can find him."

"So you can go kill him."

I shrugged, "So I can go kill him."

"Before you walked in here I was going to put this gun into my mouth and blow my stupid brains out the back of my head."

"Yeah, I put that together."

"When these Detroit fuckers rolled in, I had no idea this shit-storm would blow up in my face like a fucking nuke. But I should have known better. The moment I made the deal with them, a time bomb began to tick, tick, tick away to this night."

"How did they get their hooks into you?"

"I thought, what's the harm, you know? They bring in some drugs, sell them to the people who are going to get high anyway, and I give them a heads up if they're getting a little hot, if they need to back off a location or a sell, let them know if any warrants go out, whatever. At least that way I could maybe keep them contained, and, at the same time put a little bit of change in my pocket. Made me feel like I was getting a lot for a little. These colleges weren't going to pay for themselves."

"Nothing like a good rationalization."

Hale ignored me. Or didn't hear.

"My girl deserved to go wherever she wanted to go. She earned that. Got accepted to Notre Dame. I tell you that?"

Pride flashed across his face.

I shook my head.

"No? I wasn't going to hold her back from that. But then these Detroit boys are smart. They had bigger plans for little ol' Cain City. They started tightening the screws. The things they asked me to do kept getting bigger and bigger—cover up overdoses; keep arrests, busts, that kind of thing out of the paper, make certain evidence disappear. No press was good press. They didn't want anyone knowing they were here until it was too late for anybody to do something about it. Cain City was the perfect place for them to ruin. A little town in the middle of nowhere, on the way to a bunch of somewheres. My hometown," Hale sneered. "Remember what I said to you at the bar about how once they found out they were running the place we were all in trouble."

"Looks like they figured it out."

"Nah, they didn't have to figure it out. They always knew. It was me who didn't have it figured."

"So why Charity?"

Hale closed his eyes.

"After the debacle at the high school, I told them I could be of no further service. There was nothing more I could do for them, which was pretty much true. The cat was out of the bag. But they didn't like that. How am I supposed to cover that shit up? They expected me to be a miracle worker or something. They said if I left them hanging now, they would push the button on this town, kill every police officer on the force if they had to. Whatever they had to do, they would do. Very matter of fact. Hell, they may still do it."

"They, meaning Cupcake."

"Jesus." Hale opened his eyes. "You know everything, don't you?"

"What's his story?"

"Knows what he's doing, that one. Don't see him flaunting his power around town or anything like that. Shows his face for business, real business, and that's it. He's clinical. Once he had me under his thumb you should have seen how fast he took over the majority of the trade in town. Two weeks, tops. Laid out seven bodies, all the real players, and the place was his. Doesn't come anywhere close to the drugs either. Has a handful of trusted lieutenants who handle the street-level shit, while he sits back and runs the show from afar. Tremaine Miller was one of the local lieutenants. That's why they came at you so hard. By the way, Tremaine didn't kill the girl."

"Yeah, I know. Nobody did."

"What do you mean, nobody did? Somebody killed her."

I told him how Trisha Cammack overdosed in her parent's kitchen and her father thought it best for her mother's sanity to make her vanish, but chickened out in the end.

"Jesus," Hale said. "To think none of this would have happened if it hadn't been for a damned whore junkie."

"Something would have happened."

"But not Charity."

"Maybe not Charity. What are you going to do now?"

"I don't know." Hale expelled the oxygen from his lungs. "I've got to put my little girl in the ground." He closed his eyes and grinded his head into the back of the chair. "I want to kill them all. I want them the fuck out of this town and I want them to leave in body bags. You up for that?"

"Come again?"

"I'll get you what you're asking for on Kincaid. I'll track his credit card. I'll lead you right to him. Hell, I'll be your alibi. If I do all that, will you help me take down Cupcake?"

Fury filled me from the bottoms of my feet to the crown of my head. Blood thrummed at my temples.

"You son of a bitch," I seethed. "You dangle a proposition like that in front of me and then tell me the only way you'll do it is if I help you murder somebody?"

"Not just somebody, Nick." Hale sprung forward in his chair. "The man who killed my daughter—the man who is tearing this town apart. The man who sent a kill squad after you. That is who we are talking about here. I'm not talking about Joe fucking Citizen."

"Where were you when I needed your help?"

"I'll help now."

"And if I won't?"

Hale averted his eyes.

"That'll make it harder for you to track Kincaid down, won't it?"

I leapt across the room and pounced on him. We toppled over the chair and onto the floor. I twisted my body to land on my healthy shoulder, bounced off the desk, then elbowed Hale in the throat and grappled until I was on top of him. I pinned his arms under my knees and started wailing on his face.

"Hit me!" he shouted between blows. I obliged him. With each punch, the back of his head cracked against the floor. Hale made no attempt to stop me, just allowed me to beat the shit out of him. His lack of fight sucked all the pleasure out of it. I hit him once more for good measure, felt the gristle of his nose crunch beneath my knuckles, screamed in his face, and rolled off of him. He stayed laying there with blood pouring out of his mouth and nose, the expression on his face a mixture of disgust and relief. I sat back against the desk, panting.

A frail voice called down from the top of the stairwell. "Bruce?"

Hale turned his head and hocked blood and a piece of tooth onto the floor before responding, "Yes, honey."

"Is everything all right?"

"Yes, baby. Everything's fine. I'm sorry, it was just me. Stay upstairs, please."

"Are you coming up?"

"I'll be up soon. You okay?"

There was a pause before Cynthia mumbled, "No."

We listened to her shuffle off and an upstairs door creaked shut. Hale pointed to a box of tissues at the corner of his desk and I handed it to him. He wadded up two tissues, plugged them into each nostril and squeezed the bridge of his nose.

"I need you, Nick. I'm a novice at this game. You're an old hand."

"It's not that hard to kill someone."

"Don't placate me. We both know I'm not smart enough to pull this off."

Hale grimaced as though this was the first bit of negative self-reflection he had ever permitted.

"He'll see me coming from a mile away, kill me before I even smell the cooking. He's insulated. I haven't the first clue how to get to him."

"How did you contact him before?"

"Before I told him to go to hell you mean? They get new pre-paid phones every couple days. Someone would let me know what the new numbers were."

"It's a small town. Only so many places a person can be."

"Maybe I'll go door to door," Hale said, managing a short chortle. "I understand, Nick. I'll get that Kincaid info for you no matter. I'm late to the party on this, I know, but I owe you that. But will you help me? You're the only person I can trust."

"No one else reliable enough to murder somebody?"

"Not a one."

"You know what Cupcake looks like?"

"Yeah, we met a couple times to set things up. He doesn't do handoffs or anything like that. Why?"

"'Cause I couldn't pick him out of a line-up with two people in it. And if you want to kill somebody you gotta know what they look like."

CHAPTER THIRTY-THREE
SOMETHING LIKE GOODBYE

The bourbon in my office was gone. Anybody could have swiped it; the kid, some hobo off the street. The swinging door and missing windows were basically an advertisement for an open house. I wandered into the bedroom and found the hobo in question.

Karla was curled up on the bed with the sheet half tugged over her. Her fingers were wrapped loosely around the neck of the bottle. The whole room smelled boozy. I switched the lamp on and found the cap on the floor, got the bottle out of her hand and screwed it shut. She had taken down a good bit of the liquor. I sat on the bed next to her.

"Hey there, pretty lady," I said, petting her head. "This is a surprise."

She stirred and moaned but her eyes stayed shut.

"I wanted to wait for you," she murmured. "Tell you to go fuck yourself."

"So not a nice surprise. You're upset."

After some thick blinks she got her eyes open and swatted my hand away from her head.

"I'm livid." She said it again to emphasize both syllables. "Li-vid."

She rolled onto her back and shielded her face with her arm, squinted out from under it to look at me. Her bottom cheek was beet red and creased from having been smooshed against the sheets.

"You shouldn't be here. It's not safe."

"No, it's not safe. I don't know what I was thinking getting drawn into you. I knew better. Sure know how to pick 'em, don't I?"

She forced herself up into a sitting position and pressed her palms into her eye sockets and made a frustrated sound.

I asked, "Where's Davey?"

She shrugged and raked her fingers through her hair to clear it from her face.

"Upstairs asleep, maybe. That's where he was before I went down to The Red Head to find you. I figured your drunk ass might be there, or show up there, so I waited for you and what do you know, in you came, and you looked right at me, right straight at me, and you didn't even flinch."

"It was crowded. I didn't see you."

"If you wanted to see me, you would have seen me. Or you would've come to see me once you got out of the hospital. We went to see you when you were in the hospital. Did you know that?"

"I heard."

"But I've got to hear it from my kid that you were discharged. You send a message through my kid that you want me to stay away from you."

"That's not what I meant."

"No?" Karla's eyes fluttered and her head lolled loose atop her neck. "What did you mean then?"

She pressed her fingertips to her temples to hold her head steady and lifted her brows in an attempt to focus her eyes.

"I can't be around you right now, that's all. Are you all right?"

She declared, matter-of-factly, "I'm going to be sick."

I brought in a wet rag and a small trash can from the bathroom. I laid the rag on the back of her neck while she held her hair to the side and vomited quietly into the can. A lady to the end. When she finished I tossed the can out the busted windows, got her to her feet and escorted her down the hallway. At the base of the stairwell she stopped and peered up the two flights as if they were some insurmountable summit, her personal Kilimanjaro. I prodded her on and she clambered up the steps.

Karla had trouble keeping her eyelids above her pupils, but, pausing on the second floor landing, she rallied the energy to light into me properly.

"I'm not the girl that just gives it away," she said, flailing a hand about as if that were the international symbol for cheap, meaningless sex. "Lets you string her along, make her feel like she means more than she does and then lets you discard her like she's expired meat or something. And you expect me not to say anything about it? Just take it like a chump? I'm not that girl."

I tried to assuage her belief that I was discarding her, but she wasn't having it.

"Could have fooled me. We came to the hospital, Davey and me. Did you know that?"

"You mentioned that."

"Because I wanted to see you. Because I was worried. Because Davey thought you were a good guy. Because I gave a shit."

"It was sweet of you to visit."

"You don't care," she muttered. "I don't care."

She glanced at my busted arm in its sling.

"How's your arm?"

"Still attached," I said, wiggling my swollen fingers to illustrate.

We climbed the rest of the stairs without speaking. The silence continued as I unlocked her door and lugged her into her bedroom. I went into the kitchen and filled a glass of water. She gulped it down like a greedy camel, thrust the empty glass back at me and requested another.

When I returned with the second glass of water Karla was tucked into a ball with her arms clamped between her knees and her eyes closed. I sat at the foot of the bed. The cat, Lucifer, leapt from the shadows of the room onto my lap, giving me a start. I shoved her off, but she was persistent so I let her stay there and nuzzle me.

Karla slurred softly, "I thought you were different. If you didn't want to see me anymore you could have the decency to tell me to my face." She took in a deep breath and expelled it with a moan. "Better to hurt a little now than a lot later."

"Hurting you is the last thing I want to do."

"It's my own fault. Funny thing is, that night when I came to look for you I wasn't wanting anything more than a hook-up. But the way you—" she stopped short. "Stay away from us. I don't want to see you again."

"You probably never will."

"That's a tad fucking dramatic."

She opened her eyes to roll them and then closed them again. I sat there for some interval scratching the cat, listening to her purr and Karla's drunken breathing. Karla didn't move and I couldn't tell whether or not she was feigning sleep.

With no prelude, preconceived thought or calculation, I began the story of my long-dead son, Jake, and of his murderer, Randall Kincaid; of the eight days Jake was missing before his body was discovered in the Ohio River; of the seven years of vengeance that consumed me whole; of the wife I alienated, and the career I lost because of the beatings I meted out as I hunted for Jake's killer.

"This man was arrested down at Redding Park for whacking off within view of the playground, the one with the replica train and the zipline, which was a place I had taken Jake a few days before he went missing. This guy, Terry was his name, was arrested about a week after Jake's body had been found. Anyway, bad timing for Terry. Turns out, he wasn't whacking off at all. No, what Terry was doing was putting on his cup for his softball game at the fields adjacent to the playground. Some old lady walked by, thought she saw something lewd, and called the cops on him. Moreover, Terry was not the only person I harmed badly, but he was the only one who nearly died."

Karla opened her eyes, but did not look at me.

"Why are you telling me this?"

"Because I need to say it out loud, all of it. I've never done that. Maybe I didn't have the vocabulary. And I need you to know that before I met you, you and Davey, I was hollowed out inside. When something like that happens, losing your son, nothing in life matters anymore. There is no meaning to be found in anyone or anything, no better day ahead. You get trapped in this emptiness that chews at you. This void. There are no short days, no days where all of a sudden it's evening and you wonder where the time has gone. You feel the length of every hour, every day. Distance is a funny thing. More days pass and I feel further and further removed from Jake, while at the same time I get closer to doing this thing that I've been devoted to. Somehow, these two notions can't seem to reconcile themselves in my head. I don't know; that's the best way I can describe it.

"Every day that I've endured, from the day they pulled my son from the river to now, has been for one reason, to kill this man that put him in that water. My life had been honed down to this one end. There was nothing left for anybody else. I shed it all. My wife, my job, all of it. But you and that boy of yours put something inside of me that has been dormant for a long time. Thank you for that. I would like it very much if the circumstances were different and you and I could do normal things like go to dinner or a movie, or go for a walk, but they're not."

"I remember when that happened," Karla said. "Davey was a grade ahead of your son. They went to the same school."

A quiet settled over the room. Karla didn't say anything else. Maybe there was nothing left to say, so I stood up and left her there on the bed, staring at the wall.

Davey was standing in the middle of the front room, waiting for me.

"Is my mom okay?"

"She'll be fine. Just needs a good sleep. Take care of yourself, kid."

I stepped past him.

"There's been a few different people snooping around your place," the kid blurted, halting me at the door. "Besides my mom I mean. Four other people."

"Any of them look suspicious?"

"*Pshhh*, all of them. A couple of them just looked nosy, like they wanted to see all the bullet holes or some shit. This one old lady looked like she was just scoping your place for anything valuable. And this one bald dude had a notepad and was scribbling shit down. Ratty looking mug."

"Ciccone. Anybody with a droopy eyelid?"

"Naw," the kid squished his face up, thinking. "Nothing like that."

"Thanks, kid. You don't need to keep an eye out anymore."

"You want me to stop."

"Yeah, you're relieved of your duties."

I went out the door. The kid followed me out into the hall and called after me, "See you around."

"Sure, kid. See you around."

CHAPTER THIRTY-FOUR
THE DANCE MAN

A little past eight the next morning Hale came round in a Volkswagen Tiguan, his sister-in-law's car, in case Cupcake and his minions were able to identify his SUV. The morning was already hot and sticky. Before I got into the car I removed the .38 and the switchblade from my coat pocket, shed the coat and tossed it in the back seat. I tucked the .38 into the back of my pants. The blade was too long and awkward to fit in my pants pocket, but it fit snugly beneath the wrist of my arm cast, so I tucked it in there.

"You got a plan or are we just winging it?" Hale asked as I lifted myself into the passenger seat. His face had absorbed the previous night's beating pretty well. His lip was split in a couple spots, but his face didn't look much more bloated than usual.

"If Cupcake only shows his face for business," I answered, "then let's fuck up his business."

"How are we going to fuck it up more than you already have?"

"Any wrench I threw into his business was unintentional. Besides that I had you trying to keep me from it. Let's see what kind of damage we can do on purpose."

"You think we can do enough to smoke him out?"

"Have a better idea?"

Hale mulled this over and shook his head.

"Where do we start?"

"E.B.'s Diner."

"What the hell's at E.B.'s Diner?"

"Breakfast. Drive."

Riding over I outlined the scheme I had in mind to flush out Cupcake. It entailed breaking every rule of law cops were sworn to uphold. Hale, being the embodiment of corruption that he was, had no qualms with that.

"Today I'm not a cop, Nick," Hale said. "Today we do what we have to do."

"Keep it in your pants, Dirty Harry."

The diner was near empty, just a few old men hunched over the counter forking slop into their mouths, and Hinkle, in that same yellow booth in the back corner.

"What's good here?" I asked him as we approached his booth. He closed his eyes and slowly lifted his head, as if he were hoping my voice were a figment of his imagination and when he opened his eyes, only a gust of wind would be in front of him. But he opened them up and there I was.

"Ain't this some shit." He dropped his fork. "I thought you and me had an understanding, man. I tell you all I know about Trish and you stay out my business. Simple. Now you come in here bringing police," he jabbed a finger at Hale. "That's just cold, man."

Hale said, "Calm down, jackass. We're not here to shake you down."

"No? Why you here then?"

Hale and I crammed in the booth opposite Hinkle. I said, "I'm hungry. You hungry?"

"Famished," Hale replied.

"We're both hungry," I smiled.

Hinkle tossed his napkin down. His hands disappeared under the table. Hale barked, "Keep your hands on top of the table." Hinkle made a stink about it, rolling his eyes and smacking his lips in disgust, but he laid both hands flat.

I said, "We have a proposal for you."

"I ain't doing no deals with y'all. Snitches are bitches."

"We're gonna lay it all out—see what you think then. But first you're going to buy us breakfast because you make more scratch than we do. Then the three of us are going to have a conversation. At the end of that conversation we are going to walk out of this diner together, side by side like the three amigos. Choice you have to make here is whether or not you want to walk out of here in handcuffs or if you want to walk out of here free as a bird."

Hinkle's jowls twitched.

"I thought this wasn't a shakedown."

"It's not," Hale said. "Man said choice. You help us out today, you can stick to your low-level shit. I'll never bother you. You stay off my radar, I'll stay off yours. But if we don't like what we hear from you, if you aren't a hundred percent forthcoming with us, enjoy your pancakes because I'm going to put so many years on you, you'll be a crusty old man before you get another quality meal the likes of E.B's Diner."

"Yo, that big threatening talk is all good, but here's the thing y'all don't take into account. I might be in jail if I don't snitch for y'all, but I'll be alive, won't I?"

Hinkle lifted a satisfied eyebrow as if he had just dropped some serious truth.

Hale said, "If you call deep-throating prison cock being alive, then sure, you'll be living the dream. Who knows, you might even grow to enjoy the sensation of a dick-shaft on your tongue. Maybe you'll close your eyes as you take a salty mouthful and dream about the beach."

"Fuck you and fuck you," Hinkle pointed at each of us. "Y'all sleazy motherfuckers can't do this to me, man. This is bribery, blackmail, all that shit. I'm not stupid."

"Debatable," I interjected.

"I'll get a lawyer, don't think I won't. I'm going to file a complaint against both your asses for police harassment."

"I'm not police."

"Your word versus ours," Hale said. "Who do you think is going to win?"

"Shoot cuz," Hinkle frowned. "I say it's at least fifty-fifty."

"C'mon, Norman," I said. "You say you're smarter than that. Prove it."

"Man, if the wrong person sees me talking to y'all right now you're looking at a dead white boy. How do y'all not get that?"

"You know Aisha Bryant?" I asked.

"Ol' Gum Drop? I knew her before she got ganked."

"She was shot for talking to me. Did you know that?"

Hinkle nodded in the affirmative.

"Wouldn't it be a shame if word got to floating around that not only did you talk to us, but you even helped us get pointed in the right direction tracking down Cupcake?"

"That's jacked up."

"How about Tricky Jackson? You know him?"

"Yeah, I knew the motherfucker before you whacked him."

"I offered Tricky a way out, much the way we're offering you a way out right here, right now, but he bet against me and look what happened to him. Now, you say you're not stupid. Okay, don't be stupid. Don't bet against me."

"Or what, you going to shoot me?"

The waitress came around to take our orders.

"What's good here besides the pancakes?" I said. "Steak and eggs?"

"It's steak and eggs, man," Hinkle snapped before the waitress could answer. "Tastes the same everywhere. Shit probably tastes the same in prison."

Hale smirked, "You don't get steak in prison."

I asked the waitress again what she thought of the steak and eggs. She shrugged noncommittally and agreed with Hinkle that they were fine. I ordered them. Hale ordered biscuits and gravy with some bacon and potatoes on the side and an orange juice on top of coffee. I looked at him.

"What? Told you I was famished."

As we waited for the food to be delivered we briefed Hinkle on what we needed from him.

"You know how these guys operate. You know how they make their drops, where they run their product."

"Yeah, so."

"So, you need to tell us who their biggest street level earners are."

"The ones closest to you geographically. Ones who, if they were removed from the game, their clients would buy from you instead."

"*Pshh*, I still don't see nothing in this for me."

Our food came out. The steak was too tough to cut with one hand. Rather than have Hale cut it for me, I picked it up and ate it like a sandwich. The meat tasted vaguely of burnished leather. I put the steak down, forked some eggs into my mouth and then pointed the utensil at Hinkle.

"When this thing goes down, you're not going to have to look over your shoulder for these guys ever again. You can go back to doing things the way you did them before this Detroit faction arrived."

Hale said, "I can make you a C.I. if that sweetens the deal."

Hinkle snorted, "Man, for sure I ain't no company snitch."

"Think about it. Four hundred a month for the next year."

"I'm going to have to give people up and shit for a whole year?"

"Nope, just give us what we need today and the rest of the year is on the house."

Hinkle did the math on four hundred times twelve, counting on his fingers and mouthing the numbers.

"It's four thousand, eight hundred," I said to speed him along. The idea of an extra five g's sunnied his disposition.

"All right then," Hinkle agreed, and voila, Hale had himself a brand-spanking-new criminal informant.

"Who is their biggest earner in your neck of the woods?" Hale asked.

"They got a couple places. They got one dude roves around over on the West End. Never in the same place twice. They got a word of mouth type thing so junkies can figure out how to find them. All them honkies over there on smack."

"You know how to find the rover?"

"Yeah, it's not like they can make the shit too hard, know what I mean. Crackheads got to be able to work it out."

I asked, "How do you get a hold of them when you run out of product, when you need a drop? You got a number or something?"

"Naw, nothing like that. They got burners, but I'm not high enough on the totem pole to get those numbers. They get rid of them too fast and I don't need new drops that often. When I do, I got to go see a guy."

"What guy?"

Hinkle hesitated. Once a name was revealed there was no turning back. His eyes darted around, panicked, like he was looking for an escape route to miraculously appear. Realizing he was quite literally cornered, Hinkle wagged his head in surrender.

"You know that goofy looking dude with the dreads always standing on the corner by Timbo's Pizza, the one dancing all crazy and spinning that sign with the big arrow."

"Yeah."

"Him. He's the one I go see."

"The dance man?" Hale said. "You mean Leonard Lippman? You got to be shitting me."

Hinkle said he didn't know the dance man's name, but if Leonard Lippman was the crazy dude with dreads that spun that sign for Timbo's, then that was him. Their system worked like this: Hinkle pulled up to the corner and placed his order with the dance man, who never stopped twirling the sign and making a big show as if he were trying to recruit a customer.

Once the order was placed, the dance man pointed his sign in the direction Hinkle was to drive. The direction was never the same from one visit to the next and there was no discernable pattern. Hinkle followed the arrow in the allotted direction, peering down the alleys until he spotted a pair of shoes hanging from the power lines above one of them. Hinkle drove to the middle of that alley, stopped the car, shut the engine down and lowered the window. Eventually someone would materialize beside the car and hand Hinkle a paper grocery bag. Hinkle handed over the money cut and drove away flush with new provisions. Hinkle didn't think Timbo's was a front. He reckoned the dance man used the job to coordinate the drugs.

After a while of working it out in my head, I told them, "Okay, this is how it's going to go."

Hinkle was to lead us to Cupcake's top street-level earners who sold in the same general vicinity as Hinkle. We take those competitors out, let those losses sink in for a few hours, and then Hinkle visits the dance man, tells him customers were coming out of the woodwork; the demand has caused him to sell out a week's worth of product in one day.

Hinkle has no explanation as to why or how this is happening, but he's not going to look a gift horse in the mouth, and needs the supply to fit the demand. He tells the dance man it's an opportunity he can't pass up and is ready for a bigger piece of the game.

Hale asked, "If you want to switch up your arrangement, will they want a face-to-face to renegotiate?"

"Hell if I know—probably. They're particular about every deal they work, but you two got to be out of your heads if you think I'm going to do what y'all are talking about."

"Don't be a pussy," Hale said. "You do this, everybody wins. That bigger drop goes through, you can keep it, keep any scratch you make from it. I don't give a shit. Call it a perk."

I said, "We'll see if this will get Cupcake out of bed, or at the very least bait us somebody who can lead us to him."

"And then," Hale stared at Hinkle and brushed his hands together as if to wipe them clean. "Both our problems are solved."

I put on a shit-eating grin.

"What do you say, partner?"

Hinkle threw his fat head back against the padding of the booth and moaned, "Fuck me."

I said, "Buy me a drink first."

Hale told him, "Hand over your phone."

CHAPTER THIRTY-FIVE
SALT LICK

The mobility of the rover was a problem. If we botched our attempt to nab him, we'd lose the advantage of surprise, so the decision was made to let the rover alone. The simplest way to disrupt Cash City's trade would be to hit them where they had established roots.

Norman Hinkle directed us to two different locations on the West End; the first a strip of stores next to the viaduct that housed a pet shop called Furry Friends, a sandwich place, and a barber shop. We staked the building out from half a block away on the other side of the viaduct. The traffic moving through the sandwich place and the barber shop seemed normal, but Furry Friends was different. In the first half hour we were posted, thirteen people entered the pet store. Of that thirteen, Hinkle identified eleven as junkies. None of those eleven came out of there with a thing in their hands, no kitty litter, chew toys, or goldfish in a baggie. Nada.

The second location was a two-story rectangular warehouse that operated as a glass factory until it went belly up and was converted into a bingo hall. When the bingo hall petered out the place was left to squatters and the homeless. Now, apparently, it functioned as a Cash City drug emporium. The warehouse was located off an isolated road west of Redding Park on the other side of the creek. It sat at the far end of a gravel parking lot and backed up to a steep hill and woods.

As we cruised the road parallel to the gravel lot, Hinkle slouched low in the backseat like a petrified child, my jacket tugged up over his nose.

"What are you doing?"

"I heard these dudes be using heavy-duty binoculars and shit. Peep every car that rolls past." He stretched his neck to peer out the window. "That's a good looking place to set up shop. Shit is tight. See anybody coming from a ways away and gives you time to take 'em on if need be. Lots of cover in back if you need to skedaddle out of there. *Pfft*, good luck taking that place."

I told him to shut up and put down my jacket.

Down the road, beyond view of the warehouse, Hale pulled the car onto the shoulder and told Hinkle to step out so that we could have a private conversation. Hinkle obeyed and stood outside my passenger door where we could see him.

"What do you think?" Hale said.

"Who do you trust?"

Without blinking Hale said Willis Hively. A scowl rolled up his face as he deliberated on who else to add to that list. "Red Lewis and Jerome Kipling."

"Say it like you mean it. You sure they're not on the take, too?"

"No, I would have recognized the patterns if other detectives were involved. I would have known."

"No uni's?"

"Wasn't close enough to any of them. Can't risk it."

"That's four. You think four's enough?"

"I think we gotta keep it a tight circle."

"Warrants?"

"Cummings will sign blank warrants for me."

"Blank warrants?"

Hale nodded. "Talked to him this morning."

"Jesus," I shook my head. "What a town."

I knocked on the window and signaled for Hinkle to get back in the car. Hale put the Tiguan in gear and started down the road. Hinkle leaned forward between the seats.

"So what now?"

I said, "Now son, you and I are going to spend some quality time together."

"Fucking peachy. Just me and the guy with a bounty on his head."

"You know about that, do you?"

"Man, everybody knows about that."

"Don't go getting any ideas. Wouldn't want you to get hurt."

"I look like a killer to you?"

"You don't want to know what you look like to me."

"Whatever."

Hinkle settled back into his seat.

"Where do you want me to drop you?" Hale asked.

I craned my head around to address Hinkle.

"What do you think? Maybe get a drink somewhere real public where everybody can see us together?"

"Fuck that jazz. I ain't going to be sitting beside you when the bullets start whizzing. Take my ass somewhere ain't nobody gonna see us."

"How about your place?" I offered. "It's big and fancy. Bet your parents keep it stocked with all kinds of good shit. Bet they got sparkling water."

"You don't know nothing."

"I know your parents had to pander to your ass all these years for you to turn out so spectacularly ridiculous."

Hale said, "Who still lives with their parents at your age?"

"An entrepreneur such as yourself. Cut the cord already."

"You two can suck my nuts."

I hiked a thumb toward the backseat.

"Got a tenner says this guy's never had a drink of tap water in his life."

Hale pitched his voice high.

"My baby drinks sparkling water, only the best for Normie."

"You guys are real comedians. Don't quit your day jobs. Let me ask you this, funny guys. What am I supposed to tell my folks if they come home and I'm chilling out with stumpy here, huh?"

"Tell them you finally made a white friend," I said. "They'll probably be thrilled."

Hale pulled to a stop out front of the Hinkle home and I asked Hinkle to wait for me by the stoop.

"Can I get my phone back?"

"Nope."

Hinkle, displaying an impressive amount of petulance, hopped out and flung the door shut. I turned to Hale.

"Any word on Kincaid?"

He shook his head in the negative. "Not a peep." As if reading my mind, he added, "I'll tell you the minute anything comes up, I swear. By the way, I called the impound lot. Told them to find some good tires, slap 'em on your car. They're going to tow it back to the high school. Should be there sometime today."

"Thanks."

"That car is an all-time piece of shit. You gotta get rid of that thing."

"Ah, she's still got a good engine."

"An eighty-five-year old woman still has a pussy. Know what I'm saying?"

I laughed, couldn't help it, and told him to get going.

To this point in the morning Hale had come off sturdy and unwavering, but presently his hands began to tremble on the steering wheel and his knee commenced to bouncing up and down. In general terms, he looked like he was about to lose his shit.

"You okay?"

"What if this doesn't work?"

"Then we try something else. Simple."

I grinned to appease him.

"Yeah, simple. What if I'm wrong? What if one of the detectives is working on their side, too? What if I can't trust any of them and I can't see it because my head is all fucked up?"

"Well, we'll find out soon enough."

"Yeah," Hale nodded. "Get the fuck out of the car." He tightened his grip on the steering wheel to stop his extremities from shaking. "Go babysit that derelict."

"You got your backup set of cuffs on you?"

"Yeah, why?"

"Let me borrow them?"

"What are you going to do, have your way with the poor bastard?"

"Just give me the irons, asshole."

Hale fetched the cuffs from the console and handed them over. I told him to keep me updated, grabbed my jacket from the back, and followed Hinkle into the house.

The front door opened to an enormous room that served as a foyer, kitchen, living room and study all in one. In back of the room, a double set of massive French doors provided a view onto the manicured backyard. The walls were crammed with pictures of little Norman Hinkle at every stage of his young life. From toddler to his teen years to now, he had always looked ridiculous in one way or another. His father's WVU medical school diploma was also up there.

Hinkle kicked his shoes off into a basket next to the door and asked me to do the same. I laughed.

"So what do we do now?" Hinkle asked.

"Where do you normally hang?"

"Basement."

He led me through the kitchen and down a hallway to a stairwell that wound down to a basement. The place was decked out: wraparound leather couch, stocked bar, mini-fridge, poker table, neon signs and sports memorabilia plastered on the walls. A giant television was propped in the corner.

"Jesus, how big is that?"

"Hundred and ten inches. What do you want to do, play video games or something?"

"Sit down over there."

I pointed to the seat at the end of the couch. Hinkle plopped down. I walked over beside him and yanked the lever. The chair reclined and the leg-rest sprung out from beneath him.

"What the hell you doing?" he asked.

"You comfortable?"

"You trying to make a move on me or something?"

I pulled the cuffs out of my back pocket and snapped one around Hinkle's ankle and the other around the metal axis beneath the leg rest. Hinkle cursed me and thrashed around like a dry fish. Wore himself out pretty quickly. I flopped into the seat at the opposite end of the couch.

"Man, what if I have to piss?"

"I'll get you a bottle."

"How you going to do this to me? This is so fucked."

"You and I are going to sit here nice and quiet-like until the man calls us. Now, I'm beat, so I'm going to get some shut-eye. Feel free to do the same."

"Can I at least watch TV?"

"Nope."

"Fucked. What do you think, nobody's going to miss me if I can't be found all day?"

I held his phone in the air.

"It may be touch and go, important as you are, but the world will have to find a way to survive for a few hours without you."

With that, I closed my eyes and was slumbering soundly within the minute. The next time they opened my phone was vibrating in my pocket.

Hinkle stared at me miserably.

"Your phone's buzzing."

"No shit."

"That's the fifth time. I was hoping maybe you were dead."

"Still here. Sorry about your luck."

I fished the phone out of my pocket, checked the time, 2:18, and answered it. Hinkle watched me as I mumbled a few responses into the receiver, but mostly listened.

"What's happened?" he asked after I'd hung up.

"The raids went down. We're up."

"Oh, shit," Hinkle groaned.

The design was for Hale to swing back round to pick us up and head back to E.B.'s Diner to retrieve Hinkle's car, but the raids on the warehouse and Furry Friends netted five arrests and Hale was jammed up at the station booking them.

"You got another car here we could use?" I asked Hinkle.

"Um, no. You left mine at the diner. Sorry about your luck."

I grunted and pulled my phone back out. The cabbie wasn't thrilled to hear from me, but he livened up when I promised to pay the fare for his services.

"Well, shit fire," Dennis Maynard exclaimed. "I never thought I'd see the day."

"Don't get too excited," I told him. "You're picking me up at the house where you dropped the girl off."

"The girl that died?"

"She's the one."

"Shit fire," he repeated, with far less enthusiasm.

I uncuffed Hinkle's leg and let him piss and clean himself up. We sat on the stoop waiting for the cabbie to show up.

"Your pop's a doctor?"

"Orthopedic surgeon," Hinkle clarified.

"Apple fell kind of far from the tree."

"I was never going to be like my pop. Knew from the get-go I didn't have it in me. Never too good at school or anything like that, found out I was dyslexic and shit. Listen, I could hear y'all talking a little when I was outside the car."

"Hear anything interesting?"

"What was all that about people being on the take?"

I explained to Hinkle that some cops were suspected of being on the Cash City payroll and Hale had to make sure the personnel used to secure the raids were on the level.

"Damn," Hinkle whistled. "That's some serious problems. Were they straight?"

"No hitches. Somebody tipped off the guys at the warehouse, likely because we hit the pet store first. But we had the warehouse covered and caught them trying to steal out the back."

"Damn. Why you being so honest with me?"

"Who you gonna tell?"

"True. So that's that. Now me."

"Now you."

Maynard's cab came rolling down the street and into the driveway. I climbed into the front seat and Hinkle got in the back. Maynard gave Hinkle the stink eye in the rearview mirror.

"Nuh-uh," he shook his head vehemently. "I ain't giving no ride to no stinking murderer."

"What the fuck are you talking about, old man," Hinkle snorted. "Only thing that stinks in here is your skank ass."

Maynard twisted around to face Hinkle.

"Relax," I said before they could get going at each other. I nodded to the back. "He didn't murder the girl."

"I don't believe it," Maynard insisted. "He's all wrong."

"I agree with you there, but he didn't kill anybody. In fact, seeing as you're probably on the same dose of antibiotics, you two should know each other. Hinkle, Maynard—Maynard, Hinkle."

Hinkle's face sagged.

"What the fuck does that mean?"

Maynard tilted his head back haughtily and sniffed the air.

"That's right, motherfucker," he crowed. "I got there first! How's my salt taste?"

CHAPTER THIRTY-SIX
LOCAL COLOR

Hinkle sulked the whole way to E.B.'s Diner. I assured him that Maynard had never touched Trisha Cammack, that we were just cracking on him. Maynard played along, apologized about the salt comment, said he always went a step too far when pulling someone's leg, and offered up a decent lie about how Trisha paid her fare, not with her mouth, but with a wad of one dollar bills.

By the time we reached E.B.'s, Hinkle's spirits seemed improved. She always did have a lot of singles on her, he admitted. I got out of the cab with Hinkle, escorted him to his SUV and put him in it. We reviewed the plan.

"So you want me to go up there and be like, yo, business is booming and I need a bigger piece of the action?"

"Not if you're going to say it like that."

"How the fuck am I supposed to say it?"

I shook my head.

"Something about it feels off."

"What do you mean, feels off? This is the big master plan you and homeboy came up with and now you sitting here telling me it feels off. Don't give me that when I'm about to be face to face with these mugs."

"Try this instead. Tell them you know the police are cracking down and you're getting too much business. It's freaking you out a little bit because your whole game is staying under the radar. Now you're afraid the pigs are going to come for you next. And besides that, you don't have enough supply for all the new demand."

"Man, you trying to get me killed."

"Think about it. If you go to them acting like you want to be a big fish, which is a complete one-eighty for you, that behavior is out of the ordinary. That might tip them off. But if you go there acting worried about what's going down, that puts you on their side, sharing their concerns. Before, they kind of tolerated you as long as you played by their rules, sold their product, and lined their pockets. Now, who else do they have working the West End? Some roving delivery guys maybe, but that's not enough. Now, they need you."

Hinkle let that ping around his brain for a minute.

"I get what you're saying. Feels like a gamble though."

"This whole thing's a fucking gamble."

I handed his phone through the open window and, with my phone, called his number.

"Oh, I get this back now?"

"Yup."

His phone blared some hip-hop noise.

"Somebody's calling me."

"No shit, answer it."

Hinkle put the phone to his ear.

"Hello?"

I shook my phone at him.

"It's me, asshole."

"Why are you calling me, man?"

"I want you to keep this line open the whole time you're driving over there and the whole time you're talking to whoever it is you're going to talk to. I'm going to be listening to everything that's said. You try to pull anything funny, turn up the radio, the line goes dead, anything, I'm going to hang you out to dry, you understand me?"

"Man," Hinkle pouted. "Lines go dead all the time.

What am I supposed to do if the line goes dead? Say excuse me, the fuzz is eavesdropping on this conversation and they're going to be mad-pissed if I don't ring them back right away, just hold on to your britches for a second."

"That's exactly what I want you to say." I started back for the cab. "I'll keep my end muted unless you need to speak for some reason."

Hinkle yelled after me, "Man, this is a ghetto-ass setup for a ghetto-ass plan."

I gave him a thumbs-up and climbed into the front seat of the cab. We followed Hinkle's SUV up Clifford Avenue and under the East End viaduct to the outskirts of downtown. Hinkle was quiet on the line, no radio, only the hum of the SUV in motion.

A block before we reached Timbo's Pizza, Hinkle leaned down and spoke into the phone, "We about there."

I unmuted my cell.

"No shit. Try not to act like there's a phone on in your pocket."

The next intersection Hinkle hung a right onto Fourteenth Street. Timbo's was visible on the next corner. The dance man, Leonard Lippman, was boogying down at the curb out front, a wide grin spread across his face as he twirled the neon sign. Maynard turned onto Fourteenth and parked the cab in the middle of the block. From there we had a clear sight line on Hinkle's SUV as he pulled up to Lippman.

Everybody who was over the age of forty in this town knew Leonard Lippman. Back in his day, before he'd gotten expelled from high school for peddling grass, he was a basketball phenom. Popular lore had him pegged as the heir apparent to Jerry West in the state of West Virginia. His sophomore season, the last full season in which he participated, Leonard Lippman led Southside High to its only state title.

Two years later, despite the fact that he was already serving his first stint in prison for armed robbery, his graduating class voted him most likely to succeed. That was Cain City for you. Nobody under forty gave two shits where Leonard Lippman came from. For them, he was simply the dance man, a dreadlocked oddity to gawk at and catcall as they rolled past Timbo's.

Lippman still had that lean, long-limbed basketball body. He worked the neon arrow like it was an extension of his arms, whipping it in fluid arcs around his head and torso and spinning it like a top on his fingers.

I listened in as Hinkle slowed to a stop in front of Timbo's and lowered his passenger window. Lippman kept the grin wide and the sign spinning as he took two steps toward the SUV. His mouth moved about a half second before his voice came through my phone receiver.

"Well, well, well, look who it is." His words were a tad muffled, but intelligible. "Good to see some local color pop in for a visit. How you doing youngin'?"

"Living, man," Hinkle replied. "Things been good for me. They might be going too good, know what I'm saying. I'm already dry up, but I hear tell the police been coming down hard around here. Rounding up all kinds of folks."

"I hear your concern, I sure do, but those questions ain't for me to be hearing or answering. All I do is point the way. You know the drill, look for them shoes."

Lippman took a few steps backwards, and instead of twirling the sign, pointed it east down Fifth Avenue. Hinkle eased back into traffic and started in that direction.

"You get all that?" Hinkle said in a hushed voice.

"Good job, keep it going. We're tailing you."

Before Hinkle was away from the curb, Leonard Lippman was pulling out his burner, presumably to announce Hinkle's imminent arrival in the alley. I instructed Maynard to follow Hinkle down Fifth Avenue. We cruised past the dance man. He didn't give the cab a second glance. Too busy tossing the arrow into the air and catching it. Two blocks in front of us, Hinkle's SUV hooked left into an alley between Seventeenth and Eighteenth Streets.

"Don't slow down," I told Maynard. "Just roll by where I can get a look-see."

A pair of high-tops were strung over the power lines at the entrance to the alley. Hinkle's SUV was creeping halfway down the alley when suddenly its brake lights went red. Then we were past. I didn't spot any lookouts, but that didn't mean they weren't there. I directed Maynard to go straight for two more blocks and then turn left to circle round for another pass by the alley. The only sound coming across the phone line was the idling engine of the SUV.

On the second drive-by, traveling east to west on Fifth Avenue provided a clean view on the backside of Greenleaf Manor, an old five-story apartment building. Perched in a window frame on the fourth floor was a man with a pair of binoculars gazing out over the alley and streets. The lookout. As we coasted past the alley a second man emerged from between two buildings and walked toward Hinkle's vehicle. His face was in shadow. I couldn't make him. I ordered Maynard to turn right on Seventeenth and drive past the front of the apartment building.

"Oh shit," we heard Hinkle blurt into the phone. Then came what sounded like clothes rustling against the receiver followed by a thick voice. "What's this I hear about you having second thoughts, son?"

"No, sir," Hinkle's voice cracked. "Not second thoughts or nothing like that."

"That's good to hear because there ain't no getting out of this thing alive, you hear. Once you Cash City, you Cash City to the grave."

"Yeah, I hear you. I'm just a little freaked out is all because it seems like the pigs is cracking down hard on some West Side operators. And I don't want to be next in line to get snatched up, you know what I'm saying."

"Listen," said the thick voice. "You're flattering yourself to think the police give a motherfuck about your petty little operation."

He must have been leaning into the car now because I could hear him as clear as if he were speaking directly into the phone. I recognized the voice instantly. Hinkle was right to be afraid. This was no normal drop-man he was dealing with. This was Cupcake himself.

There was no action in front of the Greenleaf Manor. I yelled for Maynard to speed up and pull around the corner.

Cupcake continued, "But don't you worry about that, we're taking steps to remedy that shit as we speak. You ain't never going to have to worry about the police round here again. That being said, as you now know, we have a temporary shortage of vendors on the West Side."

"Yeah, I sold my whole package in like three hours. Usually takes me like four, five days."

There was a pause on the line.

"More like two weeks. Nigger don't you ever lie to me again or it'll be the last lie you tell, you understand me? Don't even embellish shit."

"Yes, sir," Hinkle whimpered.

"I know everything about my business. Everything." Another pause. "You scared of me?"

"Yeah."

"That's because you're smart. Here's what's going to happen. My man Leviticus, who you know, is going to come down here with two packages to start you off, and we're going to spread the word that you're now a main player down there on the West End. Start with two, see how you do. You do good, the sky's the limit. You going to make more money than you ever dreamed of, and you dreamed big, I can see it in your eyes. That sound amenable to you?"

"Yeah. Good."

"Don't let me down now. And don't worry about them

police. Mix red and blue and you make purple. A whole lot of them blue police uniforms are going to be purple before this day is over. That problem is going to be squashed before you close your eyes tonight. You hear me?"

"Cool, I hear you."

"Stay here."

The line went silent again save for Hinkle gulping air like he'd been holding his breath the entire conversation. I had Maynard swing around the block and into the alley north of the Greenleaf Manor. He angled into a nook where we were hidden from the lookout, but still able to observe the alley.

"Give me your phone," I told Maynard.

"I only got like seven minutes left for the entire month."

"Give me the fucking phone right now."

He grunted and handed it over. I dialed Bruce Hale's number.

"Who is this?" he answered.

"Me."

"What do you got?"

"Your man Cupcake in the flesh."

That was not the answer Hale expected. It took him a beat to disseminate the information.

"Where?"

"Clocked him in the alley behind Greenleaf Manor."

"Downtown?"

"Yeah, I think he's back inside the building now, but I can't be sure until I can talk to Hinkle. He's still dealing with a courier in the alley."

"This is going down as we speak?"

"Right now."

A different man, Leviticus, I'm assuming, entered the alley and passed two large plastic-wrapped bags through the window of the SUV. I continued briefing Hale.

"Cupcake was already on the premises because all we

did was plant a seed with the dance man and two minutes later our boy and Cupcake are face to face, striking a deal."

Nothing was said between Hinkle and the courier, just the exchange of goods. Hinkle put the car in gear and drove north up the alley.

"Hold on," I said to Hale. "I'm working two phones with one hand here." I sat Maynard's phone on the seat, picked mine up and switched off the mute. "Hinkle?"

"Holy shit, man. That was him. That was goddamn Cupcake."

"Yeah, I know. You did great, kid. Look straight ahead in the alley across the street. That's us. We've had eyes on you the whole time. Now listen, when Cupcake approached you, it was from between Greenleaf Manor and the building next to it. Which building?"

"The back of the Chinese restaurant."

"When he left, did he go back through that same way he came?"

"Yeah, I think he went back in the exact same way. What do I do now?"

"Thank Jesus for making it through this thing alive, kid. If you want to stay that way, never tell another living soul about a single thing that happened today."

"No fucking problem there."

"Go home."

I hung up and switched to the second phone.

"He's got to be in Greenleaf Manor, but I can't know for how long."

Hale asked, "What kind of set-up do they have?"

"This may be their main base of operations. I spotted one lookout back of the building on the fourth floor. I'm sure there are more. They will see most anything coming from a mile away, literally."

"You got a visual on him now?"

"Nope."

"Can you get a visual on him?"

"What do you want me to do, stroll in there whistling a tune? I'll be dead before I make it to the elevator."

"All right, all right. What about if he leaves? You able to tail him?"

"Iffy, I'm in a cab. There must be six ways out of that building. If I catch him leaving it'll be dumb luck. I've got the alley covered, but you need to get someone down here to stake the front. If we're going to move, we need to move soon. I don't know what Cupcake has planned, but something is going down today. He insinuated to Hinkle that they were going to squash the police threat, maybe by killing cops. This is your best shot."

Hale's breathing went fast and shallow, as if he were about to hyperventilate.

"I don't know what to do. I don't know what to do," he sputtered. "If they see us coming they'll have time to flee and if they get away and they're planning something we have to stop them now."

"Calm down. We just have to find a way to pin them in before they realize it, make it too late for them to leave. We need to keep them in this building."

"How the hell am I supposed to do that in the next ten minutes?"

I looked through the cab's windshield at the north side and rear of Greenleaf Manor and thought about the lookouts. What would they notice? What sight would alarm them and what sight would they dismiss? The raids on both Furry Friends and the warehouse were good old-fashioned shows of force. This incursion needed a bit more finesse.

Hale said, "Are you there, Malick?"

I said, "Shut up, I'm thinking." Then, "Can we get a hearse?"

CHAPTER THIRTY-SEVEN
RED AND BLUE MAKE PURPLE

Fifteen minutes later, Willis Hively walked into the Chinese restaurant next door to Greenleaf Manor and sat at a window table where he could scope the length of the street. In the alley, Leviticus appeared again to distribute another package to a dealer in a red Range Rover, but that was the extent of the action; thirty seconds worth. I jotted down the license number of the Range Rover so Hale or Hively could round them up later.

For the next half hour, Maynard and I sat there twiddling our thumbs in the cab wondering aloud what the hell was taking so long. Then, in his rearview mirror, Maynard glimpsed a man edging along the alley toward the cab.

"Uh-oh," Maynard cautioned, shifting the car into gear. "Time to go. We got company."

Maynard let go of the clutch and started to pull away. I twisted round, saw that the man in the alley was Bruce Hale, and directed Maynard to stay put.

"I ain't cut out for this bullcrap," Maynard griped, shifting the cab back into park.

Hale cracked the door of the cab and squeezed into the backseat. He got on his walkie-talkie and relayed his position.

"Anything stirring?" Hale asked.

"Nada."

"Good. We're two minutes out from your fake funeral procession."

"You found a hearse?"

"Wait 'til you see this puppy."

The silver hearse emerged from the East End viaduct and took a left onto Sixth Avenue, rumbling past the mouth of the alley. Behind the hearse was a convoy of ten unmarked vehicles, each with a bereavement flag planted at the right front corner of the hood. The first five cars in the procession followed the hearse up to Seventeenth Street where they turned left and halted abruptly in front of the apartment building.

Before anyone in Greenleaf Manor had a chance to react the back half of the fleet broke off into the alley, cutting off the two main escape routes from the building. Hale got on his walkie and instructed both teams to stay put and wait for the SWAT team, ninety seconds out. For a solid minute there was no activity from either the police or Cash City.

I kept my eye on the lookout in the fourth floor window. He stared down at the team of cars in the alley, calmly took out his phone and called someone, then shut the phone and faded into the interior darkness. The whole block was still, as if time had frozen. An unsettling feeling worms into your gut when you find yourself on the cusp of real violence. Presently, I recognized the sensation.

"C'mon," Hale clenched his teeth.

His walkie crackled to life.

"We've got a problem up front," came Willis Hively's voice over the transmission.

"What is it?" Hale responded.

"A bunch of women and children are fleeing the front of the building."

I said, "They're getting ready."

From where we were set up in the alley, we couldn't see the residents escaping the building, but we heard the commotion. They must have blocked the street because soon a small traffic jam had backed up to our alley.

"Shit." Hale got on the walkie. "Clear those people out of there. Grab any men and detain them."

"Roger that. SWAT is here."

A SWAT van entered the alley from the south end and halted between Greenleaf Manor and the blockade of unmarked vehicles. Five men emptied from the back of the van and positioned themselves around the rear entrance. One opened the door and another tossed a flash grenade into the entryway. After a muted blast, SWAT moved swiftly into the building.

Hale spoke into the walkie, "SWAT has breached the back entrance of the building. No engagement."

A few seconds later, Hively confirmed that SWAT had encountered no resistance on the front side either.

"You think they're waiting to get us inside before they engage?" Hale asked. "Get us enclosed?"

"They cleared the building. They have something planned."

Hale ordered teams One and Two to enter the building, then addressed Willis Hively.

"I'm coming around front. Wait for me to go in."

He opened the back door to get out of the cab.

"You should go home, Nick. You've gotten us this far. That's enough."

I said, "You're not getting rid of me that easy."

"I'll let you know as soon as I hear anything on . . ." Hale glanced sideways at Maynard, "your situation."

"Something happens to you, who is going to let me know where Kincaid lands? You're not going in that building without me."

"Fair enough," Hale conceded.

We crossed the street and made our way up Sixth Avenue, staying tight into the side of the buildings. Seventeenth Street was deserted save for Willis Hively, who was waiting for us under the canopy of the Chinese restaurant with two men sitting against the wall, their hands cuffed behind them. The women and children who had fled the building were gone.

Hively explained that these were the only two men who came out of the building with the mass exodus. He passed their ID's to Hale. Hale skimmed the ID's, walked over to the men and kicked them lightly on the legs.

"You live here in the Greenleaf?"

The tubby white one with thatches of black hair sprouting from his shoulders grunted that he did. The second man, a gaunt Mexican with a thin mustache and long black hair, also said he lived there. In garbled English, the Mexican explained that he worked as a cook at the Rio Bravo a few blocks over on Third Avenue, and asked if he could leave because he was going to be late for his shift.

Hale laughed at him and asked the fat guy if he had somewhere pressing to be as well.

"Nah, cain't get no job in this economy."

Hively pulled me aside and asked how it came to be that Hale and I were buddy-buddy overnight like it was the goddamned good old days.

"We came to an arrangement."

"You want to clue me in?"

"Not really."

"Did he admit to working with Cash City?"

"Didn't come up."

Hively leaned back on his heels and marveled at me like I was someone he had once held in high esteem.

"You sure change your tune quick."

"How about you do what you do and not worry about me."

Hively's mouth tightened. He squeezed the pet rock in his fist.

"So the fact that we now have the clout to go directly at these guys all of a sudden, after all the shit that's gone down, that's just coincidence?"

The vitriol came spitting through his teeth.

"The man lost his daughter. This is his response. I told him I would help him. You got a problem?"

"No," he shook his head. "I don't have the problem."

Hale was still badgering the two Greenleaf residents for information.

"I told you," the fat one exclaimed. "They ran down the halls screaming for everybody to get the fuck out or else we was going to get killed."

"You know what kind of business they were doing in the building?" Hale asked.

"I didn't, like, *know* know. I wasn't going around asking them what they did to make ends meet or nothing like that."

Through some open windows above us we could hear SWAT and the police units sweeping the building room by room, floor by floor. It sounded like every room was empty. Hale told the two bystanders they couldn't go anywhere and we walked into the lobby of the Greenleaf. The place looked old and smelled older. The floor was covered with ornate rugs that were probably colorful once, but now just looked like a million shades of puke brown. Two large potted plants, drooping like they'd lost the will to go on, stood at the base of a wood-banister staircase. Beside the staircase was an old elevator with a gate.

"This doesn't feel right," Hale said as he pushed the button for the elevator. "The other two raids, the guys at least tried to run."

I noticed the unlit elevator button beneath its glowing counterpart.

"We're on the first floor. Why is there a down button? Is there a basement?"

"Aw shit," Hale looked at Hively. "Did we clear the basement?"

"I don't think so."

I went back outside and asked the two guys cuffed on the ground what was in the basement. Just the laundry room and the trash room, they replied.

"A trash room?"

"*Si*," the Mexican said. "For the garbage."

"This building didn't used to have no elevator," the fat one clarified. "They have a trash shoot on every floor so you don't have to lug it all the way down."

I went back in the lobby.

"I think I know why they cleared the building."

"Why?"

I punched the down arrow button.

"I'll show you."

We rode down one floor, slid the gate open and stepped from the elevator into the laundry room, guns drawn. A woman with her back to us was folding laundry and swaying to the music coming through her earbuds, oblivious to our presence. We left her to it and moved down a short hallway to the trash room. The door was shut. Hively tried the knob. It didn't twist.

Hale told us to stand back and aimed his Glock at the door.

I said, "Put that thing away," and dug the switchblade out of my cast. The lock on the door was a shoddy little latch job. I jammed the blade into the lock and popped it loose. The door creaked open. "Magic," I said, tucking the blade back into the cast. I peered into the open dumpster beneath the trash chute.

"They weren't clearing the building to ready for a firefight. They were clearing it to get rid of any witnesses."

"Witnesses to what?" Hively asked, as both he and Hale looked into the dumpster and saw what I saw; a motherload of drugs. Coke, pills, meth, H, speedballs, Motor Seventy-Five, piled to the rim of the can. Mixed in with the drugs was an assortment of firearms: a few Magnums and G18's, an M9, four assault rifles, and two shotguns.

"Pretty clever," Hively admired.

"Not clever enough," Hale said. "We've got the Hinkle kid as a witness and it's a matter of time before we pick up that Range Rover. And you'll be a witness if we need you, right, Nick?"

"Why not."

"Guarantee these weapons will match some of the shootings that have gone down."

We headed back upstairs. Red Lewis was pacing in the lobby with a look of consternation on his face.

"We got a problem. We've got seven guys up there, including your guy, Cupcake. His real name is Walter Simms."

"Where's the problem?"

"They're all clean. No guns, no dope."

Hale ordered Red to get the crime techs into the basement and we took the elevator to the fourth floor where six of the men were being held in one of the vacant apartments. Cupcake was being detained separately in an apartment at the end of the hall.

All six of the men in the first apartment hailed from Detroit. I recognized the lookout and Leviticus, the courier from the alley, but didn't make the other four. Hale Mirandized them and, one by one, they were marched out of the building into waiting squad cars.

"I've heard some funky names in my time, but who the fuck names their kid Leviticus?" Red Lewis asked

Leviticus, the last in line, as he hauled him into the elevator.

"It's biblical, bitch."

"No shit," Red said, straight-faced. "Your mother must be overcome with pride."

The elevator doors shut leaving Hively, Hale, and myself alone in the middle of the hallway. Hale addressed Hively.

"Hive, you go down to the station, oversee the bookings and start the interrogations."

"What about Cupcake?"

"I want to ask him a few questions before we bring him in. Make sure we got him on the hook."

"A few questions here?"

"That's right."

Hively nodded to indicate me.

"But he's staying?"

"He's staying."

Hively bowed his head, nodded solemnly, then looked Hale hard in the eye.

"This is how we do things now?"

Hale didn't budge.

"Bookings and interrogations, Hive."

The two of them held an impromptu staring contest that looked downright intimate if you didn't know they were silently telling one another to go fuck themselves.

I said, "Anybody see anything they like?"

Hively broke it off, turned his back on us and flung his pet rock down the hallway. It bounced off the walls and clanged against the elevator door. Hively walked slowly down the length of the hall, picked up the rock and pressed the down button. After he got in and the door slid shut, Hale stared at it trance-like for half a minute. Sweat ringed his hair and trickled down his face and neck. Some kind of frenetic current ran through his body and snapped him from the daze. He shook the current out through his hands, ran the hands over his face and through his hair and flung the sweat from his fingers onto the floor. Then he moved toward the apartment at the end of the hall.

When I didn't follow he stopped.

"Let's go."

"This is your show."

"You don't want a shot at the guy who put a bounty on your head?"

I shrugged.

"That's your devil in there, not mine."

"C'mon," Hale goaded. "You don't even want to get a look at him?"

I gazed beyond Hale to the apartment where Cupcake was being held captive, then down the long end of the hall to the elevator, and finally back to Hale.

"I'll take a look at him."

CHAPTER THIRTY-EIGHT
CASH CITY

Cupcake was lying face down on the floor of the vacant apartment, hands cuffed behind his back. Jerome Kipling had his boot heel ground into Cupcake's spine at the base of his neck. Cupcake was built like a fat woman with bulgy hips and thighs. His limbs and his torso looked like they had come out slightly shorter than they were designed to be.

Hale walked a slow circle around Cupcake, came to a stop above his head and lorded over him silently.

I hung back by the door, watching and waiting to see how Hale would play it. Did he want to talk to Cupcake? Stomp his skull? Put a bullet in it? Kick his face in until nothing was left but bone and gristle? Light him on fire? None of the above would surprise me in the least.

All Hale's ire was concentrated on the back of the drug dealer's head. Just when I started to wonder if Hale had gone stiff, he rocked back on his heels and gave a quick nod to Kipling, who lifted his boot from Cupcake's spine, grabbed hold of the cuffs and yanked him backwards onto his knees. Cupcake sneered over his shoulder at the detective, then turned and realized that the man standing in front of him was Hale. Cupcake's mouth stretched into a wicked grin.

Hale flicked his eyes to Jerome Kipling.

"You can go."

Kipling said, "Me?"

"You frisk him?"
"Yeah."
"You search the apartment?"
"Yeah."
"Find anything?"
"No."
"Then what do we have to take him in on?"
"But—" Kipling muttered.
"Go help Red process the rest of the scum."

Kipling looked to me as if I had answers to his unasked questions.

"You want me to uncuff him?" he asked Hale.

"Leave 'em on."

Kipling glanced at everybody again, trying to make sense of the directive.

"You sure you don't want me to stay?"

Hale peeled his eyes off Cupcake to look at Kipling.

"Get out."

Kipling brushed past me and exited. We listened to his footsteps dissipate down the hallway.

Cupcake's fat head twisted on his short neck to face me. He growled, "You must be Malick."

"How do you figure?"

He gestured at Hale.

"This silly bitch don't have the balls to pull something like this by his self."

Hale launched forward and grabbed Cupcake by the head, clamping down with such force you could hear Cupcake's face squish between his fingers.

"Why did you kill her?" Hale screamed, viciously shaking Cupcake's head.

"I ain't kill nobody," Cupcake hissed.

Hale brought his knee up into Cupcake's nose. Blood splooged down from Cupcake's nostrils over the lower half of his face.

"Lawyer," Cupcake whispered through a mouthful of blood.

Hale addressed me.

"Get a good enough look at him?"

"Yup."

"Good."

Hale took out his gun, flipped it over in his hand to where it was butt-up, and conked Cupcake on the temple. Cupcake fell on his side and released a sound that rated somewhere between a wolf's howl and a vulture's squawk. Hale grabbed him by the ear and dragged him back to his knees. Cupcake spit blood at Hale's face. It missed. Landed on the shelf of Hale's gut. Hale walloped him again with the butt of the pistol.

I turned my back on the two of them and walked out of the apartment. As I shut the door behind me I heard Hale calmly state, "Before we leave this room you will confess to my daughter's murder."

Apart from three curious Chinamen pressing their noses against the glass of the restaurant next door, the world had resumed its complacency. The police were gone. Traffic was moving. A few of the tenants from Greenleaf Manor were hanging around down at the end of the block, unsure of whether or not they should re-enter the building. I told them the fourth floor wasn't cleared, but the rest of the building was safe.

The cabbie was still parked in the alley, meter running at ninety-six dollars fifteen cents and counting.

"Thought you might have made a break for it," I said, scooting into the back seat.

"After all this stress you put me through? Shit, I ain't letting you stiff me now. Where to?"

I told him to just drive.

"You got it," Maynard said, jerking the cab into gear.

I laid my head back and shut my eyes. I felt the car veering right when Maynard gasped and stomped on the breaks, pitching me forward. My head banged the partition.

"Son of a bitch," I yelled. "I've got a fucking concussion." The atoms in my brain felt like they were sizzling around and colliding with one another. Flares of light streaked my vision. I clamped my eyes shut until the pain abated to its standard throb. I dabbed my fingers on my forehead. No blood, just a hard lump.

Maynard pointed through the windshield to the upper stories of Greenleaf Manor.

"A man just jumped out of that building," he said slowly, as if he didn't quite fathom what his eyes had witnessed.

"Keep driving."

"I don't think you understand. A man just jumped out of that building from the . . ." he counted the stories from the bottom up, "fourth floor."

"I heard you."

"Looked like he was taking a nose dive 'cept his legs was flapping like he was trying to walk on air or something. We got to get them cops back here."

"Keep driving," I said again. "You want your money or not?"

That got him moving.

Nowhere to go, nowhere to be. Maynard ran me by the bank and I withdrew my last two hundred dollars. He dropped me off out front of The Red Head. I paid the fare and told him his debt to me was settled, I wouldn't be calling him anymore.

"Thank Christ," he exulted, and peeled out of there.

Tadpole was alone, sitting on a stool watching the Reds-Braves game on TV.

"Wrong side of the bar," I told him. "No friends left?"

"It's Sunday," he said, yawning. "Most people try to be respectable for a couple more hours."

"Fill me up."

For two hours the place was all mine; no people, no music, just bourbon, baseball, and my very own personal bartender. Ten days previous I would have called this paradise. But now, no amount of alcohol could sand the edges of my soul or dull the images in my head. Kincaid was out there, free to do whatever his lecherous heart desired, jaunting off to destinations unknown. Doubt snuck into me, that I might never find him, or before I did, his predilection for small boys would surface and ruin more children, more families. What if he got locked away again before I got my shot at him? I checked my cell every few minutes to make sure I wasn't missing a call from Hale. All that accomplished was to drain the battery.

"Tadpole, let me ask you something?"

"Shoot."

"You ever notice a man with a beard come in when I was here, maybe sit back there in a booth. Maybe was watching me?"

"What are you talking about?"

"The guy who told the police I was defending myself when I cracked Teddy with the bottle."

"Oh, that guy. Yeah, he's been in here quite a bit. Weird dude. Never orders a real drink. Just Sprite."

"He been here any since yesterday? Beard might be shaved now."

"Nah, haven't seen him around for a bit. Why?"

"No reason."

Around dusk the door swung open. Teddy the one-eyed drunk sauntered in, got one look at me, muttered something incomprehensible, and turned right back around.

"You're bad for business," Tadpole complained.

"How many people has that Cyclops run out of here with all his blathering?"

Tadpole admitted I had a valid point. Teddy did seem to knock the hex off the door though, because after that it kept opening. The Sunday stragglers, the people who had no people, gradually filled the place. I clocked the door every time it opened, holding a small hope that maybe Karla would show up to forgive me one last time, to give me one last night. But I knew better. Karla never came through the door, but my old buddy Bruce Hale did. He saddled up next to me and ordered a beer.

"You get your confession?" I asked.

"Doesn't matter," he said. "Cupcake tried to escape. Went nuts and ran through the window of the fourth floor. Must have thought there was a fire escape or something. Landed right on the crown of his head."

"That so?"

"You should know. You were there."

"That's right," I nodded. "I was there. Saw the whole thing."

Hale related the details of Cupcake's final minutes so that our stories would be clean for the police inquest that was sure to come. "I'll get away with it," he said, not from some misplaced confidence, but because he knew how shit in this town worked, even more than I did.

"You ask him how he got that name?"

"Slipped my mind."

"You feel better?"

"I don't feel worse."

"Kipling going to give you trouble?"

"Nah, that pussy won't open his mouth."

"Hive might."

"He's a sharp one, our Hive. He'll hawk me to keep me honest, but I don't think he'll take it further than that. If I slip up again he'll be all over me."

"But those slipping days are done."

"Finito."

Hale lifted his glass.

"To our children."

We drank.

As was his custom, get some alcohol in him and Hale began his vexing. Cain City was now a known entity, and with Cash City out of commission, the place was up for grabs. Word on the street was that gang factions from Atlanta, Columbus, and Tallahassee were eager to stake their claim.

"We're gonna be swarmed. I could use you back," Hale said. "If you want to come back. I'll put a word in with the chief, tell him what kind of role you played today and you're set."

"Nah, you can handle it. This time you'll see them coming."

"I don't know, Nick. I don't know."

Hale downed the last of his beer and stood up, tossed a couple twenties on the bar, told Tadpole my drinks were on him.

"We got a hit on Kincaid's credit card."

"Where?"

"St. Louis. Three hours ago. Thirty dollar charge at a truck stop restaurant. Just came through the system."

Hale studied me to gauge my reaction. I sipped my bourbon.

"I thought you'd be a little happier at that news."

"Well, I'm not gonna shit myself over it."

Hale wrinkled up his face.

"Fair enough. What's your move?"

"I'm going to buy a ticket for the first plane out in the morning to St. Louis, or, if you get another hit, whatever the closest airport is. There I'll rent a car and chase him to the edge of the fucking earth."

"Okay." Hale rapped his knuckles on the bar. "Your car's back at the high school, by the way."

"Better not have a scratch on it."

"Oh, yeah. That'd hurt the value. Anyway, I'll call you if the credit card pops up somewhere else. Nick—"

"Yip."

"Good luck."

"Yip."

Hale left. I tossed the last of my drink down the hatch, waved adios to Tadpole, and walked through the clear night to the high school. There, I fished a duffle bag out of the closet and stuffed in some clothes and toiletries, tossed in my bottle of antibiotics. I would have to find another gun once I landed, wherever I landed.

Despite Karla's best efforts a couple nights previous, she hadn't put too big a dent in my bottle of Maker's. I snagged it off the nightstand and ambled over to my desk where I sat in the chair and nipped at the bourbon and, for what might be the last time, gazed down onto the street lit by the pale bright of the moon. No more waiting. The thing was finally here, one way or another. I don't know if I was nervous or scared, or if the electricity coursing through my body was the natural high of anticipation, but I knew there would be no sleeping that night. I would stare at the moon until it was replaced by the sun, and then I would get on a plane to go kill a man.

My tongue felt fat in my mouth. I tried to wiggle it and found that I couldn't. I tried to speak, but words didn't form. I tried to sit forward, but the synapses didn't fire. The bottle of bourbon fell from my hand onto the floor. My entire body went numb. All my senses became distorted. The moon multiplied into five moons. I didn't panic; something about the delirium felt smooth and free and strangely removed from the chaos in my head. I listened to the bourbon glug from the bottle onto the floor.

A figure appeared in front of me, blocking out the light of the five moons. He leaned in close. I felt the pungent heat of his breath on my face, and I looked into his pupils, and I knew.

Before I faded into oblivion, one final, vivid thought flitted through my mind.

He got me first.

CHAPTER THIRTY-NINE
IN WALKS THE DEVIL

"I know you are awake."

Perceptive fucker.

I had been conscious for a few minutes. But, on the off chance he was just testing to see if the dope had worn off, I kept my eyes shut and my head lolling against my chest. He hadn't moved me from the desk chair. My wrist was hogtied to the armrest and my ankles were tethered to its legs. My feet were flat on the floor. As far as I could tell he hadn't fooled with my gimp arm; it still dangled in its sling. My head was thick with the remnants of the drug and my body felt like a numb, detached mass beneath me. The cool night breeze coming in from the win dows chilled the left side of my body.

"I know you are awake," Kincaid repeated softly.

The proximity of his voice was no more than a few feet away, maybe less. I listened to the faint whistle of air going in and out of his nose. A sour odor permeated the space between us. He must have been sporting the same soiled clothes for the past week. His coughing had brought me to. He had suffered three coughing spasms in the short time I had been awake. The spasms racked his throat and hoarsened his speaking voice.

In an effort to provoke me from my ruse, Kincaid clapped his hands in front of my face. I didn't flinch.

"You are good. But the moment you woke up, your breathing quickened and the slackness in your shoulders vanished. I've sat here watching you feign sleep while you wiggle each finger and each toe ever so carefully as to avoid detection. Amusing to a point but let's end the charade, shall we?"

So the gaff was up. I pried my eyes open, lifted my head and came face to face with my own personal phantom turned to flesh. Two feet in front of me. The light of the moon illuminated the right side of him, his drooped eyelid, pitted neck and scrawny arm, and put the rest of him in shadow. He had the black market .38 I had purchased from Vada leveled casually at my chest.

"Also while you were unconscious," he said, bemused, "you moaned and moaned. You sounded vaguely like a deaf seal. That noise ceasing, mercifully, was a pretty dead giveaway."

Kincaid cleared his throat and put a closed fist over his mouth to suppress another cough.

"I must admit," he said, lowering the fist from his mouth, "I have the utmost admiration for the fervor that you have maintained all the way to the dire end. The conviction it must have taken to persevere over such a length of time—it's quite a testament to the endurance of the human spirit." He assumed a mocking, triumphant tone. "Forever striving to wring the world into proper balance, to stay the course of justice, to win the day, to exact revenge at any cost to your personal well-being."

He paused to let the compliment register. When I didn't show any reaction Kincaid frowned and assessed me from top to bottom before proceeding with his monologue.

"After witnessing the abandon with which you live your life—it's truly shocking that you have made it this far."

"Yet here I am."

"Here you are, thanks to me."

"Thanks to you? That's rich."

"Oh yes, Nick, thanks to me. Don't play dumb. It is thanks to me and me alone that you are physically sitting right where you are. If not for the statement I made to the police exonerating you, this very second you would be wasting away in the Cain City jail awaiting trial for assault with a beer bottle."

"Gee, thanks. This is so much better."

"Save your false gratitude. Really I could not help myself. You are such a fascinating spectacle to behold, like some Greek tragedy enacted right in front of my eyes, purely for my benefit. I was concerned that saving you would be a fatal indulgence; my fatal flaw, so to speak. But I had to see how all these dramas in your life would play out, what with the search for the girl, the vendetta with me," he waved the gun around as if to illustrate the absurdity of the situation. "But in the end I knew we would be right where we find ourselves, having this chat, in this manner. It was easy, really. You're such a creature of bad habit. What brought you to this town anyway? A woman? The doctor?"

"Who cares?"

"I care, Nick. I used to be so envious of people from other places. Anywhere but here," Kincaid rolled his eyes dramatically. "I was clawing the walls to get out. A big city like Chicago, forget it. Those places were beyond dreams. No one in my family had ever left the tri-state. Everyone in this town looks stupid, acts stupid—the accents alone are enough to drive you insane. But then I realized something that made all these stupid people not only tolerable, but desirable. I realized there was no better place on the face of the earth for me than in this piddly town. Here I could do anything I wanted, and I could get away with it."

"But you didn't get away with it."

"Didn't I? In this moment I am a free man. Can you say the same? You know, when I was released from prison, I expected to be very put out by this whole vendetta of yours. All I wanted, truly, was to move back into my mother's home and start a quiet, unassuming life. Find a job. Keep to myself. To be the target of a revenge crazed fanatic, well, thanks but no thanks. Who needs it? But I have to confess, I have relished participating in our cat and mouse game these past weeks."

"Game was rigged, you got a head start."

Kincaid shrugged, squished up his face.

"I am no monument to fair play. I had to find out if you were who you said you were. If your intentions to cause me bodily harm were real, or if you were just a sad, zealous man who jumped off the deep end when he lost his family."

"Bodily harm is a polite way to put what I intend to do to you."

"Ah yes, I know. Thus, we find ourselves here in this moment. When I determined that not only did you intend to put an end to me, but accomplishing this task was your primary reason for existing, well, there was only one course of action to be taken."

Kincaid sighed as if he deeply regretted this conclusion.

"How do you think you would have felt upon achieving your goal? What would you have done when I was no more? When it was all over?"

"Oh, I would have figured something out."

"Let me ask you a question. Have I lived up to the expectations of what you thought I would be or have I exceeded them? You've surpassed my expectations in so many ways. Our interactions have been a true thrill. Tell me, how did you plan on killing me?"

"Any which way would do."

"Oh, I don't believe that. You must have fantasized about it endlessly. When you envisioned the specific act, how did you see it?"

I looked down at the gun, pointed in the general direction of my abdomen.

"You know how to use that thing?"

"Point and pull the trigger. I think I can manage."

"It's not quite that easy. You gotta hold the gun firm but not too firm. You jerk the trigger and the shot'll go wild, not to mention the recoil. Probably hit yourself in the face. No, what you wanna do is take it nice and slow. Breathe. Don't rush."

Kincaid sat up straight and re-adjusted his grip on the gun.

"You are giving me advice on how to shoot you?"

"I don't want you to botch the damn thing. In fact, when you get up to it, go ahead and press the barrel right into my skull."

Again, Kincaid implored me to reveal just how I imagined killing him.

"I pictured dropping you off the bridge and watching you plummet into the river."

"That's not a very reliable method. Do you know that fifty-seven people have attempted suicide by leaping off that bridge in the ninety-odd years since it was built? Out of those, thirteen died. The rest were injured or maimed, sure, but the bridge is not high enough to guarantee death. I would have to fall just right."

"Not if I slit your throat just before I dropped you over."

Kincaid smiled and nodded.

"That's more like it. I'm sorry you will never get the opportunity."

The image of a sharp knife dragging across Kincaid's jugular, a stripe of blood blooming on his neck and cascading over like an infinity pool, sparked a crucial piece of information in my mind. The switchblade had been tucked into the cast of my mangled arm. I flexed my wrist. The blade was still in place; he hadn't found it.

"You know," Kincaid carried on, "you were a legend to the inmates in my prison. Word of your antics spread, about how you frequented every correctional facility in the tri-state area, terrorizing all the pedophiles, suspected pedophiles, rapists, murderers, kidnappers, jaywalkers—everyone."

I tensed my forearm and wrist in an effort to inch the knife's handle up into my palm. Kincaid reached into his pocket and withdrew a piece of paper, unfolded it, and brushed his fingers reverently over the words.

"I kept your letter. I've read this single economical sentence thousands upon thousands of times. '*Randall Kincaid, if you murdered my son, I am going to be waiting for you when you're released from prison and I am going to kill you. Nick Malick.*' Those words burnished themselves into my brain."

"I kept your letter too."

"I know. I've seen it in your desk. It must be hard for you now, knowing that these last weeks the man who destroyed your son has been right there beside you, behind you, smack dab in front of your face at times. I even stood next to you at that dingy bar you frequent and ordered drinks, tolerated the bartender's inane jokes. If you had been able to see past your own nose you would have found me right there, close enough to smell my breath."

"God, you talk a lot. Why don't you shoot me already and get it over with?"

"And spoil all the fun we are about to have? What would be the pleasure in that? The party has just begun. And rest assured about your little pal Davey. He's a tad too old for my proclivities."

At the mention of Davey I bristled. Kincaid saw it. The corner of his lip twitched and his mouth drew back into a delighted smirk.

"That's true," I said. "You like them before the grass is on the field, don't you?"

Kincaid's smirk dissipated and he looked away from me, out the busted windows into the cool pale night. I worked the knife higher up my wrist, but the exertion caused my hands to sweat and the knife kept slipping back down into the cast.

"Are you a sinner, Mr. Malick?"

"What?"

"It's a simple question. Are you a sinner?"

"I don't know. I've practiced enough."

A wan smile came into Kincaid's face. He turned and put his eyes on me again.

"There was a priest who came to visit me every other Wednesday while I was in prison. He paid me one hundred and seventy two visits over the course of seven years. And every one of those Wednesdays he asked me the same question: 'Would you like to confess your sins?' One hundred and seventy two times he repeated that question. I was weak, I admit, and bored, so I pandered to the priest on occasion about various topics: my childhood, my mother, or whatever headline was in the news, or baseball—I always loved baseball. I mean, that ballfield was so close to my house. But I never confessed. Not a single sin. Never felt that it was necessary. But now, here, tonight, I am ready to confess my sins to you."

"Don't do me any favors."

"Oh, I'm certain you will not consider what you are about to hear a favor. I expect it will bring you an extreme amount of pain. That's the thing the children did not realize, at least not at first—the transcendent relationship between pleasure and pain. They were too young, I suppose, to understand the pleasure they gave, and I received, from making them suffer. Your son, Jacob . . ." his voice turned reverent. "What a beautiful boy he was. My very favorite boy. Do you know why?"

I didn't respond. I wasn't going to help him get nostalgic over the depraved shit he inflicted upon my son, but the pervert recognized the hate roiling inside of me and fed off the energy. If my body had been numb before, lightning now burned through it. Every heartbeat felt like a bomb exploding in my chest. The bindings of my wrist and ankles lacerated the skin from my straining against them.

"I'll tell you," Kincaid said, as if he were about to regale me with some fond story from his youth. "He was my favorite because he was the meekest of them all. Do you watch nature shows? Lots of those to watch in prison. A predator always preys upon the weakest of the herd, the runts of the litter, the easiest of pickings. Have you heard the saying, *if it's in the cat, it's in the kitten*? See, I no longer know if I believe that. I look at you here in front of me, so committed, so stupidly defiant. I recognize the amount of trauma you've suffered to bring yourself to this moment, sitting with me. The ferocious will it must have taken. And I appreciate it very much. But the aforementioned cat and kitten axiom didn't apply to Jacob, did it? The boy was very different from you. He had no fight in him, no will to speak of. Even the boys younger than him, at some point, put up some form of resistance. But not Jacob, he succumbed to my every wish. He was so . . ." Kincaid paused and gazed upward to craft the perfect word. "Malleable. I remember he used to say the cutest things. He used to say, 'please don't touch my hurting spot.' The softest, most exquisite voice. My God, how could I resist that whimper? Who could? They all lose their luster, but I kept Jacob alive longer than the others. He was so—exceptionally fragile."

Kincaid reveled so fondly in the memory he nearly forgot to breathe. A sharp intake of air prompted another coughing fit. He wrenched forward with his head between his legs and clutched at his chest. I took the opportunity to drag my arm against my ribs and secure the switchblade into my palm.

"Excuse me," Kincaid said, upon recovery. "I have been sleeping in my car for the last few nights and seem to have caught a cold."

"Just kill me."

"No more fight left in you either? That's disappointing."

"Congratulations, you've won. Enjoy the spoils."

Kincaid tilted his head to the left and studied me.

"That's exactly what I'm doing. I will kill you, don't you fret about that. But not for a while. The wonder of it is that no one will suspect me. It seems any number of people would like to see you dead, and I, as far as anyone knows, I am currently somewhere in the Midwest. All I had to do was leave my wallet in the right truck stop for the right trucker traveling in the right direction and, *voila*, off I went, for all intents and purposes, exploring our vast wondrous country. As far as anyone knows, I could be anywhere."

Kincaid shrugged and fluttered his eyelids.

"So I've violated probation. Who would blame me, having been locked away for so long?"

"How many boys were there?"

"Is that what you want to know?"

"Yeah."

"Not why I did it? You don't want to dissect my childhood, my mommy issues, find out what deranged me? Or when I figured out that I was different from every human being around me, and how I came to appreciate the beauty in that difference?"

"Not even a little."

"Do you want to know how I picked the boys up? How I picked Jacob up?"

"Why always the river?"

Kincaid's shoulders shrugged as if the question bored him.

"The river is good at getting rid of DNA."

"How many boys?"

"Nine. One in Ashland. One in Proctorville. Two in Charleston, one in Morehead . . ."

"Four in Cain City."

"And four in Cain City." A tinge of satisfaction came into his voice. "There are many ways to coax a child into one's car. I knew Jacob's route home from school, walking all by himself those three short blocks. The first block was in plain view of the school and the third block was in plain view of your neighbors, leaving me just the second block to work with, which could not have been more fortuitous because that middle block had all those thick oaks to screen the view of any onlookers. I'm sure you are wondering what I said to these boys, to your son, that convinced him to ride in a car with a perfect stranger? The beauty is in its simplicity. Do you have any idea?"

"I don't think like a sick fuck."

Kincaid leaned forward as if disclosing some ancient, holy wisdom.

"You use their love of their parents against them. You tell them a story about their parents being in a car accident and how you have been sent to fetch them to the hospital. *Pfftt*," Kincaid sat back and nonchalantly flicked his hand into the air. "Into the car he came."

"You think you're the first pedophile to come up with that piece of brilliance?"

His top lip arched into a nasty sneer.

"When it finally dawned on Jacob that I was not the kindly stranger advertised, when he understood that something was very, very wrong, and it was too late for him to do anything about it, you know what he said to me?" Kincaid let the question hang in the air in case I cared to respond. "He said, 'My daddy will come get me.' He repeated this sentiment often in the beginning. 'My daddy is a policeman. My daddy won't let you hurt me.' However, once that belief was shattered, his pleas changed. They sounded more like, 'I promise I will not tell my daddy if you let me go.' It's too bad he did not have your decisive instinct. Once again, proof. A trait in the cat does not mean the same trait will be in the kitten."

"Do you think you're hurting me?"

"Very much so."

"Nah, you're not hurting me. I already know what you did to him. I've lived with it for seven years."

"Well then," Kincaid showed his teeth. "You won't mind hearing it out loud."

Presently there was a soft knock at the door. Kincaid's eyes snapped in that direction. With him looking away from me I maneuvered the switchblade between my middle finger and my ring finger with the base of it fixed against the heel of my hand. Whoever was out in the hall attempted to push door in, but Kincaid had boarded it shut.

Kincaid hissed, "Who is it?"

"How the fuck should I know?"

"Not a sound," he warned.

Then the kid spoke.

"Yo, you in there? It's me, Davey."

I hoped that if I didn't respond Davey would think me gone, give up and walk away, but that was dashed when Kincaid forgot to breathe again and broke into another hacking fit.

"You okay? I know you're in there. Heard you coughing just now and talking before that. I got something I think you'll want to know. Fell asleep waiting for you to get home or I would have been down here earlier."

I looked to Kincaid for a cue.

"Get rid of him," he whispered. Kincaid stood up and pressed the muzzle of the gun into the middle of my forehead. "Or I will shoot you in the head and then I will shoot the boy, and after that I will walk upstairs and strangle his mother."

"Hey," Davey called. "You got somebody in there?"

"No kid, it's just me."

"Let me in, man. I got something to tell you."

Kincaid positioned himself to where I was between him and the door.

"It's going to have to wait 'til tomorrow, kid. What the hell are you doing up anyway? Go to bed."

"If you got a woman or something in there you can just tell me. I won't tell my moms or nothing."

"It's not that, kid. I'm just beat is all. Come back tomorrow, all right."

"But I did what you said, I kept a lookout or whatever, and I got some dope shit I think you wanna hear right now."

"I don't want to hear anything," I yelled, trying to sound mean. "You hear me. I don't give a fuck what you have to say. Get the hell out of here and don't come back."

Everything was quiet for a few seconds and I thought the kid might have been insulted enough to get lost. But then Davey thwacked the door violently. Kincaid hopped back.

"Fine. I was just trying to help your ass. You said to look out for anybody coming around that looked funny so I did that shit for you because you made it seem like it was important. Like I don't have better things to be doing. I watched this place all goddamn day and night and if you don't want to know what I saw then fuck you!"

"Ask him who he saw," Kincaid whispered.

"What?"

He pressed the muzzle deeper into my forehead.

"Ask him."

I turned my head to face the door.

"Who did you see, kid?"

"How the fuck should I know?"

Kincaid fed me another line.

"What did they look like?"

I jerked my head clear from the barrel. Kincaid jammed it hard against my temple. I glared up at him.

"Say it!"

"What did they look like?"

"Oh, now you wanna know?"

"Yeah. Now I wanna know."

I prayed the kid would tell me to fuck myself raw and then get as far away from this shitty office as fast as he could.

"C'mon kid," I whispered.

But he answered. And like a perfect little snoop, described Kincaid to a tee: spindly body, round face, features slightly askew from the drooped lid, receded hairline combed straight forward, bushy eyebrows, everything he was wearing down to his fresh Asics sneakers. I peered down at those crisp new shoes, out of place with the rest of him, and wondered absently if he had gotten them across the street at Sole Brothers.

"Is that the guy you were looking for?" Davey said, attempting to mask the eagerness to please in his voice.

Kincaid stared at the boarded-up door, disbelieving, mouth agape. The moment lasted no more than a breath but felt infinite. He lowered the gun from my temple and steeled himself for what he meant to do next. His eyes flashed violent. He cocked the weapon and started past me toward the door. All at once, I flicked the blade open and lunged from the balls of my feet at Kincaid.

Our bodies collided. I careened off of him and wrenched sideways to avoid landing on my fucked arm or the knife. The impact against the floor sent a shock of pain down the length of my skeleton. My brain screamed. Vomit spewed from my mouth. My vision wobbled and objects skewed oblong. Suddenly there was six of everything. I glanced down at my hand in the sling and saw six hands, but zero knives. The knife was gone.

Kincaid's shadow loomed over me. Those sporty new tennis shoes of his, all twelve of them, edged right up to the moat of vomit surrounding my head.

I squeezed my eyes shut and gave myself over to the bullet about to enter my skull. A comfort settled over me—a recognition of the end. The choice to die had been made a long time ago, when I started down this path. The image of my son's face materialized behind my black eyelids, like a pixilated photo rushing into focus. I had never seen him so clearly. In my mind's eye he had never aged—forever six years old. I smiled and his face became animated. He cracked a sheepish grin in return.

Maybe I'd be proven wrong. Maybe there was a God and I was about to see Jake, touch him, talk with him. As good a thought as any to go out on, I reckoned. I seized upon the concept in my head, the image of Jake cracking that grin, and I welcomed the end: the end of struggle, the end of pain, the end of meaning.

But nothing happened.

CHAPTER FORTY

HEAVY WHEN THEY'RE DEAD

I peeled my eyes open. The shoes were still there, but they were back to being a single pair, not six, and they were no longer white. They had been doused in crimson. The ring of puke surrounding my head had extended further and was crawling up his toes.

I twisted my neck to look up at Kincaid, who was tottering back and forth like a skyscraper in the wind. His eyes were fixed on the handle of the switchblade protruding from his abdomen. The knife had caught him just right, piercing his torso at the inside of his right ribcage. As I fell, the blade had cleaved down through his stomach, struck his hip bone and stayed lodged there, buried to the hilt.

Dark blood glugged from his wound out over the knife's handle. Kincaid pressed his palm against the gash, then held the blood-soaked hand in front of his face and examined it as if it were some peculiar artifact. He lowered the hand back to his side. A red bead dangled from the tip of his middle finger and dripped to the ground. Kincaid studied that single red splotch for some duration before his focus shifted across the floor to me, bound helplessly to the chair.

"Why did you do that?" he asked, giving me no time to respond before lifting the .38 and pointing it in the vicinity of my brain. The gun quaked in his hand. His eyes narrowed to focus and before I could say stop, or wait, or no, he squeezed the trigger. The shot reverberated through the room. The pistol snapped back and nearly struck Kincaid in the face. The bullet whizzed above my ear and splintered the desk behind me.

Kincaid staggered backwards into the wall and almost fell through one of the busted windows. His hand slackened and the revolver thunked down onto the hardwood. He braced against the windowsill and scanned the floor for the pistol. Found it at his feet. Gingerly, he bent to pick up the weapon, but in doing so, inadvertently kicked it further from his grasp.

Kincaid lurched for the pistol. The movement caused his body to seize up and he tipped over head first like a felled tree. Landed on the knife and yelped in pain. He attempted to roll from his belly to his side, but his arms and legs had given out and he couldn't get enough of a boost. Desperate, he ground his head against the floor, which gave him the leverage to tilt himself onto his shoulder. We lay there in our shared puddle of blood and vomit, facing one another.

"Not like this—not like this," Kincaid muttered to himself. He flung his arm above his head and pawed for the revolver. When it dawned on him that the pistol was out of his reach, he bore down and began worming his body, inch by inch, across the floor toward the pistol. All I could do was lie there and watch death crawl at me in slow motion.

At the far corner of the room I glimpsed a flash of movement. Davey had gone around to the outside of the building, scaled the wall and was now squirming through the absent windows. Kincaid didn't see him. He was wholly focused on retrieving the gun. Another foot and he would do just that.

Davey got through the window, got to his feet and took in the carnage around him. I nodded my head at Kincaid, who was now clawing for the pistol, and said, "Get that gun."

The kid scuttled around Kincaid and kicked the gun away from his outstretched hand. This sound I'd never heard from a human before, like the shrill whine of an animal going to slaughter, rose from Kincaid's throat. He rolled onto his back and lay there heaving.

Davey picked up the gun and set it on the desk.

"What now?"

"Should be a steak knife or something in the top left drawer in the kitchenette. How 'bout cutting me free."

The kid found a knife, sawed the zip-ties and assisted me to my feet. I jiggled my extremities to get them working.

"What the hell do you think you're doing coming in here like that? Trying to be a hero?"

"I thought you might be like—I don't know—trying to hurt yourself or something."

"Hurt myself?"

"I dunno," he shrugged.

I motioned toward Kincaid.

"Is this the guy you saw earlier?"

Davey peered down at the man on the floor like a person afraid of heights would peer over a high cliff. Kincaid's breathing was calm now as he lay there beneath the windows, dazed, blood pouring smoothly from his gut. His head was tilted toward us, but his eyes were transfixed on something beyond our shoulders, something faraway.

Davey nodded.

"That's him. Was he trying to kill you?"

"Yes."

"Is he gonna die?"

"Yes."

"Should we call the police?"

"No."

That stopped the kid asking questions. We stood there in silence. I half expected sirens to come bearing down on the high school at any moment. I didn't care. Let them come, I thought, but nothing sounded and nothing came. The amount of havoc this neighborhood had witnessed, no doubt a hollow little potshot from a .38 sounded like a dull illusion.

"What now?" the kid asked again.

"Any chance you know how to drive a car?"

"Yeah, I can drive a car."

"For real?"

Davey said his mom let him drive in the grocery parking lot all the time. I gave him my keys, told him to pull the Skylark around to the front of the school and back it in beneath the windows of my office.

"Keep the lights off," I told him. "And don't hit the building."

"Thanks for the tip."

Davey gave Kincaid a wide berth as he stepped around him, swung his legs over the windowsill and hopped down, disappearing from the world.

"Alone again," I said, as I knelt next to Kincaid. The moonlight slanting in from the window cast an eerie blue complexion over his clammy face. In an effort to stave me off, he lifted his hand and groped at my head. I swatted his arm away.

I wrapped my fingers around the handle of the knife and unsheathed it from his gut. Blood spurted up like a geyser. Kincaid's mouth ratcheted open into a wide, muted scream. Gradually, his mouth closed and he glared at me with an expression that vacillated between agony and repugnance. A tear dripped from the corner of his eye and streaked his cheek.

I held the knife to his throat and said, "Don't have much to say now, do you, you fuck? Well, this is how you end."

Kincaid grit his teeth. The muscles in his neck stretched taut. His lips parted as if to speak. He tried to get a breath to carry the words, but the air snagged in his throat and he coughed up a spray of blood. His eyes blinked once, stiltedly, and then opened wide. Blood oozed from the corners of his mouth, bubbled onto his lips.

I set the knife aside and watched Randall Kincaid die. Then, for a good while, I watched him stay dead. I don't know what I expected, but there was no great release of emotion, no catharsis. I didn't feel anything. Ambivalence maybe. The whole thing was over.

From outside the window, the kid whisper-shouted up to me. I got off the floor and peered over the sill. He had the Skylark backed up to the building. No one else was visible on the street and the parking lot across the way at the strip mall was empty.

"Any lights on up there?"

He looked over the facade of the building and said no. I went in the bathroom and tore down the shower curtain, tossed it out the window to Davey and told him to pop the trunk, lay the curtain down in there and stand aside.

Kincaid was a little man but even little men are heavy when they're dead. It took me a bit of time, with the one arm, to hoist him up over the sill. I dropped him out the window and watched him float down. His head cracked against the side of the car. The upper half of his body landed in the trunk. His legs were jacked out over the side.

"Lights?"

Davey scanned the upper floors of the building again. "Nothin'."

"Don't touch him. I'll get him."

I kicked off the boards that barred the door, got outside as fast as I could, stuffed Kincaid into the trunk and shut the lid, then ordered Davey to go home.

"You don't need me to drive?" Davey asked.

"No, I got it."

"Can I ask you something?"

"Why not."

"If this man tried to kill you, then why you gotta hide him? Why don't you just call the police?"

I closed my eyes and massaged my temples with my thumb and my middle finger.

"That's okay," Davey said. "You don't have to answer."

I took my hand away from my face.

"It's just—in this world, you have the truth and you have the law. The two are mutually exclusive."

I don't know if Davey understood what I was getting at, but he said, "Oh, okay."

"I'm sorry you had to see this, but I'm damn glad you were there or else it would have been the end of the road for me."

Davey brightened.

"So I like, saved your life and shit."

"Let's not go crazy, but yeah, something like that."

"Can I ask you something else?"

I nodded for him to proceed.

"Why does everybody want to kill you?"

"Well," I started to explain, but his question sparked an impulsive fit of laughter. The kid laughed, too. When the laughter waned, I said, "I guess they all have their reasons."

Davey gestured at the trunk, serious now.

"What was his reason?"

"He killed children, and he knew I wasn't going to let him get away with it."

Davey worked this out in his head enough to say he believed me.

"One of them kids was yours, wasn't it?"

"Yeah. One of them was mine."

"Maybe I won't tell my mom about this."

"I think that'd be best."

He climbed the portico steps and went inside. I slid behind the wheel of the Skylark and steered her under the viaduct and through downtown to the riverfront, past the flood wall down to the end of the parking lot and over the curb through the dark field to the edge of the wood where I stopped the car and cut the engine. I got out and opened the hatch, took hold of Kincaid's belt and yanked him out of the trunk; got him situated onto the shower curtain and dragged the curtain by the rungs down through the wood to the clearing at the river's edge.

I stood there for a moment and watched the river's placid current slide by so smoothly it seemed not to move at all. The hills on the other side of the river were dark and blurry. The tree tops cut a jagged outline along the ridges. To the west, the bridge into Ohio loomed over the river. The stars and the moon shone intermittently through drifts of gray clouds. I closed my eyes and listened to the pure quiet of it all.

Then I walked Kincaid's body into the shallows. I waded out until the water was to my chest, until the power of the river enveloped me, and I let go of him. Kincaid floated away until he became nothing more than a dark blot on a dark river.

And then the river took him.

CHAPTER FORTY-ONE
THE STRAGGLERS

I don't know how long I stood there in the shallows, or how long I sat on the shore after that, wondering where to go and what to do, not caring for the answer. I made it back to the high school just before dawn, showered, shaved, popped some antibiotics and changed into some fresh clothes. By then the sun was full in the sky.

Bruce Hale left a message on my phone. Randall Kincaid's credit card purchased gas, food, a bottle of tequila, and a hotel room late the previous night in Montgomery, Alabama. He would keep me posted on any further movements.

I went out to the front of the high school and sat on the steps and watched the world go by. The day was pleasant, warm in the sun, cool in the shade. The pain in my arm wasn't too severe. I was starting to get used to it. Down the block I saw the neon sign for The Red Head flicker to life. Tadpole opening up. When I turned back around Davey was sitting there next to me.

"Jesus Christ! What are you, a ninja?"

"That's right," the kid said, enjoying the distinction.

"You get some sleep?"

"Eh," he lifted his shoulders and dropped them. "What you doing out here?"

"Nothing much."

The kid squinted against the sun.

"Everything all good with like, all that shit last night?"

I nodded.

"All good. How's my cat?"

"Oh, it's your cat now? I don't know, Mom loves that thing. You might have a hard time getting it away from her."

"She can have it. On a scale of one to ten, how pissed off would you say she is?"

"Forget it, off the charts. I ain't never seen her get *that* mad at anybody 'cept me. She'll cool off, man. You just gotta give her some time. Probably a *lot* of time."

Okay, I thought. Time. I can do that. Across the street a handyman was erecting bars over the windows of the shoe store, Sole Brothers. High above us, a plane traced a white line across the sky. I wondered if it was bound for St. Louis.

We watched the cars go by on the avenue.

"You hungry?" I asked Davey.

"I mean, I could eat."

"All right, let's get some hot dogs."

"Aw, man, don't come at me talking 'bout hot dogs."

"What do you want, a bunch of fuckin' Ding Dongs?"

"Last time I had a hot dog I puked it out."

"That was your own fault."

"Variety is the spice of life, man. All you ever eat are hot dogs. If you're not careful, you're going to turn into a damn long, flimsy hot dog."

"Hey smartass, are you paying?"

"*Pfftt*, no."

"Then we're eating hot dogs."

"It's like that?"

"Yup."

We got up and started walking down the street. Davey stuffed his hands in his pockets and kicked at the crabgrass sticking up from the sidewalk.

"So what are you going to do now?" he asked. "Go back to Chi-caa-go or something?"

The question struck me.

I thought about Chicago, the place that made me, and Cain City, the place that changed me, and I thought about the rest of it: the Cammacks' and Hale's dead daughter, Gum Drop's five orphaned children, Randall Kincaid at the bottom of a river. I thought about Joanna pregnant with a new child, and Karla's bluesy eyes and fierce nature, and I thought about my dead son. The image of his grinning face that came to me the night before had stuck in my mind's eye. I liked it there.

I hooked an arm over Davey's shoulder and answered his question the only way I knew how.

"Kid, I got no idea."

ACKNOWLEDGEMENTS

Firstly, I owe an immense debt of gratitude to my agent, Renée C. Fountain, whose unwavering belief and support is the reason this book exists in the world instead of being consigned to the proverbial desk drawer to collect dust for all eternity. To Steve Feldberg at Audible, who has been a joy to work with at every turn, and whose deft editorial touch makes everything that much better. A big thank you to Otto Penzler and his team at MysteriousPress.com for making the leap of faith to publish these books in print and quite literally make a childhood dream come true. I'd also like to thank the first people to lay eyes on this book and give me the confidence that I might be onto something: Greg Taylor, Champ Clark, and Tom Epperson.

To Chandra, who encouraged my artistic endeavors for many years when it must have seemed like none of it would amount to much. To my father, who maintains a bottomless trove of cornball jokes, a few of which finally came in handy. Along with him, to my wonderful mother and the many friends who have supported me along the way, and spurred me on both personally and creatively—you mean the world to me.

ABOUT THE AUTHOR

Jonathan Fredrick is the author of the Cain City Novels, which were inspired in-part by his hometown of Huntington, West Virginia. After working in Los Angeles as a writer, filmmaker, and actor for more than fifteen years, Fredrick now resides in Columbus, Ohio, with his wife and three sons.

THE CAIN CITY NOVELS

FROM MYSTERIOUSPRESS.COM
AND OPEN ROAD MEDIA

MP